The Werewolf's Mask

K. S. Gerlt

Copyright © 2023 by K. S. Gerlt. All rights reserved. This book or any portion thereof may not be reproduced or used in any manner whatsoever without the express written permission of the author except for the use of brief quotations in a book review.

This is a work of fiction. Names, characters, places, and incidents are a product of the author's imagination. Any resemblance to actual persons, events, or locales is entirely coincidental.

Cover design by K. S. Gerlt

Cover creation by Lesia

Special thanks to my first reader and biggest cheerleader, Aly. Thank you for all of your support and encouragement.

Prologue

Are monsters born or made?

Through the eyes of a child, the answer is as clear as day and night; the bad guys are bad, and the good guys are good. The good guy beats the bad guy, becomes a hero, and lives happily ever after.

It is only when that child grows to understand adults and the world around him or her that such a simple, clear-cut answer starts becoming ever fuzzier, fading into murky hues.

That line between good and evil, right and wrong, starts to blur. It blurs until maybe the bad guy isn't absolutely evil, and the good guy isn't purely angelic.

A child given wealth but no love can become cruel, but a child given a little love and nothing else can become resilient. Do circumstances make the monster? Or personal choices? Or perhaps, a little bit of both?

It's all about perspective, the way you see the world. If you look for the darkness, it's all that you will find. Glance around for some light, and you will be showered in its radiance. That is the choice each person makes every day. And those days add up to a lifetime.

So, are monsters born, or are they made?

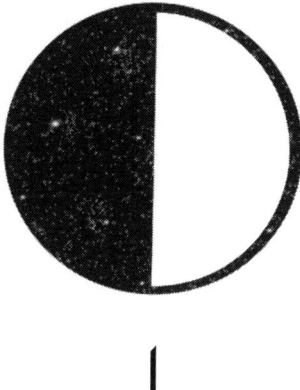

1

My heart pounded in time with the rhythmic beat of my horse's hooves striking the earth as we flew across the fallow field. I never felt so free as I did on horseback; all my worries would slip away, until only me, my horse, and the endless azure sky remained. *This must be what flying feels like.*

The silver crescent moon necklace that had once belonged to my father had worked its way out of my shirt, sparkling as it caught the light of the setting sun. It was my most treasured possession, one that very few people even knew about. I gripped it momentarily before tucking it securely back into its hiding place and returning my full attention to the race.

A second set of hoofbeats was closing fast behind me, but I wasn't worried.

The lone oak tree at the end of the field was fast approaching, its vast branches filled with verdant green leaves rustling in the wind. I closed my right hand on the reins, sat deep in my saddle and whipped my head around as we made the turn around the oak. As we finished the turn, I shifted my weight forward over Soren's withers and smirked at Chris, who was only just approaching the oak tree on his bay mare as I flashed past him.

The sun painted the sky with streaks of red and gold as Soren and I raced back to our starting point by the field's gate. I savored these last few moments of elation, tucking them deep inside myself, before slowing Soren down as we passed the finish line. I turned him around and ran my hand down his velvety neck, thanking him for a good run.

"So how did my dust taste?" I called to Chris triumphantly as he came to a halt in front of me, his mare puffing from the exertion.

"Tastes like extra chores for me," Chris replied good-naturedly. He gave Bella a few pats on her neck, and then fell in beside me as we started walking back towards the barn.

"I'll beat you next time, Serena LaRoux!" he grinned as he ran his hand through his tousled golden locks.

"You always say that, Chris Ranger, and yet somehow I always beat you anyways," I quipped back. "Race you back to the barn?" I suggested with a grin.

"You're on!" Chris yelled, and we both urged our horses into a canter.

As I closed Soren's stall door, I could hear him happily munching away on his hay. I paused for a moment and leaned against the door, deeply inhaling the peace of the barn and savoring the quiet sounds of the horses swishing their tails and eating their hay and grain. Their quiet whickers settled deep in my soul. If only this was my home too.

Sighing quietly, I pushed off the door and walked down the compacted dirt floor of the barn aisle, aiming for Bella's stall. I glanced into some of the stalls as I passed, smiling softly at the new foals. I was looking forward to training them in a few months' time. Chris was just closing Bella's stall door as I approached.

Turning to face me, he said, "Thanks again for your help today. I'd never be able to take care of all the horses myself." He took my hand and dropped a handful of copper coins into it, but his fingers lingered a few beats longer than normal.

Smiling gratefully, and maybe a little nervously, I replied, "Thanks. It hardly feels like work to me. I hope I'll have a place like this someday."

"I'm sure you will, Serena. Soren is a very lucky horse. Only one year left before he's yours, right?"

"Yes! I'm so grateful to you and your parents for letting me work here to help pay for him. These last four years have been like a dream," I responded, my eyes misting slightly.

Seeing my expression, his own softened, his chocolate eyes turning into molten pools. Hesitantly he asked, "Would you like to stay for dinner tonight?"

I hesitated, mulling it over. Having meals with Chris and his family was always wonderful. Lately though, Chris kept looking at me...differently. I had the sneaking suspicion that he was starting to see me as less of a friend and more of a...well, as something more than a friend. And I had absolutely no idea how I felt about that.

I sighed, then straightened and said, "I wish I could. But I really should check on her tonight. She's been...worse, lately." An image of dirty hands with ragged fingernails clutching a bottle of cheap alcohol rose unbidden to my mind's eye.

"Ah...alright, I understand," he said softly. We both headed out of the barn and towards the road that led into town. Chris closed the gate behind me as I exited.

"Get home safe, and don't let the monster of the Forgotten Forest get ya!" he playfully exclaimed with a wink and a wave.

I smiled at his superstitious nature, shaking my head to myself as I waved and called out, "I will. See you tomorrow, Chris! And don't forget that you get to do all the mucking out for the rest of the week!"

Grinning at his mumbled grumblings, I picked up my pace, the coppers I'd earned today clinking together in my pouch. The wind lifted my scarlet hair around me, and the sun seemed to set the tips ablaze with ruby light as I made my way into town.

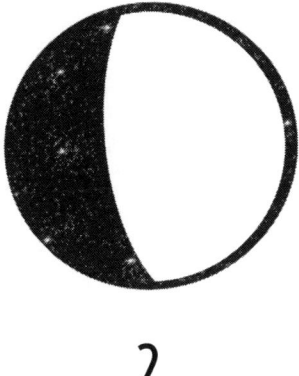

2

The small town of Verdain bustled with activity, the setting sun gilding the ordinarily drab buildings a brilliant gold. Villagers rushed along the main road, occasionally calling greetings to each other and popping in and out of the stores that lined each side. The fragrant aroma of baking bread floated in the breeze, and the bell-like laughter of little barefooted children rang out as they scampered about, playing one last game before the inevitable call to dinner.

I smiled at the familiar scene, reveling in the general happiness that I could practically feel all around me. My nose caught a whiff of something deliciously sweet in the air. I breathed it in greedily before following the delicate aroma further down the street and straight into the bakery shop.

A little brass bell tinkled as I opened the sturdy wooden door, and warmth from the massive stone oven enveloped me in a comforting embrace. The baker, Mrs. Thompson, was busy attending to a couple of customers by the front counter, so I made my way over to the display shelves.

Fluffy loaves of bread and sticky buns lined the shelves, each with a little sign indicating the price of each item. The signs were mostly there for the benefit of the rare traveler that passed through town, since most of the locals preferred to barter or trade for their bread, myself included.

The two ladies who had been at the counter passed me on their way to the door, fresh loaves packed safely in their woven baskets. One of the ladies' full skirts momentarily caught in the door as it closed; I smiled to myself as the offending fabric was quickly tugged out. Though I sometimes envied the ladies their lovely dresses, my riding breeches served me well, despite the occasional snide comment I could hear muttered as I passed. At least breeches couldn't get caught in doorways or on bushes.

"Serena dear," Mrs. Thompson called out, "how are you? Have those ranchers been treating you well? Has that Chris asked for your hand yet?"

"You know they treat me like family," I replied, blushing slightly. "I don't think Chris sees me that way, Mrs. Thompson." *Well, at least that's what I had thought until recently...*

"Oh nonsense, that boy is head over heels for you. You're all he ever talks about–well, you and his horses that is," Mrs. Thompson went on.

"H-he does?" I stammered. "Well, of course he does. Surely he has to complain to someone about how frequently I win our little races!" Mrs. Thompson raised an eyebrow. Before she could say anything more, I rushed on, "And since today I got my wages for the week, I thought I might buy a treat," I hinted not-so-subtly. The only real way to stop the endless questioning was by turning the conversation to buying something.

"But of course! I just so happen to have something extra special today," Mrs. Thompson exclaimed, a big grin lighting up her face. She turned and hurried into the back room, where the stone oven and cooling trays were located. She returned a few moments later, her flour-covered hands supporting a wooden tray laden with a very special kind of pastry.

I couldn't help but grin with delight at the cinnamon buns on the tray. They were my absolute favorite, and Mrs. Thompson always seemed to have a fresh batch right around pay day. The wonderful aroma I had followed in from the street wafted from the tray, and I could already feel my mouth watering.

I reached for my pouch, and carefully withdrew four of the twelve coppers Chris had given me today. Unfortunately, my favorite food also just so happened to be one of the most expensive; both sugar and cinnamon were difficult to come by.

"I'll take two of them," I told Mrs. Thompson, handing her the coins.

"Is the second one for that mother of yours?" she asked kindly, though her brows furrowed in concern. Whether that concern was for me or my mother, I wasn't quite sure. Perhaps for both of us.

I stiffened slightly at the mention of my mother, and conflicting emotions rose to the surface once more. Still, I managed to reply evenly, "Yes. They were...I mean, are, her favorite too."

"You're a very sweet girl, Serena," Mrs. Thompson told me softly. "Now if only my little rascals were so considerate. Those boys will be the death of me some day, you mark my words, missy." She wrapped up the two buns as she spoke before handing the fragrant little bundles to me, her warm, calloused hands squeezing my own.

"Now you get on home safely, dear. Don't you go walking too close to that there forest!" she warned.

"Don't worry, I'll be careful. Thanks, Mrs. Thompson!" Relaxing a bit, I smiled as I headed out the door, the little bell chiming softly behind me and my precious bundles clutched tightly to my chest.

When I was little, mom used to hold my hand as we walked to the bakery to get a treat. It'd been our little tradition for as long as I could remember. Whether we needed a little something to lift our spirits or wanted to celebrate the end of the week, a cinnamon roll had always been the go-to.

I remembered one night in particular, when mom had been arguing with a well-dressed stranger in our house, I'd run to my room and hidden under the blanket. That's where she'd found me, hours later, once the man had left, curled up in a ball with my hands over my ears. She'd taken my hand and led me to the bakery, and we'd stuffed our faces with sweet and sticky goodness, laughing and telling silly stories well after everyone else had gone to bed. I smiled at the memory.

As I strolled down the main street, I noticed that the atmosphere had changed while I was in the bakery. The children had been ushered indoors, or were being tightly held by their mothers. The general din of a typical evening had been replaced by a tense quiet, punctuated by the muted but excited whisperings of the townsfolk. Not even the local official of our town elicited such a response from the townsfolk.

On high alert now, I scanned my surroundings, searching for hints to indicate the reason for everyone's attention. Near the end of the street, I could make out a few clumps of people excitedly talking and pointing towards the local inn.

In front of the inn, groups of servants and uniformed guardsman worked on unloading two red carriages, each one decorated with swirls of gold and emblazoned with an elaborate coat of arms, in which a serpent twined around a sword. A team of four stunning Arabian horses stood harnessed to each one. Their snow white coats positively glowed in the gathering twilight, despite the sweat marks earned from a long day of pulling such heavy carriages.

I sucked in a quick breath. I had never seen such gorgeous creatures. The way their necks arched gave them an air of grace, and their glossy tails were held high. Nostrils flared in delicate faces with expressive eyes, and elegant ears flickered this way and that as each horse examined their surroundings and the actions of all of the servants. Even if I worked for the rest of my life at Chris' ranch, I could likely never afford to buy such a fine-looking Arabian horse.

As I approached the edge of one of the larger groups, I could make out Mrs. Smith, the blacksmith's wife, talking in hushed tones to several of her neighbors.

As soon as she spotted me, she animatedly gestured for me to come over, so I quickened my pace until I had joined the group. We were well acquainted, since I frequently visited her husband to request his services, shoeing the ranch's many horses every couple months or so.

"Serena, have you heard the news?" Without waiting for a response, she rushed on, saying, "The Duke's son is staying at the inn!"

I started, taken aback, before managing to get out, "Duke Lindora? *The* Duke Lindora's son?"

Duke Lindora was one of the kingdom's three dukedoms–the others were the Verdania Duchy and the Windsom Duchy. The Verdania Duchy currently sat vacant, since the previous duke and his family had mysteriously vanished about a year ago, and his Imperial Majesty had yet to appoint a replacement. Duke Verdania had been in charge of Verdain; since his disappearance, the forest where his estate was located had become forbidden to the townspeople, supposedly due to a monster infestation, and Verdain had been under Duke Lindora's temporary control ever since. The thing was, Duke Lindora and his family had never set foot in Verdain even once, though he must have thought we were doing well for ourselves since he kept demanding more and more taxes. All we knew of his son, Lester, was that he was more interested in grand feasts and women than learning the sword or governance from his father.

"I heard one of the guardsmen complaining about being dragged all the way out to 'some backwards town,' as he put it, because his lord is looking for some beautiful girl," Mrs. Smith continued.

"Oh my! What a fortuitous opportunity!" Mrs. Weaver twittered excitedly. "He *is* older than my Maria by a decade or two, but that's not uncommon for the nobility! This could be her chance–dukes often take several concubines. I must arrange a meeting!" And with that, she scurried off in the direction of her house, her voluptuous skirts swishing with each step.

"Why would he come all the way out here? Surely a noble would be more than satisfied with one of the other noble ladies, all decorated in silks and jewels," I mumbled to myself.

The other ladies and Mrs. Smith gave me a sharp look. "Serena, you of all people should be aware of this. Nobles, especially those with the highest titles, are particularly enamored with rarities. Rare fabrics, rare animals, and rare people, especially women with uncommon physical traits, like unusual eye or hair colors. Just like what happened to your mother."

I flinched, annoyed at my own carelessness. This wasn't exactly a topic I wanted to be conversing about with the biggest gossips in town. They'd already beaten the topic of my mother to death years ago, and I'd rather not have it dredged up again. My mother was already so sensitive about the whole thing. In the past, a few whispered words from some finely-dressed ladies was all it took to send her on a drinking binge for days. I shuddered at the memory.

My face paled, and I mumbled my goodbyes as I hurried off in the direction of home, past the noble's entourage, my little packages clutched to my chest. But I wasn't quick enough to miss hearing Mrs. Weaver murmur to Mrs. Smith, "What's gotten into her?" Mrs. Smith's reply was lost to the wind as I broke into a run, quickly moving out of earshot. But I couldn't possibly outrun the thoughts swirling in my mind like a maelstrom.

As I rounded the last bend in the road, the small home I shared with my mother came into view. The edge of the Forgotten Forest came right up to the edge of the house, which was the only reason we could afford it. The sun had now fully set, and the twilight air had a bite to it, indicating fall was not far away. The full moon hung low in the sky, just visible above the treetops.

But I was surprised to see an Arabian stallion, even finer than the ones I'd seen in town, tied to a tree next to my house. He stood tall and regal, his tasseled bridle standing out against his satiny black coat. His glossy mane and tail were a deep ebony, and he held his tail up high, like a silken flag. My first thought was: *Everyone knows tying a horse to a tree with the reins of its bridle is dangerous–the horse could spook and get tangled in the reins and hurt itself!* And my second thought was: *Why on Earth is there an Arabian stallion tied up in front of my house?!*

Resisting the urge to pet the beautiful creature's velvety nose, I quietly padded past it and around the back of the house, my footfalls silent on the thick layer of soft leaves that blanketed the ground. I crept stealthily to the back door and eased it slowly open so it wouldn't creak and give me away.

Passing through my plain but clean room, I moved into the short hallway and paused, listening. I could hear the murmur of voices. One was definitely the rasp of my mother, but the other one sounded distinctly male, though somewhat whiny and nasally.

I moved very slowly, hardly daring to breathe as I arrived at the door to the kitchen and living room area. The door was ajar, so I peeked into the room. I saw my mother, her hair unkempt and oily, dress ragged at the hem, facing in my direction and talking with the man whose voice I'd heard and whose back was to me. His obscenely rounded figure was swathed in a red tunic with ridiculously puffy sleeves and gold stitching. The coat of arms of the Lindora Duchy was emblazoned on the cape he wore, which hung down to his calves, which were ensconced in supple brown leather boots. Rings of gold glittered on his pudgy fingers as he gestured, making his cape ripple and revealing a fat leather coin purse on his hip.

My mind flashed back to what the gossiping ladies had been chatting about. My heart pounded in my chest in response to the sudden icy fear that ran its clawed fingers down my spine. *There's no way*, I thought. *There's no way a noble would be interested in my mother!* But then I remembered what Mrs. Smith had said. There was already a noble whose eye had fallen on ruby red hair.

I focused in on what they were saying.

"You drive quite the hard bargain, Helena, but since I'm in *such* a generous mood this evening, I'll indulge you. Alright, I will give you 10 gold coins *and* 3 barrels of our finest Lindora wine, in exchange for your daughter," he purred.

My mother's bloodshot eyes met mine as a wicked grin split her face. She held my horrified gaze as she replied, "You have a bargain, Lord Lindora."

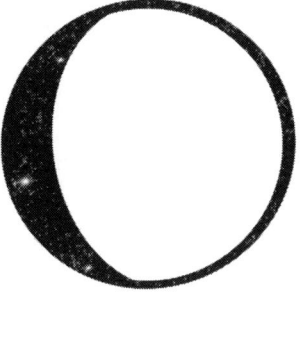

3

The pastry bag slid from my numb fingers, thudding softly on the worn wood floor. Shock and horror warred within me, despair and rage swiftly replacing them.

She'd referred to him as Lord Lindora—so the man in front of me must be the visiting son of Duke Lindora that everyone had been talking about in town! So the girl he was supposedly looking for—could that truly be me?

My own mother—after everything I've done for her, after everything she's put me through—that's what it was all worth?! Ten gold coins and some alcohol?! All the late nights wiping the vomit from her face after another drinking binge, all the harsh words, the abuse? THAT'S ALL?! She sold me...she sold my future to some stranger?

Both of them had heard the bag hit the floor, despite how quiet it had been and how loudly they had been talking.

"Oh, look who we have here," my mother crooned, stepping forward and tugging the door all the way open.

The noble had slightly turned at the noise, but now fully faced the open doorway. I got my first full look at him and almost wished I hadn't. His small, upturned nose in a rounded face reminded me of a pig, and his extra chins did nothing to dispel that impression. Stubble coated his chins in uneven patches, and a sad, wispy little mustache disgraced his upper lip. His curly blonde hair hung in greasy ringlets, and a small gold cap sat atop his head, a red feather tilting jauntily to one side.

A wide grin wormed across his face, his soulless brown eyes alight with greed. "She is as beautiful as I've been told—though she'll be much better once she's out of those rags," he chuckled, looking me up and down in a way that made my skin crawl and set his extra chins jiggling. He waddled closer to me, near enough for his extremely unpleasant odor to waft toward my nose. Horse manure smelled like roses compared to his stench.

There was not a single thing about this pig that did not wholly repulse me. My eyes flicked back to my mother, and without thinking, I blurted out, "How could you?" My voice cracked under the weight of my emotions.

"This fine gentleman has asked for your hand in marriage, and I gladly accepted on your behalf, since you were late coming home today. You are nearly seventeen, Serena, and it is long past time for you to settle down and raise a family, instead of chasing ridiculous notions of horse breeding," she scolded, her eyes slitted.

She had always spat on my dreams so easily, even when I was a little girl. Not that I'd let that deter me for long.

"You are much too fine for such mundane and dirty work," scoffed Lester. He reached out one of his swollen hands, his gold rings flashing in the flickering candlelight, and lifted a lock of my fiery hair to his nose, before inhaling deeply. He licked his lips.

"Yes, you'll do nicely, once you're cleaned up a bit," he leered as he let the strands of my hair slip through his fingers.

I stepped back involuntarily at the absolute promise I saw in his eyes. *I'm to be wed...to this, this pig? A life of luxury and abuse, a gilded cage? But what about the future I dreamed about, the one I've been working so hard towards for the last four years?*

The image in my mind of the future I so desperately wanted, of me riding tall on my beautiful Soren, my own sprawling horse ranch behind me, a small herd of mares grazing peacefully in my wide, grassy pastures, with a blurry figure standing next to me, of some future loving husband, seemed to be melting, slipping right through my calloused hands.

I heard it then, the sound of the door leading to the future I so desperately wanted, slowly creaking shut. This was a crossroads, and if I let that door slam closed today, I might never be able to open it again. The crossroads of destiny sat before me, paths diverging in very different directions, one paved in gold and misery, the second in grit and opportunity.

I let the hurt and the fear flow out of me, straightening my spine as I let a new resolve fill me to the brim. It was not like I was afraid of a little hard work. It was my bread and butter, always had been.

My previously slack expression hardened into one of fury and determination. I took a step forward, allowing the noble to reach his hammy fist out towards me again. Just before he could touch my cheek, I slapped his hand away with as much force as I could muster.

"Don't touch me," I snarled, staring him dead in the eyes, back erect and head held high.

"Wha—," he faltered, staggering back a step, the shock plainly evident on his face. But a moment later, the look of shock was swiftly replaced by one of rage.

"HOW DARE YOU STRIKE ME, YOU PEASANT!" Lester bellowed, his multiple chins jiggling in a humorous imitation of his fury. "Don't you know who I am?! I could have you—"

"You will NEVER have me!" I declared. Pivoting on my heel, I spun and bolted back out the door I'd come through, not bothering to spare so much as a glance at my treacherous mother and leaving Lester to sputter in his self-righteous indignation.

I dashed through the short hallway I had so timidly crept through mere minutes ago, though it felt more like a lifetime. Once in my room, I paused to grab my winter cloak from where it hung on the wall, and then sprinted out through the back door.

I nearly ran straight for the Forgotten Forest before coming to an abrupt halt. I grinned as a perfectly, wonderfully, wicked idea popped into my head.

I turned on my heel and sprinted around to the front of the house, making a beeline for the beautiful black stallion tied (incorrectly) to the tree. It only took a moment to untangle the magnificent creature's fine leather bridle. I vaulted into the finely wrought saddle, which was stiff from disuse. The horse startled and huffed at the sudden motion and weight on his back, so I patted his neck and made soothing noises to settle him before turning him to face the game trail into the forest that I had frequented as a child.

As I shortened the reins and squeezed his sides to urge him into a canter, I could hear muffled shouting and cursing coming from inside the house. Lester finally managed to make it out the front door, my mother barely visible behind his large frame, just in time for them both to watch me disappear into the Forgotten Forest, the stallion's silky black tail giving one final swish as we dove into the trees.

4

The stallion's powerful legs pumped beneath me. Branches whipped across my face as we raced through the dense trees in the near pitch-black darkness. Even the light of the full moon and a sea of silver starlight could not reach us down here. My breath rasped in my chest, coming short and fast, in time with my racing heart and mind.

Had it really only been an hour since last I sat astride a horse, racing the wind during a golden sunset? Now I was racing for my future and my freedom into the dark unknown. Tears blurred my vision, only partially caused by the sting of the wind. I'd just left everything and everyone I'd ever known behind, and I hadn't even gotten the chance to say goodbye. My heart ached at the thought of Chris' warm brown eyes filled with confusion and hurt and sadness. I thought of his mother and father, who had given me refuge; and his younger brother, who never failed to put a smile on my face; even Mrs. Thompson and Mr. Smith—I would miss them all. It felt like I was leaving a part of me back there with them.

I knew that Lester and his guards would be after me in no time. I was lucky that he hadn't brought guards with him-he probably didn't want his "purchase" to be widely known. But it would only take so long for that priggish noble to waddle his way back to the inn. If any of his servants knew anything at all about tracking, I was in big trouble. Horseshoe tracks weren't exactly difficult to follow. My main advantages were my head start, the cover of night, and the superstitions surrounding the forest. My best bet would be to cut through this forest and get to another town somewhere.

And then...what? Live in hiding for the rest of my life? Would I have to flee to a neighboring country just to escape a noble and preserve my freedom of choice?

The stallion skidded to a sudden halt, sides heaving, just in front of a spring. I had been so wrapped up in my own frantic thoughts that I hadn't been paying attention to where we'd been going. I wasn't even sure how long it had been since I'd entered the forest. Maybe two hours? Three?

We were in a small clearing with the spring at its center. The spring itself almost seemed to glow under the light of the full moon, which was now almost directly overhead. Water lilies bloomed in the shallows, and delicate silvery moonflowers ringed the spring. The whole area was covered in lush greenery, and fireflies twinkled in the warm air.

I dismounted and led the horse to the spring. Small frogs hopped out of our way, and chirping crickets quieted at our approach. We splashed into the shallows, the stallion lowering his graceful head to suck up some water. His sides were streaked with sweat, so I decided to let him rest for a few minutes before pressing onwards.

Crouching down, I cupped some of the spring water in my hands, momentarily entranced by the moonlight sparkling on its rippling surface. I slowly sipped, letting the cool water ease my dry throat.

Movement at the corner of my eye caught my attention, and I looked to the left side of the spring. Staring back at me across the calm waters were a pair of icy-blue eyes. I froze, narrowing my eyes to try and make out what manner of creature was so intently watching me. The rumors I'd heard about a monster residing in this forest flashed through my mind, sending a chill down my spine. I had always dismissed those rumors as superstitious nonsense, mere stories to scare young children into behaving.

But right in front of my eyes, I could just make out the silhouette of a large, black-furred, wolf-like *something*. Its ears were pointed in my direction, but at least I couldn't see its teeth. It was absolutely silent and still, which was either a really good thing or a really, really bad thing. There was no warning growl, which was good. But didn't some predators crouch right before they launched themselves at their prey?

Suddenly, the stallion whipped his head up and around, ears pricked forward and nostrils flaring. Except he wasn't looking at the beast in the shadows. He was looking back the way we had come, at the snarling hunting dog that stood just inside the tree line. The dog raised its sleek head and howled.

My face paled in horror as I realized that Lester had hired woodsmen to hunt me down like an animal. The faint voice of a huntsman calling out to others, "This way! She must be close by!" snapped me out of my shock.

I stood up from my crouch and immediately put my left foot into the stirrup, vaulting onto the stallion's back. I turned him towards a faint game trail, and a sharp kick from my boots had him swiftly moving forward into a canter, then a gallop.

I could hear a group of men crashing through the underbrush behind me, but I didn't dare turn to look. Instead, I urged my horse on faster, faster, faster through the trees, dodging left and right to avoid tree limbs that tried to take me out of the saddle.

The indistinct forms of towering trees rushed by me in the darkness, blurring together into a stream of monsters, jagged branches reaching for me. I thought I caught a glimpse of icy eyes in the shadows, but I blinked and they were gone. Hopefully the racket the men were making had scared it off. Though I might have preferred my chances with the beast than with whomever had been hired to hunt down one girl in the Forgotten Forest at night.

The hunting dog's panting grew louder as it closed the distance between us. The brief rest at the moonlit glade hadn't been enough; I could feel the stallion starting to tire. After walking all day along rough roads, and now having to sprint on uneven ground, it was losing steam fast. But the baying of the dog at our heels spurred him on with another burst of fear-induced adrenaline.

The dog lunged, his fangs snapping shut inches from the stallion's hind leg. The horse kicked out at the dog in terror, then shied away from it. Straight into the low-hanging branches of a large tree.

One of the branches caught me right in the shoulder, knocking me off the horse and over empty air. I plummeted, slamming hard into the rocky earth on my back, driving the air from my lungs. My head struck a rough rock, and darkness devoured the sky.

5

I struggled to regain consciousness, fending off the darkness that had just barely receded to the corners of my vision. I must have only been out for a few seconds, judging by the pounding in my head and the way I had to gasp for air after my unplanned dismount. I could still hear the heaving breaths of the horse nearby and the barking of the hunting dog as it circled, snapping at the poor horse's sides.

Suddenly the beautiful stallion reared, screaming in pain and terror, as the dog clamped down on one of its legs, before shaking it off and galloping off into the foreboding forest. I felt my hope fading along with the pounding of the horse's hooves, the yapping of that horrid dog going with it.

A sob ripped from my chest as I forced myself up into a sitting position. The sudden motion sent my head swimming for a few seconds, turning the dark shadows around me into moving monsters. It cleared after a few moments, allowing me to focus on the pinprick of light I could now see coming towards me, accompanied by the sounds of a large group of men trampling through the undergrowth.

"I see her! Over there!" one gruff voice called out. They ran straight towards me, the light of the torches they carried illuminating their features.

I was able to get my first good look at my hunters. Each face was rough and unshaven, most bearing jagged scars and eager expressions. They were dressed crudely but practically, and each one carried a motley assortment of weapons: daggers, knives, axes, even a few short swords and maces. These were no noble guards or servants. A vicious gang of mercenaries for hire now towered over me.

"Well boys, looks like we've caught ourselves a live one!" jeered a mercenary holding a curved dagger, with a scar on one cheek.

A rough, dirty hand grabbed my tightly plaited braid, yanking me up onto my feet. I cried out, shutting my eyes against the stabbing pain in my scalp, my hands clawing desperately at my captor.

"Let me go!" I shrieked.

I opened one eye, grimacing at what had to be the mercenaries' leader. He stood several heads taller and several times wider than me. A double-headed axe was strapped to his back, and corded muscle stood out on his brawny arms, most of which were criss-crossed with stark white scars on tanned, leathery skin.

His face belonged in the stories used to scare children into behaving. A long scar ran diagonally from his scalp, across his milky right eye and crooked nose, and disappeared into his thick brown beard. I noted dazedly that a couple of leaves were tangled in it.

He shook me by my hair before bringing his face down to mine, close enough that his foul, alcohol-tinged breath made my stomach curl in disgust. That stench only ever preceded pain. And large amounts of it.

He retorted with a wicked grin on his face, "Oh, I'll let you go...to that pompous noble. But only after me an' me men 'ave 'ad our fun with ye."

The other men guffawed and laughed, leering at me and cracking disgusting jokes amongst themselves.

"Leave some fer the rest o' us, Bruce," called one of the men, a chorus of agreement following from the others. I was right; this was indeed their leader.

Despair swirled around me; how was I ever going to escape from these men? If only I could find that horse...But I'd need to get this monstrous man to release me first. Somehow, I didn't think that reasoning with him would be very effective. There was one trick in my arsenal I sometimes resorted to when Chris or his little brother were being especially rough or pig-headed that worked like a charm. It was a very rare kind of man who was immune to taunts from a girl.

"Men? All I see is a pack of lousy drunken curs!" I sneered.

In one swift motion, I grabbed the silver moon pendant from under my shirt and brought it down in one vicious arc on his face. Adrenaline surged through me, pushing back the darkness at the edges of my vision and dulling the throbbing ache in my head and limbs, at least for the moment.

Taken by surprise, Bruce stumbled back a step, releasing me to bring one massive hand up to his face. It came away red with blood from the gash that now split his left eyebrow in half, stopping just short of his one good eye. Oddly enough, the wound was blistering like a burn, the skin around it flushing a bright red.

I landed with a soft *oof* on the ground, my already bruised backside complaining loudly at its second unplanned meeting with the earth in the last few minutes. I struggled to my feet, my scalp aching from the rough treatment.

I gripped the silver crescent even tighter as Bruce curled his bloodied hand into a fist, his face contorting into a look of rage. The other men, who had also frozen in shock, now stirred angrily, scowling and muttering darkly. Though a few seemed to be chuckling at their leader.

"You stupid *wench*," he growled, his lip lifting into an animalistic snarl. "You'll pay fer that!" He lunged towards me, hands outstretched, the others close behind.

A low, menacing growl echoed all around us, stopping the mercenaries cold in their tracks. They looked around nervously, whispering quietly, hands straying to their weapons.

I also looked around wildly, uncertain of what new threat awaited me. Today was just *not* going my way at all. Scanning the shadowy trees around me revealed only deeper shadows. For the first time since I'd entered it, the forest was still. Before, I'd heard bird calls, the rustling of small critters, and the chirping of insects. Even the trees had gone silent, not so much as a breath of air disturbing their leaves. The air itself seemed charged with primordial danger.

Suddenly, Bruce froze, his single eye riveted on something behind me, his wound all but forgotten. All eyes turned in that direction, every hand frozen to a weapon.

"It can't be," Bruce breathed. "They were all...unless you..." His face hardened into a mask of fear and confusion.

Hardly daring to breathe, my heart thudding loudly in my ears, I turned my head just in time to see a massive black shadow with piercing blue eyes leap over my head to crash directly into Bruce. They went down in a whirlwind of flashing fangs and flailing limbs, blood spraying in a wide arc, growls and grunts of pain mixing in a cacophony of sounds.

I stood transfixed by the battle, man grappling with beast. At this point, I couldn't even distinguish where one ended and the other began. Snarls and whimpers punctuated the night air.

Why was the beast fighting the mercenary? It had completely ignored me—perhaps because I didn't seem to offer any kind of threat to it? But what timing! It almost seemed as if...the beast was protecting me. I shook my head in denial, wincing at the answering pain, the black at the edges of my vision creeping closer to the center.

I staggered, dizzy, as the beast disentangled himself from Bruce, who sat panting on the ground, deep gashes bleeding freely on his broad chest. The wolf-beast planted one clawed paw on his back, shoving him back down, before lowering his head and softly closing his fangs around Bruce's neck. Bruce froze, the teeth pausing centimeters from his jugular, as the beast gave a low, meaningful growl, his icy gaze roving over the other mercenaries, his threat made clear.

The men, one by one, dropped their eyes in submission. I marveled at what had just happened: the so-called beast was intelligent enough to identify the men's leader, strong enough to defeat him, and wise enough to use him as a hostage to keep the other men from attacking him as a group. If I had had any remaining doubts as to the existence of a beast in the Forgotten Forest, those doubts were long gone now.

Once the last of the men had lowered his eyes, the wolf-beast gave one final growl before slowly opening his powerful jaws and releasing Bruce, who remained as still as a statue until those teeth were a safe distance away from his neck.

But then the beast turned towards me, padding slowly forward, as silent and graceful as a dancer. I stumbled backward, my boot catching on a hidden root and sending me tumbling to the ground once again, the darkness reaching ever farther over my eyes. I desperately scooted backwards, my hand clutching the silver pendant to my chest. Then my back hit the rough bark of a wide tree, and I held the pendant in front of me like a little dagger, my breath coming in rasping gasps. I hadn't thought it was possible to become even more terrified than I already was.

    The wolf padded closer before coming to a stop directly in front of me. He towered over me, a regal and dangerous shadow, silhouetted by the full moon, his icy gaze piercing my own. The hand that held the silver crescent started trembling, and the last thing I saw before the darkness dragged me into the deep was the sadness that seemed to soften those glacial eyes.

6

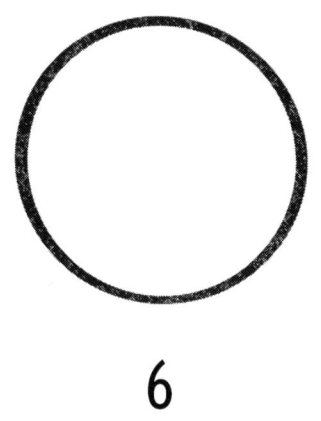

I picked my way carefully through the shattered glass, wincing as a small shard I had missed scraped my little toe, leaving a fine red line. My torn and stained dress, if you could still call it that, fluttered around me from the chilly breeze coming from the broken window in the kitchen.

Today was a very special day. I was officially five years old, which was old enough to ride a pony! Tomorrow, the nice rancher family had promised I could ride one of their ponies as a special birthday treat. But first, I needed to make it to tomorrow, so I headed into the kitchen, despite the cold.

Carefully, I eased open each cupboard in the kitchen, searching every dim nook and dusty cranny for something I could eat to dull the ache in my belly. Finding nothing but dust bunnies and cobwebs, I mustered up what courage I had left and hopped my way through the broken glass, avoiding all of the shards this time. I didn't have far to go, just to the big bedroom.

I listened intently at the door. Satisfied that I couldn't detect any sobbing or breaking glass, I peeked around the door, wrinkling my nose at the sour smell of the bad drink. Still, my empty belly urged me on, so I padded softly into the room, my eyes glued to the lump in the blanket on the bed.

As I approached, I got a better view of the occupant of the bed. My mother lay propped up on a pillow, a glass of the bad drink in her hand. She was vacantly staring at the unpainted wooden wall, her long red hair appearing dull and disheveled against her gaunt, pale face, stray wisps standing out in random directions. Her threadbare dress was hardly in better condition than mine, the stains mainly from the bad drink instead of dirt or mud from the forest, where I spent most of my time these days, playing and exploring. Mama wouldn't go into the forest, so I was always safe there.

"Mama?" I asked, voice quavering. No reaction.

"Mama?" I tried again, a little louder this time. Nothing.

"Mama! Mama I'm hungry! There's no food left," I cried worriedly. My mother slowly turned her head towards me, ungluing her lifeless blue eyes from the wall with some effort.

I smiled timidly at her but was met with that same blank expression. The smile fell from my trembling lips when she finally spoke.

"You want food?" she said. "Go ask your father for some."

"But," I hesitated, "Father's not..." I trailed off nervously.

"Here?!" she shrieked, her face suddenly contorting in rage. "No, he's not! He saddled me with you and ran!"

She hurled her glass, which shattered against the wall, narrowly missing me. I flinched instinctively, covering my eyes with my hands. Shards rained down, a few landing in my hair, a larger piece scratching my chin. She then threw something shiny and silver at me, which bounced off of my forehead before clattering onto the ground. I raised one trembling hand to my forehead and was horrified to see the shiny red splotches now covering it.

"Get out, and take that stupid thing with you. Stop reminding me of him already," she yelled.

Without looking, I closed my little fist around the shiny silver thing, before pivoting and dashing out of the house, tears streaming down my face, and straight into the welcoming darkness of the forest.

I slowly bubbled up towards the light from the comforting darkness. The first thing I noticed was the throbbing in my head. *Why did my head hurt so much?*

It all came back to me in a rush; the noble, the stallion, and the mad dash through the Forgotten Forest, followed by glowing eyes and being hunted by mercenaries. The mercenaries! Had I been captured?! Was it all over for me?

My eyelids felt like they were glued shut, so I used my other senses to figure out if I was in trouble. I quieted my breathing, listening intently. The only sound I could hear was the slight rustling of fabric, but since I also felt a corresponding breeze, that must've meant there was an open window, with curtains. It felt like I was lying on either a bunch of really fluffy clouds, or the softest bed I'd ever encountered. I shifted my wrists and ankles slightly; no ropes or shackles bound me. So either I was under guard, or locked in a room.

With no small effort, I managed to crack open my eyes, blinking them into focus. I was indeed alone in a small room on a bed, a delicate lace curtain fluttering over a partially open window. The room was large and could have easily fit half of my house in it.

Not that that place is my home any longer, I thought bitterly.

I gripped my pendant nervously, half-expecting some guard or servant to come bursting in at any moment.

Ornate furniture filled the room, and an elaborately patterned rug graced the floor. Swirling vines and flowers made up the pattern on the wallpaper, and oil paintings of landscapes filled the walls. This kind of wealth was something a peasant could only dream of. I felt my heart sink as I realized I must be in a noble's residence. Except something was off; a thick layer of dust coated everything, and cobwebs hung in the corners. Though the room was magnificent even under all the grime. I could only imagine how stunning it would look after a thorough cleansing.

I slowly sat up, pausing a moment so my eyes would quit throbbing. I ran my hand along the bed sheet, reveling in the feel of such a soft, smooth fabric.

Could this be silk? I wondered.

I carefully pulled the equally soft covers back, and grimaced at my dirty breeches, which seemed so out of place against the silk. I swung my legs out of bed, burying my toes in the thick rug, despite the dust. Someone must have taken off my socks and riding boots.

I scanned the room until I noticed the tip of my boot peeking out from beside the dresser that stood next to the bed, against the wall. I reached over to grab them, and then put them on, discovering several new bruises and scratches as I did so. My left forearm was swathed in bandages, courtesy of the wickedly sharp rock I'd grazed when I fell off the horse. I hadn't even noticed it right away. I shuddered to think of what would have happened had my head hit that rock, instead of my arm.

My whole body felt like one big bruise. *That's just great,* I grumbled inwardly. *How was I supposed to make a daring escape in this sort of shape?*

Nevertheless, I needed to see what I was up against and if I could figure out where I was. I padded quietly over to the window, the rug absorbing the sound of my footsteps, and braced my hands against the windowsill, leaning into the fresh breeze. I closed my eyes for a moment, inhaling deeply, before opening them again. I was on the ground floor, looking out at a rather overgrown garden. The tall lawn was a vibrant deep green, and a large bed of overgrown roses still boasted several beautiful blossoms in reds, pinks, whites, yellows, purples, and even a few multi-colored ones. I could just make out stone steps leading into the roses.

What looked like the Forgotten Forest had grown quite close to the garden; it was almost as if the grounds hadn't been maintained for some time. From what I had seen, the Lindoras were far too prideful to let any of their estates appear so unkempt. Was I not at the Lindora Estate? If not, then where exactly was I? I highly doubted mercenaries would live in a place like this, unless perhaps they had taken up residence in an abandoned home.

I made my way to the ornate door on the other side of the room, past the comfy-looking couches in the sitting area. As I passed a dressing table and the mirror that was on it, I paused, bringing a hand to my cheek. Someone had bandaged my cheek where that especially big branch had hit it. *I supposed both the mercenaries and Lester wouldn't want their prized brood mare badly damaged, huh?* I scowled, turning back towards the door. *Now, for the moment of truth,* I thought.

I placed my hand on the gilded door handle and turned it.

7

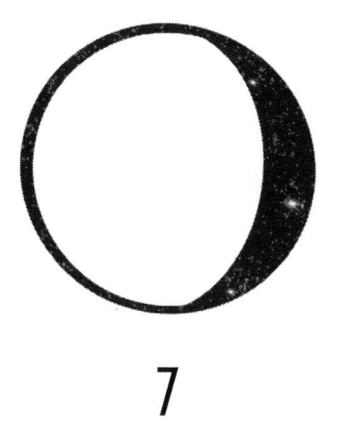

The door wasn't locked! I eased the door open and looked out into a hallway that had the same decorations and same layer of dust as the bedroom I had woken up in.

Fear spiked through me, and for a moment I thought I'd been discovered. That is, until I took a closer look, and realized I'd just had a mild heart attack thanks to the figures standing by the walls.

The spacious hallway was guarded by dull suits of armor that must have once gleamed in the midmorning light filtering in through the large stained-glass windows. Apparently I was now scared of inanimate objects.

Great.

In the remaining spaces on the walls, large oil paintings were proudly mounted in intricate gilded frames. Unlike the ones in the bedroom, these paintings depicted people.

Since no one besides the creepy suits of armor seemed to be around, I stepped out into the hallway and approached the closest painting. An austere and regal man stared back at me, his gray hair standing out against the dark background. Laugh lines radiated out from the corners of his eyes, which were a deep cobalt blue. He wore a formal military jacket, which was adorned with a number of medals that looked very important.

I moved on to the next painting, this one of an older woman with similar features to the man, including her beautiful blue eyes. Although she wore a gown instead of military dress, she seemed every bit as brave and kind as the man.

I stepped past another couple of paintings, each depicting what I assumed to be more heads of the family, and paused in front of a different kind of painting. This one was a family portrait, and judging by the thinner layer of dust and cobwebs, this was a relatively more recent addition. It showed a mother and father seated on ornate chairs, with three children standing beside or behind them. The father wore a military jacket so crowded with medals and ribbons that there couldn't possibly be room for another. I could see a strong family resemblance to the older man in the first portrait I'd examined, with a sharp jaw and piercing blue eyes. It looked like there was some sort of crest or emblem on the ring he wore, but the brush strokes were too indistinct for me to make it out clearly.

The mother smiled softly, her light brown locks pinned back in an elegant bun, with a few strands escaping to frame her delicately pointed face. Her light green eyes were alight with contentment and seemed more stunning thanks to the deep emerald gown she wore.

There were two boys and one girl arrayed around the two, all with rosy cheeks and fine outfits. The girl seemed to be the youngest. She stood next to her mother, her dark blue eyes shining out of a sweet face. Her puffy pink dress and wavy black hair gave her the air of a princess. The second oldest must've been the boy who stood in the middle, between his parents. He had inherited his mother's features most strongly and wore a rather lopsided grin. I would've pegged him as the trouble-maker of the family.

My eyes were drawn to the oldest son, who stood next to his father, a solemn look in his ice-blue eyes. He took after his father, with a shock of dark hair and defined jawline. All of the children were very young, the oldest son likely no more than ten or eleven.

The line of paintings ended at this one. Did that mean this family lived here, or had once lived here? They obviously must have been either nobility or very successful merchants, to be able to afford such a lavish house.

It certainly didn't seem like I was being held captive in the Lindora Duchy, and neither the Lindoras nor any other high-ranking noble would permit their possessions to languor in dust like this. Their sense of pride would never allow it. Unless some minor noble was helping them in return for some favor—but then I would have been locked in the bedroom at the very least.

My fear fizzled out, to be replaced with overwhelming curiosity and a little wariness. At the end of the hallway stood a pair of massive doors, their once shiny handles now dull with age and disuse. I walked toward them and tried lightly tugging on one of them. It barely budged, so I put both hands on the handle and really put my back into it. The massive door creaked open, its hinges protesting noisily.

The door opened to reveal a grand ballroom, complete with dusty marble floors, a sweeping grand staircase, and high stained-glass windows. Tables and chairs had been pushed to the edges of the room and covered with sheets to protect them from dust and damage. The sunlight filtering in through the windows painted the floor in vibrant reds, greens, and blues. Below them, several doors led out to a terrace overlooking the overgrown garden I had seen from the bedroom window.

My footsteps echoed in the cavernous space as I crossed the room to the doors. I marveled at the sheer size of the room. I could almost imagine the balls that must have once been held here, ladies and gentlemen swirling around the floor in their finery and jewels, peals of laughter and conversation filling the room with joyous sound. Perhaps a group of musicians would have been stationed in the corner on that raised platform, their lyrical notes weaving between the dancers. The crystal chandelier would have dazzled all below it, hundreds of candles filling the space with light. Liveried servants would have elegantly circulated around the edges of the ballroom, trays of sugary confections and fruity wines held high. All of the guests would have been able to glide onto the terrace to watch the sun set and the moon rise, the stars spilling across the night sky like scattered diamonds.

This ballroom looked like it had come straight out of a fairy tale. I shook my head to clear it of such fanciful daydreams. I thought I would have found someone by now. Was this place deserted? Had someone brought me here, bandaged my wounds, and then just left?

I headed out onto the terrace, and decided to wander towards the rose garden. I found the stone step pathway I had noticed from my room, and followed its meandering course through the bushes, stepping high or ducking low to avoid reaching thorny stems. I paused every now and then to smell a rose that wasn't too closely guarded by thorns, admiring the wide array of colors and inhaling each delightful fragrance.

My mother used to love roses, especially the deep red ones. She'd said that my father had brought her a rose that perfectly matched her fiery red hair. There had been a time when we'd gone on walks together just to smell the roses.

After a while, the steps ended at a white pavilion, which stood on a raised stone dais. Ruby red and sky-blue roses twined around the white columns holding up the tiled roof. I walked into its center, noting the scuff marks on the ground where a table and chairs likely used to sit. This must have been someone's preferred spot for afternoon tea. Perhaps the lady in that painting used to come here, to sip tea and enjoy pastries surrounded by her roses.

I braced my arms against the half-wall of the pavilion, gazing absently over the roses. From this vantage point, I could clearly see how close the forest had grown to the estate. It might be overgrown now, but perhaps if I walked around the perimeter of the estate, I could spot a road. My ankles throbbed at that thought, reminding me what kind of shape I was in. Even if I *did* find a road, I likely wouldn't make it very far on foot. I sighed wistfully, thinking of the beautiful stallion that had bolted off into the forest. Plus, those mercenaries were likely still hunting for me on Lester's orders. He didn't seem the sort to tolerate failure.

"Do you like them?" asked a deep voice behind me.

I whirled, my heart nearly jumping out of my chest, to face the man who had spoken. I had been so caught up in my thoughts that I hadn't even heard him walking up behind me.

He stood a good two heads taller than me, his messy black hair hanging down past his ears. If I had to guess, I'd say we were about the same age. He wore simple clothes, his shirt sleeves rolled up to his elbows. He carried no weapon that I could see. His jawline could probably cut glass, but it was his eyes that startled me. They were a stunning shade of icy-blue, and were currently boring into mine.

I blushed, realizing I'd been staring, and said lamely, "Do I like...oh, the roses? Yes, I've never seen so many different kinds."

The stranger didn't say anything, and I began to fidget nervously. I had never been a big fan of the awkward silence.

"Do I have you to thank for this?" I asked, holding up my bandaged arm.

He gave a short nod, but made no other reply. *Dark brooding type, much?* I mused to myself sarcastically. He didn't seem like a mercenary. He was certainly muscular, but lacked that arrogant and threatening air that the mercenaries had exuded. Did he know what had become of the mercenaries? Had he seen the wolf-beast in the forest? Why hadn't the beast attacked me too? Maybe he had come across me lying on the ground while hunting or something. But it was still strange to find another soul who was willing to enter the Forgotten Forest. Either way, I owed this man my life.

"Thank you so much for helping me, um... I don't know your name. My name is Serena," I told him.

"You're welcome," he replied. "...Call me Fenn."

8

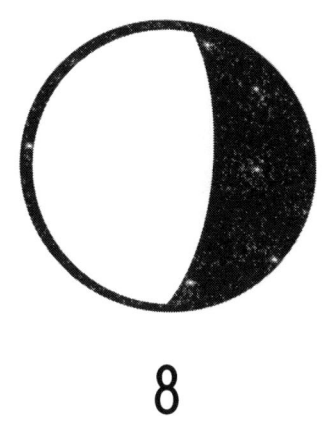

After the rather stilted introductions were made, we stood facing each other in the pavilion. Judging by the fact that Fenn seemed to be the only person in this huge estate, it made logical sense that he must be the one who found me in the woods.

Though it was a little strange-what was this man doing at this otherwise abandoned residence? I supposed this would explain the mystery of the state of the place—I had never known a boy to take to dusting and cleaning all that enthusiastically. Chris had been the exception, as far as horse–related chores went at least.

The thought of Chris sent a pang through my chest. He was probably worried since I hadn't shown up for work today. Would I ever get the chance to see him again?

Refocusing on the conversation, or lack thereof, I asked tentatively, "So, Fenn, I never knew anyone else lived so close to Verdain. How come I've never seen you in town?"

The uncomfortable silence stretched on long enough that I wondered if I shouldn't have asked, when Fenn shifted a bit and replied, "...Not a fan of people."

Clearly.

"Oh, is that why you live out here then?" *By yourself?* I added silently.

Fenn turned his head slightly to gaze at the encroaching forest, his eyes softening slightly.

"Yes. It is quiet. Peaceful."

"I've always felt the same," I agreed, shifting to look at the forest as well. "It feels like you're the only person in the world. And there's an endless number of places to hide," I added with a slight grin. Before Chris' family had taken me in, the forest was where I went to find sanctuary from my mother, from reality.

I started a little when I realized Fenn was staring at me now, instead of the forest. He looked surprised. Again, his vivid blue eyes reminded me of something, but I couldn't quite put my finger on it.

"I guess we both really like the forest then," I said a little self-consciously. I tried to smooth out my hair a little, only to find snarls and a leaf, which I picked out and let fall to the floor.

He nodded. I squirmed.

"Oh, but what do you do for food?" I inquired. His face was so hard to read!

"...Hunt. In the forest. Just what I need," he said stiffly, his eyes once again guarded. If I didn't know better, I'd say he was hiding something. Then again, we were strangers.

"Then did you find me in the forest while you were hunting?" I asked.

He nodded. "You could say that."

"Where you found me in the forest, did you happen to see...anything odd? Like strange tracks, or a large...animal?" I asked tentatively.

The events of last night had become a little hazy, but I knew for absolute certain that something had saved me from the mercenaries. Something powerful, with cold blue eyes.

Fenn hesitated, then opened his mouth to respond. Suddenly, his brow furrowed, his eyes narrowed to slits, and he whipped his head toward the forest, tilting it as if he were listening to the faintest of sounds. I strained my ears, trying to figure out what it was, but I couldn't hear anything besides the sigh of the wind through the rose bushes.

"Fenn...?" I whispered, unsure of what was going on. Why was he acting so strangely?

"Human—Hunters. In the forest. Coming in this direction," he said, his gaze still riveted on the trees, or perhaps what lay beyond them.

I paled at his words, my wounds and bruises giving a throb, reminding me of what, or rather who, was coming for me. Fingers trembling, I clutched at my pounding heart. If they found me again...I was lucky enough to have escaped the first time. Escaping again seemed too much to ask for. And Fenn! There was no telling what a bunch of mercenaries would do to him if they spotted him! Had Lester given orders to keep this whole ugly affair quiet? Would they hurt or even kill someone who helped me escape him? Despite his gruff demeanor, Fenn had bandaged me up, and asked for nothing in return-I couldn't let him get dragged into all of this.

I clenched my hands into fists, already trying to determine in which direction I should run. Maybe if I could make it to the next town over...

"Fenn, I-" I began, my voice wavering in fear.

Fenn turned to stare at me, the suspicion clear on his face.

"You! Did you lead them here on purpose?!" he snarled, stepping closer.

"What? Of course not! I never even knew this place existed!" I snapped back hotly, taken aback by the accusation.

He glared at me, clearly unconvinced.

"But...I am what they are hunting," I said, trying to keep my chin from quivering. "I had hoped...that if I could escape into the forest, I could outrun him, and start a new life far away from here, somewhere he would never find me. Somewhere I'd be safe," I whispered. "I guess I underestimated just how much he wants to own me."

Fenn stiffened at that, his expression changing into one of barely controlled rage.

"Own?" he asked quietly, forcefully.

"My mother sold me to him," I replied to the question in his eyes. "But I would never walk meekly into a life of slavery, no matter how jewel-encrusted the shackles are!" I exclaimed, letting a renewed sense of determination fill my heart, until there was no space left for the fear.

"I'm sorry I brought trouble right to your door, Fenn," I continued, looking down guiltily, "Especially after how you helped patch me up. I should go."

"His name," Fenn demanded.

I hesitated. If Fenn knew the man hunting me was nobility, would he be tempted to hand me over for a reward?

"Tell me his name," he ordered more firmly.

I bit my lip, uncertainty filling me. Could I really trust this eccentric man with my freedom, my future? But if I refused to tell him, wouldn't I be putting Fenn in greater danger? Helping me unknowingly was one thing; Lester would show no mercy to someone who purposefully aided my escape. Could I live with myself if the cost of my bid for freedom was the misery of this man?

"Serena," he said, his voice softening.

"He's...someone powerful," I said before I could change my mind. "The only son of Duke Lindora."

"*Lester* Lindora?" Fenn questioned, an edge of steel entering his voice.

I nodded silently, clasping my hands together. My view of the floor showed his feet close the distance between us. His hand reached out, and I flinched, bracing for a blow that never came.

I felt him grip my chin, his fingers rough with callouses, and gently lift it. I opened my eyes to see him looking at me, something akin to understanding, or respect, in his eyes. My breath caught at his nearness. This close, I could smell his woodsy scent of pine and sunlight.

Staring deeply into my eyes, he told me, "Never apologize for fighting for your freedom."

Gently letting go of my chin, he moved to the entrance of the pavilion. He turned back slightly and said over his shoulder with a lopsided grin, "Stay hidden here. I'll give ol' Lester something to chase." And with that, he was gone.

9

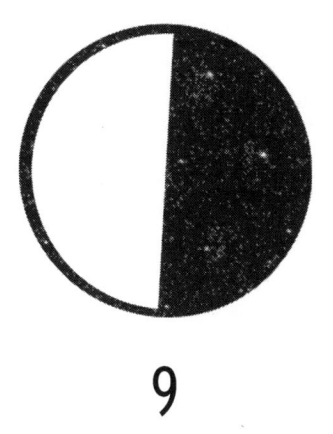

Waiting had never really been one of my strong points. Standing and staring off into the forest didn't make Fenn reappear any sooner. Pacing back and forth like a caged animal didn't seem to be working either.

I sighed in frustration, pausing my pacing once again to glare into the forest, searching for the tiniest of sounds or the slightest movement to indicate his return. The rustle of leaves in the wind and bird calls were my only answer.

What am I even doing? I wondered. I'd never been one to just wait around idly. *Should I go after him?* I took a step, then winced at the answering throb of pain. I was in no shape to go traipsing through the forest again. And even if I was, it was not like I could help fight hunters or mercenaries. Besides, I'd probably just get lost. *I'm enough of a burden to Fenn already,* I thought with no small twinge of regret and irritation, biting my lip. *For now, I should focus on my strengths, and what I can do to help out as I am, with the skills I'm confident in.*

My mind made up, I slowly made my way back through the rose garden and towards the estate. The ridiculously *large* estate. I gave a little sigh. I was bound to stumble across the kitchens at some point, if I kept looking long enough. Right?

⸺

Fenn crouched behind a large, thorny blackberry plant, watching the show play out before him. An extremely sweaty Lester sat on a fine horse, his frivolous, poufy, ruffled clothes looking quite ridiculously out of place in a forest as unforgiving as this one. Lester had become even more obese than Fenn remembered, and that was saying something.

Lester alone was making enough noise to scare off every animal within a two-mile radius, not to mention the racket his servants were making. After locating and following him for a while, Fenn had learned to strategically place himself upwind. The man's odor was so bad that he could hardly pick out any other scents.

The rotund oaf was currently berating his poor servants and hired goons, who looked to be at their wits' end. Fenn picked a few ripe blackberries off the bush and popped them into his mouth one at a time. A show was best watched with snacks.

"Why haven't you found her yet, you imbeciles?!" he roared, waving his pudgy little fists in the air for emphasis.

Fenn wondered how much waving it would take before he unbalanced himself and went tumbling to the ground. It did look like the poor horse could use the break. Was its back supposed to be that curved, or was it a result of having to cart around such an overstuffed load?

"W-we're d-doing our best, m-my lord," stammered what seemed to be the head servant, wringing his hands anxiously. His sad little droopy whiskers made him easy to spot.

Fenn's hackles rose at that word, "lord," and he bared his teeth, barely holding in a growl. Lester was even less worthy of that title than he had been the last time Fenn had seen him.

"Well, do it faster!" the lordling roared. "This forsaken place is unbearably hot!"

Indeed, it looked like his round face was turning rather purple, though it was hard to tell whether it was from the heat or his tantrum. Even his horse was shifting uncomfortably, though that probably had more to do with the great load on its back than the humidity.

"W-we must be cautious, m-my lord," the servant stammered. "S-several of those mercenaries you hired returned seriously wounded. I-it really m-might have been the w-work of the b-beast"

"Superstitious nonsense!" he barked. "This so-called 'beast' is a mere peasants' tale to frighten children!"

Fenn grasped one of the stones he had stockpiled earlier, lobbing it into the undergrowth behind the lordling. His horse started, eyes wide and nostrils flaring, ears flicking back and forth. The slight movement nearly toppled the lordling from his mount. He had to scramble a bit to stay upright, much to Fenn's amusement.

"W-what was that?!" blustered the noble once he had regained his seat. "You!" he shouted, gesturing wildly at the group of guards a little ways away, who seemed to be consulting with the hired hunters. "Go and investigate!"

Fenn caught one of the guards rolling his eyes, and one of the hunters muttered, "What will it be this time? Another squirrel? Perhaps a little bunny rabbit?"

Nevertheless, they all made their way over. Another guard cursed when he tripped on a root, barely catching himself in time to avoid a nasty fall. These men had obviously never stepped foot inside a forest before.

Fenn lobbed another stone, this time landing it a little farther from the first, in the direction of the town.

"There she is! Don't let her get away!" roared the aristocrat, pointing a pudgy finger towards the sound, his many rings glinting in the scattered beams of sunlight.

"S-she's trying t-to escape to V-Verdain!" cried the servant.

"We're on it," sighed the guards as they began to chase the ghost.

Fenn smirked. That's right, keep going that way. He'd give them something to really complain about. They'd wish they'd never dared to trespass in his territory.

***

Many hours and many, many rocks later, Fenn sat high in a sturdy oak tree, beholding the fruits of his labor. Lester, his servants and guards, and even one of the huntsmen, were all thrashing around in a mud pit. A cacophony of cursing could likely be heard for miles, though the high-pitched whining and shrieking of the lordling drowned out the rest.

At some additional noise-making on his part, the horse had spooked, dumping its rider into the pit. Naturally, the lordling's first words after he had regained his senses, besides the curses, were complaints about his fancy embroidered tunic and coat being ruined. The horse was smart enough to run off while it could. The servants and guards, on the other hand, were not quite so fortunate. Their attempts at rescuing their master had resulted in every one of them also winding up stuck. It wasn't just a mud pit. It was a muddy sink-hole, and extremely difficult from which to escape.

The one time Fenn had made the mistake of playing in there, it had taken both his brother and his father ages to get him out. Fenn scowled, shoving that memory back into the box he never opened. He was tired of wallowing in his grief.

At the very least, it should take these fools half a day or more to free both themselves and their master. Now that Fenn looked, he couldn't quite unsee it. The fat noble looked very much like a pig in a mud stye from this vantage point.

"This is all your fault!" screamed the pig, thrashing around and thoroughly coating himself and anyone unfortunate enough to be in range with mud.

There was no doubt in Fenn's mind that Lester would need at least several days to recuperate from his little foray into the forest. At least he'd bought the girl some time.

Fenn's sharp ears even picked up the servant muttering to himself, "A-at least we d-didn't run into t-the b-beast."

Fenn grinned to himself.

10

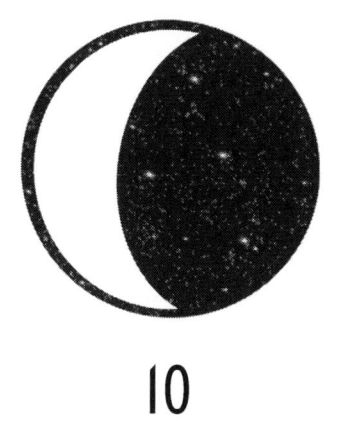

I had just finished when Fenn walked through the kitchen door, nearly stopping my heart with surprise.

"Oh, I'm so glad you're back! Are you okay? What happened?" I blurted out, scanning him from head to toe. I noticed some dirt smudges here and there, and a small tear in his sleeve. Though I couldn't quite remember if that had been there before he left or not.

"You're hurt!" I exclaimed as my eyes noticed the fine red line just visible through the tear. Definitely new then.

"I didn't notice. It's fine. I heal quickly," Fenn stated, shrugging. "Those men. They won't bother us for a while. They'll never find this place."

"Really?" I whispered, the tension I hadn't realized I'd been carrying slipping from my shoulders. "That's a relief. Thank you," I told him, really meaning it. I guess I was safe for now. It finally felt like I could breathe for the first time since I'd laid eyes on Lester.

"Let me take a look at that scratch. Come, sit down," I ordered. He looked like he was about to argue but sat down anyways at my tone.

I went and fetched the medicine bag I'd discovered earlier and took out the cleansing oil, a clean rag, and some bandages. I widened the tear in his sleeve so I could wipe away some dirt and use the oil to clean the wound. The split fortunately was quite shallow, though it was a straight line, and not ragged like it should have been if the wound had been caused by a stray tree branch or thorn. This wound had been made by a blade.

"You're not hurt anywhere else, are you?" I asked, double-checking for any injury I might have missed. I didn't see any other visible marks, at least.

"No. I just didn't expect that hunter to chuck a dagger at me. Still, he was slow. Not much of a challenge," Fenn stated matter-of-factly, with a small shrug.

I paused, taken aback. A hunter chucking daggers at him wasn't 'much of a challenge?' Who exactly was this strange man? Was I really safe with him?

"I'm so sorry. This is all my fault," I mumbled miserably, my shoulders drooping. "If I hadn't—"

"If you hadn't fought for your freedom, then I never would have gotten to meet you," Fenn said, turning his head so he could look me directly in the eyes, before glancing away again. "Besides. I've been bored. Needed the exercise."

I blinked, surprised. I think that was the longest sentence I'd heard from him all day. This huge empty house...it must have been lonely for him. "I...thank you, Fenn," I said, smiling slightly. I squared my shoulders and set about finishing up cleaning his injury.

"Earlier, it sounded like you knew Lester," I said as I tied a secure knot to keep the bandage in place. "Have you...met him before?"

He stiffened, his eyes shuttering. He stood abruptly and gave a terse, "Don't want to talk about it," before striding toward the doors.

"Wait!" I cried, reaching out to stop him, halting just short of his still wounded arm. He paused, waiting. "Fenn, I didn't...Here, take this with you," I stammered, rushing back to the stove and ladling the soup I had made into a bowl, plopping in a spoon. I held it out to him, hoping he would take it.

"To thank you for saving me twice in one day. You said you normally eat meat, so I made some meat stew for you. I used some dried meat I found in the pantry—I hope you like it," I rambled on.

He took the bowl gently, nodding his thanks, and left.

I sighed, strangely disappointed, before setting about getting my own bowl. I'd spent most of the afternoon cleaning the kitchens and cooking. At least the stew had been ready when Fenn arrived. I slowly packed up the medicine bag, stowing it back in its cupboard.

Why had he suddenly gone from chatty to stiff and silent?

I sat down with my soup and ate in silence, surveying the work I'd gotten done. Most of the dust was gone, and the floors were swept clean of dirt and dust balls. I'd managed to polish some of the pots and pans, but I'd only found two sets of silverware that had been scattered about. There was clearly storage for more, so I wondered what had happened to the rest of it.

There was even an entire row of cupboards filled with delicate fine china, glasses made of crystal, and serving platters. I hadn't touched those. They seemed too delicate, and besides, I would've never been able to afford to replace even one glass if I accidentally damaged or broke one. Not that Fenn seemed like the kind of person that would care about things like that, as evidenced by the dust.

At home, we'd always used our one pot and pan, and we used the same bowls and utensils for every meal. There were probably enough bowls in here that I could use a different one for every meal for months before running out.

I finished my meal and cleaned my dishes, drying them and putting them away. I wouldn't mind washing Fenn's dishes too, but I had no idea where he'd run off to. But wandering around the place searching for him might not be the best idea.

Restless, I left the kitchens and walked out the side door to the vegetable garden right outside. The plants were crowding each other, each competing for the most light and room. I'd always enjoyed gardening, both for food and for peace and quiet. There was something about freshly turned soil and the aroma of greenery that I found calming. Even the monotonous task of watering them provided an opportunity to sort through my thoughts and daydream about the future.

So, I set to work, weeding and pruning with some tools I'd discovered in an unlocked shed in the corner. The approaching sunset cast warm golden light over the garden, coating my brow with a fine sheen of sweat for my efforts.

While pulling up crabgrass and mint, which had spread everywhere, I started wondering, what now? Hopefully Fenn would let me stay at least until most of my injuries were healed. He was certainly a strange one, but he'd had plenty of opportunities to hurt me if he'd wanted to. I think I could trust him, for now. But then what? I hadn't exactly had much of a plan when I made my escape yesterday. What felt like a lifetime had passed in the last twenty-four hours. I supposed I would just have to take it day-by-day, and figure it out as I went.

I certainly did not have enough coin saved up to purchase a horse, let alone a ranch. If only that stallion hadn't spooked and run off into the forest. If only I had finished paying for Soren. I sighed, annoyed with myself. There was no point in whining about what had already happened or wishing I had done things differently. I needed to focus on my goals for the future and the next steps I could take today to meet that goal.

The next day dawned gray and misty, in keeping with my mood. I'd tossed and turned all night, settling into a light doze in the early hours. But all the birds that lived in the forest around the estate had started warbling and singing, calling and screeching the moment the first rays had touched the treetops.

If I was being honest with myself, that wasn't the real reason I hadn't gotten so much as a wink of good sleep. My body may have been tired and sore, but my mind just wouldn't shut down. My future had seemed so certain for the last few years, and I had been making so much progress, that suddenly being back in that place where absolutely nothing, not even my meals, were set in stone was terrifying. I had almost forgotten exactly how much I despised this feeling.

For a time, the only way to get food for my mother and I had been to beg for it. From neighbors. From strangers when the neighbors stopped caring. From passing travelers when the kind strangers became irritated acquaintances.

The only person who'd never grown tired of me and my hunger was Chris and his family. And when I became fascinated with their horses, instead of shooing me away, they taught me. They gave me hope for a future, any future. And I'd run away without so much as a goodbye. Chris, at least, would understand, if he could figure out the reason why.

Maybe, after all this was over, I could visit the Rangers in secret to thank them, and let them know what was going on.

I rolled out of bed and groggily dressed, wincing as I discovered a couple new bruises. Fenn seemed like the type to rise early, so I needed to get moving.

It didn't take me too long to collect all the ingredients I needed, though I did have to make a couple of substitutions. Hopefully, what I was making would help smooth things over with Fenn.

My mother had been the one to teach me how to make a good hearty bread. She'd laughed when I'd managed to cover myself from head to toe in flour, her eyes sparkling with mirth and love. Cooking had always been our special time together, when mom could take a break from working as a seamstress. Where had our relationship gone so wrong?

Shaking my head to clear it of such painful thoughts, I focused on kneading the dough I'd been working on for the last ten minutes. I always could think better when I was doing something with my hands. Picking up the ball of dough, I slammed it into the table, pouring my grief and frustration into each repetitive motion. Normally, I could work out my frustration by mucking stalls or cleaning tack. But I didn't have a stable to go to anymore, did I?! *Whack.* No family either. *Whack.* No home. *Whack.*

"I didn't know cooking could be so...violent," commented Fenn from where he leaned against the doorframe, arms folded across his broad chest, one eyebrow raised.

"Fenn!" I exclaimed, nearly dropping the dough on the floor in surprise. I'd been so focused I hadn't heard him coming. My cheeks flamed, and I glanced down in embarrassment, noting that the dough was looking a little over-kneaded.

"You'd be surprised," I replied, laughing at myself. "Dough can be a rather tough opponent."

"I can see that," Fenn said, a smile pulling at the corners of his mouth.

"Would you like to give it a try?" I asked a little hesitantly. "It does wonders for the mood."

He was quiet for a moment, his face unreadable, before he pushed off the doorframe and strode over to the other side of the counter, facing me.

"Why not?" he shrugged, that small smile lingering. "You'll have to show me how though. It's been a while since I've tried to cook."

"I had no idea," I said drily, eyeing the spots I hadn't gotten around to cleaning yesterday. Smirking slightly, I continued, "Here. You can start on the second batch." I handed over the bowl, then moved some leftover flour in between us.

"First, coat your hands with some flour," I instructed. "Then, all you have to do is fold the dough over and into itself. You can do that slowly and carefully, but it's more fun to pound it instead."

He did as he was told. I grinned, thinking his large hands looked a little ridiculous covered in flour. Fenn delicately pushed the dough around on the counter as if it might disintegrate at any moment.

"Going the gentle route, I see," I commented with a smile. "You're a natural. Just don't be afraid to really mix it together, or we'll be here all day."

"Thanks," he mumbled softly, looking a tad surprised and putting a little more effort into the motions.

After a few minutes of comfortable silence, accompanied by the soft sounds of dough thudding onto the counter, I asked tentatively, "I noticed that there are stables near the back of the house. Did whomever used to live here keep horses?"

Fenn paused but answered without looking up, "Yes. Usually about a dozen or two."

I waited for a moment, hoping he would continue. But Fenn remained silent. I couldn't contain my curiosity, not when it came to anything horse-related.

"Do you know what kinds of horses they had?" I asked, trying, and probably failing, not to sound too excited.

This time, Fenn looked up, the trace of a smile on his lips. "Friesians. Arabians. A few Fox Trotters."

"Wow," I sighed wistfully, imagining what such a fine group of horses would look like running around a lush green pasture. "What would it be like to ride one of those?"

Fenn's eyes crinkled in amusement, a real smile lighting up his face for the first time since I'd met him.

"You must really like horses," he chuckled.

I blushed slightly, feeling a little defensive and a little pleased at the same time.

"Well, I'd better, considering I train them! Or at least I used to," I said, a touch of melancholy turning my smile a tad bittersweet. "Nothing can compare to flying across the land on the back of a horse, the wind in your face and a song in your heart. It's always been my dream to have my own stables, filled with the most wonderful horses. By working at a ranch, I was able to learn all about how to care for and train them. I was even paying off my own horse, before, well..."

"Before him," Fenn supplied seriously.

"Yes. Before him. Well, I'd always planned on having my stables in another town. I just left a little sooner than I had anticipated," I finished softly.

"That was brave of you," Fenn said, meeting my eyes. Again, I had that nagging feeling that I'd seen them before.

"Thank you, Fenn," I smiled gratefully. "And thank you for leading those hunters away from here. From me. I...I don't know what I'd do if they caught me again."

I furrowed my brow, thinking. I needed to have some sort of plan. Lester didn't seem like the type to just give up once he'd decided something belonged to him. He probably even considered my running away an insult to his pride. There was no telling what he'd do to me if he caught me. I shuddered. I didn't want to continue that line of thinking. Was it only a matter of time? Could I outfox him? Preferably without causing Fenn any more problems than I already had.

Maybe I could sneak into town to grab Soren, leaving the rest of his payment, of course, and take off for a faraway town. Though the other duchy likely could not offer me asylum from someone as powerful as Duke Lindora's son and sole heir. If I truly wanted to escape where Lester could never reach me, I would have to travel to a different country altogether.

I bit my lip, considering. I might be able to disappear into another country, but it would be far more difficult to navigate in a foreign place, not to mention owning property or working there. Eldore was the closest neighboring country to the north, but it was ruled by elves. From what I'd heard, elves weren't so fond of humans. Seahalla, to the south, was maybe my only option. At least there, I could board a ship to a country across the Zalean Sea. But bringing a horse may cost more coppers than I had. I sighed. There was no easy solution to this.

Fenn had been thoughtfully kneading the dough. At my sigh, he looked up, a determined set to his shoulders.

"Maybe we could do something about that," he declared.

"What do you mean?" I asked, startled.

"I'm going to teach you how to fight. We start as soon as that arm is healed up."

11

Several days later, when the cut on my arm had been replaced by shiny pink skin, Fenn declared it was time to start my training the next morning. But apparently when Fenn said *in the morning,* what he really meant to say was, *at the actual buttcrack of dawn.* After he'd knocked on my door to wake me up, I'd blearily stumbled around, gotten dressed and managed to stub my pinky toe on at least three pieces of very sturdy furniture. Splashing some cold water on my face perked me right up before I emerged from the manor and into the brisk morning air.

The first beams of watery sunlight hadn't yet succeeded at dispelling the mist that hung around the gardens like a silky cloud, but they sure did turn each dewdrop into a sparkling diamond. The birds were already calling to each other, but other than that, everything was still and calm.

I breathed in deeply, savoring the damp air and sense of peace that enveloped this place like a thick blanket. I locked that peace inside my heart, knowing I would need it for what came next.

I passed the rose garden and the white gazebo, turning the corner to see the expansive rolling green carpet that was considered the manor's front lawn. In the center of the long gravel carriageway that led from the forest to the front entrance stood a large stone fountain. The flowers and shrubs that had once ringed the basin were now twining around the carved statue in the middle of the fountain. It was hard to make out exactly what it was, but from what I could see, it looked to be some sort of dog, or maybe a wolf.

Fenn waved me over from where he was waiting on the lawn, casually stretching his arms. When I reached him, I could almost swear the ghost of a smile flickered across his face at my glorious bedhead. I had done my best to tame my locks into a passable ponytail to keep it out of the way, but strands still managed to escape out the sides, with two locks framing my face. At least he had the decency not to mention it.

"Good morning, Serena," Fenn said, looking much too handsome and chipper for such an ungodly hour.

"Morning, Fenn," I replied, trying and failing not to yawn.

"Since it's been a couple days, most of your scrapes and bruises should be on the mend. But just to be safe, we won't be doing anything too strenuous today."

I nodded, understanding his logic. Most of my injuries from the fall and the fight had healed enough for moving not to be too painful. As long as I didn't take another hit on top of the already existing bruises, they would fade in another few days.

"That being said, you still need more muscle before I can teach you to fight effectively. So today we're doing strengthening exercises."

Fenn then proceeded to demonstrate various moves that were meant to target specific muscle groups. First, we did a set of push-ups, followed by sit-ups, squats, and a plank.

After I was done with the plank, I collapsed on the grass, panting. Squats weren't a problem for me, since the motion was similar to what I already did on horseback, but whomever came up with the plank was simply evil.

Fenn smirked, and I sat up straight, slowing my breathing to a less embarrassing tempo.

"Ready for set number two?" he asked, grinning.

"Again?" I groaned theatrically, but I got up and moved into position anyways.

After five agonizing sets, during which Fenn corrected my positioning, I flopped dramatically onto the grass. At least Fenn was doing all the exercises too, even if he made everything look effortless.

"After a short break, we'll be running around the estate. Three times." He was definitely smirking when he said that last bit.

"You're hilarious," I gasped.

"Guilty," he quipped back.

I laughed in surprise. Fenn had a sense of humor after all! And here I was beginning to wonder.

We ran and ran until my breath came in rasping gasps. I now had a greater appreciation for how large the estate truly was. Fenn stayed just a few paces ahead of me the whole time, leading the way, and encouraging me to keep going. I was relatively fit from working on a ranch every day, but I still struggled more than I cared to admit.

"That was good for your first day," Fenn said, a hint of approval in his tone.

"Thanks. You're a good teacher," I replied, smiling shyly. At least he didn't think I was a lost cause. I actually felt surprisingly invigorated. And not at all surprisingly, I was starving and ridiculously thirsty.

"Let's take a lunch break," Fenn said as he started heading back towards the kitchens.

I jogged to catch up and fell into step beside him. I had to lengthen my stride to keep up. Looking up at him from the corner of my eye, I found myself wondering about his story. He was a complete mystery, and his expression was always so hard to read. But here and there when he was really focusing on something, his blank mask would slip, and I could catch a glimpse of the emotion beneath. I wondered, *What had made him put up that mask in the first place?*

Once we were back, we each drank a large glass of water, and then I set about making us some lunch. While I was slicing the bread and arranging some of the leftover meat from yesterday, I couldn't help but notice that Fenn had no idea what to do with himself in a kitchen. Knowing him, and considering the state of the kitchen when I first walked in, he'd probably been just scraping by with cooking meat over a fire or something. It was rather comical watching him fidget. He'd sit down, then get up and pace around.

"Lunch is ready," I announced, a smile tugging at the corners of my mouth.

I set our plates down across from each other and took a seat on a stool, Fenn doing the same.

"Thanks for the meal," Fenn said before picking up his sandwich and taking a big bite, then another.

After a few minutes of quiet munching, Fenn said around a mouthful of sandwich, "Next, let's work on the basics of fighting." He frowned, then added, "And how to break out of an opponent's hold. Especially an opponent that's bigger and stronger. With or without a weapon."

I nodded in agreement. If I had to fight again, it would likely be against a man, who would have the size and strength advantage over me.

"But fighting isn't just about fists. It's also important to outsmart and outmaneuver your opponent. Use the terrain to your advantage. Use any nearby object as a weapon. Even positioning your opponent so that the sun shines directly into his eyes can give you an advantage," he continued. "And most importantly, in a real fight, anything goes. Survival is your only goal."

I nodded seriously. But then my eyes lit up with excitement, thoughts of fancy maneuvers and weapon flourishes filling my mind. "I like where this is going," I grinned.

"Good," he said. "Then let's get started."

After grueling session number two, during which Fenn showed me how to properly form a fist so I wouldn't injure myself and throw a straight punch, I repeated the motion until I'd gotten it right. Next, we moved on to lifting weighted objects, first with one hand, and then the other. We even talked about various ways to use the environment to our advantage during a fight. Once Fenn had finally said we were done for the day, I noticed that the bandage I'd put around the scratch on his arm was askew.

"The bandage has come loose. Let me fix that for you," I offered, already reaching for it.

"No don't—" Fenn started, but I'd already unwrapped it to reveal …nothing at all. There was only a faint pink line where the scratch had been before. It looked healed, as if he had gotten the cut weeks ago.

I paused, surprised, then finished rewrapping the strips of cloth. It would still be a good idea to keep dirt and sweat off of it, at least until it was completely gone. Which, at this rate, might very well be tomorrow. He flinched when my hand brushed his shoulder, so I tried to be more careful.

"I, uh...I heal fast," Fenn said stiffly.

"No kidding," I said, laughing a little. "Well, good for you. Wish I could heal that fast. I'd never have to worry about falling off a horse again!"

For a moment, I thought I had succeeded in lightening the mood a bit. Fenn's shoulders did relax a little bit, but he wouldn't quite meet my eyes.

"Good work today," Fenn said, not too subtly changing the subject. "You should get some rest. Tomorrow will be even tougher."

I groaned. At least that familiar devilish gleam was back in his eye. That, I could handle.

12

After five days of grueling conditioning, Fenn insisted that I take a "rest day," so that I wouldn't go overboard and injure myself. In all honesty, getting to sleep in *past dawn* felt ridiculously good. I took my sweet time getting up and dressed and devoted some quality time to working the snarls out of my hair. Even completing such routine tasks left my sore muscles aching, but it was a good ache. It was proof that I was moving forward and becoming stronger.

When I walked into the kitchen to scrounge up something to eat, Fenn, who was seated on a stool and working on what was probably his second breakfast of the day, started chuckling to himself.

"What's so funny?" I huffed indignantly.

"You," he smirked.

"Me? What do you mean, me? I combed my hair and everything!" I informed him, flipping my rosy locks over my shoulder for emphasis.

"You're hobbling around like an old lady," he teased.

"Wha— why you!" I fumed, putting my hands on my hips. My arms protested the movement. "Pffft. You're right," I laughed at myself. "Muscles I didn't even know I had are sore."

"It gets easier with time," Fenn said with a grin.

"It'd better," I grumbled good-naturedly and set about fixing myself something to eat.

I slathered some jam on the last of the bread and devoured it in a decidedly unlady-like fashion. I tilted the bread a little too far and a glob of jam slid off, plopping right onto my shirt.

I glared at it for a moment, releasing a sigh of frustration through my nose. "That's just great."

"Nice one," Fenn commented, the corners of his mouth twitching upward.

"It fits right in with all the other stains and dirt on this thing, doesn't it?" I asked a little ruefully. I hadn't exactly had time to pack a change of clothes during my escape. I'd been making do by dunking my clothes in some water when the smell became a little too noticeable, but the stains were an entirely different issue.

"You could," Fenn paused, but then rushed on, "If you want, you could use some of my sister's old clothes."

"Thanks, Fenn," I said, a little surprised at the gesture but more surprised by the trust. "So...you used to live here with your family, then?" I asked tentatively. That made him a noble. I ran a hand through my hair. Fenn may be a noble, but he was nothing like Lester.

"Yes," Fenn replied, his tone a little clipped. "Though I was sent off to an academy in the Windsom Duchy when I was young. I did spend some holidays and breaks here, at least in the beginning."

I opened my mouth to ask Fenn more about his family—what had happened to them, why he was alone here in this big empty house—but thought better of it. He was just starting to really open up to me. I didn't want to push him too far and cause him to become distant again. I wasn't exactly the most forthcoming about my own family situation either.

Something else clicked in my mind, and I recalled Fenn's reaction when I'd mentioned Lester. "Is that how you know Lester? You must have run into him at social gatherings," I mused.

Fenn nodded. "He and I didn't exactly get along. It was pretty fun to mess with him, though. I remember this one time at the annual hunting tournament when I brought in three times the number of kills he did, including a bear, when I was ten and he was thirty-something. The look on his face was priceless. I heard he was so mad that that night, he got so drunk that he insisted on riding his horse around—but of course, he fell off."

"I don't have a very hard time believing that," I chuckled, picturing the scene in my mind.

"The best part was when he fell off—because he landed in the horse's water trough!" Fenn grinned, his blue eyes sparkling with mirth.

I laughed with him.

"I guess I was pretty lucky that you weren't Lester's biggest fan to begin with," I said.

"I suppose you were," Fenn replied, giving me that lop-sided grin of his that set the butterflies loose within me.

"Well, um, I think I'll go and find something a little less stained to wear," I stammered, desperately hoping my cheeks weren't as pink as they felt. "If you can rustle up some game, I'll make us something tasty tonight. Think you can manage that?"

"Challenge accepted," Fenn said confidently.

I ran my hand along the velvety soft curtains in what I assumed was the bedroom of Fenn's sister. The walls were decorated with a pale pink floral wallpaper, which stood in stark contrast to her wardrobe full of practical attire. There were even brackets on the wall where weapons would have hung.

Of course, there was still a sizable section of extravagant dresses and ball gowns made of silk and taffeta, with intricate lace patterns. I enjoyed looking at those, but couldn't quite bring myself to touch them. I'd probably get dirt on them, or wind up tearing a delicate sleeve. There weren't quite as many dresses as I'd expect a young noblewoman to own, though there were a number of empty hangers.

I turned away from the dresses and began carefully sorting through the more practical outfits. I selected several shirts and tunics and a few pairs of breeches. I tried them on and was happy to discover that they fit fairly well, though perhaps the breeches were a little long on me. But simply rolling up the fabric would solve that problem. Each garment was made of incredibly soft and lightweight fabric that was flexible and easy to move in. These would be perfect for training.

I gathered the clothes in a bundle and placed them on the large, four-poster bed. Next, I took a look at some of the practical footwear; there were several pairs of soft leather riding boots as well as cushioned walking shoes that had thick soles. I tried on a pair of each. Although they were a little too big for me, they still felt amazingly comfortable. I could always wear two pairs of socks to fill in the gaps. I added the shoes and a few pairs of warm, woolen socks to the pile.

I was about to gather up the pile to take it to my room when I paused. I didn't want to pry, but...I also wanted to learn more about Fenn's younger sister.

I walked over to her vanity table, which had a large, gilded mirror in front of it. I sank down slowly onto the cushioned chair, a small cloud of dust drifting down onto the carpeted floor. Carefully, I pulled open the drawers, which were already partially open, so I could see what was inside. The first couple contained mostly empty jars of rouge and lip paint. The rest of the drawers at first appeared to be empty, but I found a thin silk ribbon at the back of one drawer, and a loose pearl in the back of another. Of the remaining two drawers, one was completely empty and the other contained a jeweled hairpin.

Reverently, I took out the golden hairpin and held it up to the light, admiring the way the blue gemstone glittered when I moved it. Part of me was tempted to tuck the beautiful object into a pocket. An item like that could buy me a small house, months of food, or even a horse.

I sighed and gently placed the pin back into the drawer, closing each one securely. Even if Fenn never found out I'd taken it, I would know. And that shame and guilt would eat away at me. Better to leave it.

The rest of the room was much the same; a clashing battle of delicate items for a noblewoman and practical items for someone who wasn't afraid to get a little dirty.

My mind swam with various questions and theories about the former occupant of the room. What had it been like to grow up in such a wonderful place? To have siblings? Had the girl willingly left this place, or was she forced to run away? Did the entire family flee, or were they captured, or worse?

Most of the valuable, easy to carry and easy to sell items in this room were missing. The drawers and doors had all been open or ajar, meaning things had been taken in a hurry.

I grabbed my bundle of clothes and padded back to the room where I was staying, which likely must have been a guest room. I put everything away, but then stood staring out the window for a minute. It was still early afternoon: I had a fair amount of time before Fenn returned.

My mind made up, I exited my room and began to wander through the halls, peeking my head into rooms as I passed and paying more attention to the little details. The sitting rooms and personal studies looked to be in order—the ornate but heavy furniture was all covered in dust. But then I noticed that the metal candle holders in these rooms were gone; only holes in the walls and slight burn marks remained.

As I moved deeper into the estate, I noticed that there were more gaps in between the paintings that lined the halls. The nails on which the art once hung were left purposeless. All the missing items were valuable, but lightweight. Works of art, things made with precious metals and gemstones. Jewelry. Maybe even some dresses, made with fine fabrics and decorated with pearls and lace.

Soon, the hallway became wider, grander. The suits of armor became more frequent. But what stood out the most were the massive claw marks that scored the walls, faded splatters of blood accompanying them. Had whomever attacked this place brought huge hunting hounds with them? The marks grew more frequent until the walls and the floors were covered in them, and focused around one room in particular.

I moved towards the room as if I was wading through sludge, each laborious step increasing my sense of foreboding. I stopped right in front of it, caution and curiosity warring within me.

The double doors hung ajar, as if they had been smashed in. Hesitantly, I stepped inside, and found myself in what must have been the master bedroom of Fenn's parents. Heavy drapes were drawn over the windows, casting the room into a deep gloom, so it took a moment for my eyes to adjust. The room itself was luxurious, but the size of the bed wasn't what brought me to an abrupt halt.

I gasped, bringing my hand up to cover my mouth. The furniture had been smashed to pieces and feathers and stuffing from the pillows and upholstery littered the floor. But the blood—oh, the blood! It had dried to a dark brown, rusty color, but there was just so much of it. It lay splattered across the walls, the furniture, the bed. It had pooled on the fancy rugs, in the deep gouges that had been dug into the floor. Claw marks and slashes from knives and swords told the tale of the ferocious, desperate battle that had been fought here.

How was it *possible* that a noble family had been so brutally attacked and no one knew about it, not even—not even—

Fenn! Oh, poor Fenn! He must have come home, after years away, only to find his house abandoned, to have gone looking, searching for clues, only to find the horror that was this room!

A tear traced down my cheek, followed by another, and another.

"Serena...?" Fenn said softly from behind me. A strangled noise came from his throat.

I turned around slowly. Fenn stood silhouetted in the doorway. His face was in shadow: I couldn't make out his expression. But I saw his hands slowly curl into fists.

"Fenn," I said, my voice breaking on the word. "I—I'm so sorry. I shouldn't—I shouldn't be in here. I—"

Before I could finish, he'd turned on his heel and stormed away, his steps echoing in the devastated hallway.

My knees trembled, starting to buckle. What had I done? Did Fenn hate me now? How could I possibly face him? Should I give him some space? If our roles were reversed, what would I want? No, what would I *need*?

Before I knew it I was stumbling forward, forcing my numb legs to move. Then I was running, racing, tearing out of that desecrated tomb, back down the hallway full of gaps where memories once hung in gilded frames. The sound of the echoing footsteps ahead of me were becoming fainter: I had to move *faster*.

I saw his shadow dart through a doorway that led outside and followed him through it. The radiance of the golden afternoon sun made a mockery of what I'd just witnessed.

"Fenn!" I called out desperately past the lump in my throat. He was already halfway to the forest, but he faltered for just a moment at my tone.

That was all the opening I needed. I put everything I had into a sprint and grabbed onto him from behind in a hug. He froze at the contact, his spine going rigid, his shoulders tensing up.

"I'm sorry," I gasped out, pressing my forehead to the back of his shirt. "I'm sorry I went in there, sorry for what happened. I understand you may not want to even look at me right now." I squeezed my eyes shut.

"But I know that when I was hurting and alone, I would have given anything to have someone, anyone, tell me that even though maybe it wouldn't be okay, it would get better. Not right now perhaps...but someday in the future, the sun would feel warm again and the music would sound sweet. And when that day came, it would no longer hurt to smile."

I felt a tremor run through him. I hugged him harder. I could've sworn I heard him sniffle, felt him take a trembling, fortifying breath.

"I told you my mother sold me to Lester. But I didn't tell you that I can't quite bring myself to hate her for it. For all the times I had to carry her home from the bar, for all the times she spent the money I'd earned for food on liquor, for the time she nearly blinded me as a child.

My resemblance to my absent father, and the whispers and contempt of the other women only reminded her of what she had lost.

"I wish I could've introduced her to you before she began to drown her sorrows in alcohol. Her hair ringed her head like a rosy halo in the sunshine, and we'd spend hours and hours together picking daisies and moonflowers to make flower crowns for each other. We'd go crazy baking all sorts of ridiculous things, like pies filled with plums instead of apples and tarts full of eggs. We'd both end up covered in flour and laughing like loons. We'd stay up and stargaze in the summer, when the whole sky looked like an endless sea of sparkling diamonds. She'd sing me lullabies and tell me stories long into the night, and the next morning I'd find the loving little notes she'd left for me hidden all around the house."

Now I was the one who was taking deep, fortifying breaths. The tears came regardless, flowing like a raging river finally freed from a dam. I hadn't even realized how great a toll bottling up these emotions, these memories, had taken on me.

After a while, Fenn said quietly, "I used to leave notes for my siblings to find when I was little. When I was sent away, that tradition became something new. We'd write letters to each other. Getting those letters is what kept me going. After a while, my brother's letters petered out, but my sister never failed to send me a letter every week."

I opened my eyes to see Fenn looking over his shoulder at me, a hint of red ringing his bright blue eyes. I smiled, not trusting my voice just yet.

He turned his head to gaze into the forest, his gaze dimming with his next words. "That's the reason I came back here, even though it meant expulsion from the academy. One day, my sister's letters just...stopped. I had this horrible feeling—I knew something was wrong. So I got here as fast as I could, but...I was too late. I found my parents' room like...that."

"Oh, Fenn," I murmured.

"I hate staying here, knowing that room is there. But I don't...I don't know what else to do," Fenn whispered, the pain in his voice hauntingly familiar.

I pulled back and walked around to face Fenn, taking his calloused hands in mine. The pain in Fenn's eyes was reflected in my own.

"Maybe we can figure out what comes next...together," I suggested gently, giving his hands a squeeze.

His eyes softened, the defeated slant of his shoulders lifting a little. A hint of what looked suspiciously like hope entered his crystalline eyes. He nodded, and gave my hands a slight squeeze in return.

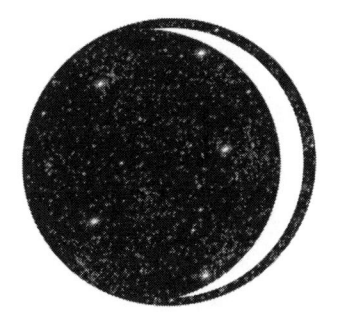

13

For some reason, even though the sunrise looked the exact same today as it had yesterday, it looked different too. Yesterday's had seemed dreary and cold. Today's seemed hopeful and warm. Or maybe it wasn't the sunrise that had changed, but me. I felt like I had captured the slightest glimmer of hope and enthroned it in my heart. And it was growing every day that I spent here. With him.

Shaking my head to clear it of such sappy thoughts, I walked out onto the lawn, toward the figure shrouded in mist waiting for me. As I drew closer, I could see the moment Fenn spotted me, and his face broke into an easy smile. I definitely preferred his smiling face to the serious and almost sad one he used to wear.

"Ready for more combat training, Serena?" he called out, a wicked tilt to his smile, eyes dancing with amusement. I was glad to see that light back in his eyes after our conversation yesterday.

"I still feel like one big bruise from our last session" I replied, hiding an answering smile of my own. "So of course I'm ready to train even harder today."

"That's the spirit," Fenn said, a hint of approval shining in his blue eyes.

For the first time, I noticed that Fenn had a few twigs and leaves caught in his unruly black hair, and there were a couple streaks of dirt on his clothes. It looked like he'd been running around in the forest. *At night! In the dark, with a mysterious beast on the prowl!* I didn't see any visible injuries at least. Maybe he'd just needed some time out in nature to settle his emotions after yesterday's...incident. A slight blush rose unbidden to my cheeks.

"Did you...go into the forest last night?" I questioned, still rather concerned.

"Ah...well," Fenn stammered, looking suddenly uncomfortable. He ran his hand through his hair, his gaze darting away and back again.

"I, uh...I got you...something," he continued, reddening a little.

"You...got me something...from the forest...at night?" I asked, incredulous. "Surely you must know how dangerous the forest is at night! Couldn't you have waited till morning?! Did you go hunting or something?"

"Something like that," he said, clearly missing the point.

"Ok, so what did you hunt? Was it something you wanted me to cook up for dinner?" I pressed when he remained silent.

"Not quite. Here, tie this over your eyes," he urged, handing me a clean strip of cloth he apparently wanted me to use as a blindfold.

"Why?" I asked warily, suddenly nervous. I certainly felt like we'd grown closer after yesterday. Surely Fenn wouldn't hurt me. If he'd meant me harm, he would have just left me in the forest, at the mercy of beast and mercenary alike. I did consider myself a decent judge of character, and he certainly seemed to be kind and genuine. Then again, I had never in my wildest dreams imagined my own mother would sell me off to a human monster. So maybe my character radar wasn't quite as good as I had led myself to believe.

"It's a surprise," he said, excitement seeping into his voice.

It all came down to whether or not I trusted Fenn. After everything he'd done for me and what we'd shared yesterday, the answer was as clear as the crystal glasses in his kitchen (after I'd dusted them off, of course).

I took the blindfold and fashioned it around my head, tying a neat little knot at the back without another thought. Perhaps he did just want a grand reveal of whatever he had caught while out hunting.

"Alright, lead the way, Fenn," I said with a smile, holding out my hand so he could guide me.

After a pause, I felt his rough calloused hand take my smaller, but no less calloused, one and tug me forward. I followed where he led. At one point, I became fairly certain that he was leading me around in circles to confuse my sense of direction, and it was working. Not that I cared at the moment. A silly giggle bubbled out of me at the thought that I was holding hands with the man who had saved my life on a dark night, and now he was leading me in circles around a lonely estate in the middle of the Forgotten Forest. And only a week ago, I'd been living like a normal-ish person.

I could hear the smile in his voice as he said, "Almost there. Just a little longer."

After a few more circles and a few minutes of walking in a straight line, Fenn stopped abruptly. I kept going and walked right into him, giving out a surprised, "Oof," as he caught me. I could feel my cheeks flame, and I laughed nervously.

Fenn gave a low chuckle as he disentangled us. He gently removed the blindfold, saying at the same time, "You can look now." I was facing Fenn as the blindfold was lifted. A gave a silent prayer of thanks that it didn't get tangled in my hair, and I gave another for the rare sight of Fenn giving me a full smile. He looked like he was beaming with pride, so I looked around to see for myself what he was so proud of.

It was staring right back at me. My jaw went slack with disbelief as I gazed at the thing Fenn had "hunted" last night. The Arabian stallion I'd stolen from Lester, escaped with into the forest, and lost when the hunting dogs caught up with us was standing right in front of me, neck arched gracefully, saddle crooked but intact.

"How did you find him?" I breathed, unable to tear my gaze away.

"It wasn't easy," Fenn responded proudly. "Tracking him down wasn't that difficult, but it took me half the night to try and catch the damn thing."

Indeed, it looked like the stallion had been running hard and long, sweat streaking his sides, and bits of leaves and twigs tangled in his silky mane and tail. But I would be overjoyed to give him a full grooming from nose to tail. I'd have him shining in no time.

"It sounded like you really love horses, and I remembered seeing horseshoe tracks near where I...found you, so I figured he couldn't have gotten too far. So I thought...today you could take another rest day and go riding," Fenn finished, suddenly looking rather shy.

I stood frozen in place, dumbfounded. He did all this for me? My eyes welled up with tears, and I let them fall, completely overwhelmed. He'd already saved my body, and now, he was saving my soul.

"W-what's wrong? Why are you crying? I thought you'd be happy!" Fenn asked frantically, a frown furrowing his eyebrows, his eyes boring into mine.

I stepped forward and hugged him, burying my face in his chest. I whispered, "Thank you." Fenn seemed startled at first, but then he hesitantly wrapped his arms around me, laying his head on mine.

Despite the greedy man I knew was still out there, hunting me, I'd never felt so safe.

"He'll need some cleaning up though," he said gruffly into my hair.

I laughed through my tears, unable to help the huge grin on my face.

"Oh, don't you worry about that. I'll have him gleaming in no time!"

14

I whipped my right leg up and kicked out, the solid *thud* sound the impact made telling me I'd done it correctly this time. Beads of sweat ran down my spine, and I quickly wiped some off of my brow before it could sting my eyes. My breath came in controlled gasps, and my muscles ached, but in a good way. Sore muscles meant a hard day's work, that I was making progress toward my goals.

"Never take your eyes off your opponent, even if sweat or blood gets in them," barked Fenn. "An experienced fighter will use that opportunity to take you down. So don't give him that opportunity."

"Right, of course," I gritted out, knowing he was right. Not that I enjoyed admitting it. When it came to fighting, somehow Fenn was always right.

"Again," he ordered, tapping his left arm, which was where I was supposed to be aiming.

The first time he'd told me to actually make contact during a spar, I'd balked at the idea of accidentally hurting him. At least, until I'd discovered the man was practically made of steel. I was pretty sure that anytime I did manage to hit him, I was doing more damage to myself. According to him, "The day you bruise me is the day you can fight those mercenaries yourself." But fortunately for me, bruising him was a very, very long way off in the distant future.

In answer to that thought, my shin throbbed, but I ignored it and dropped into the stance Fenn had taught me. I performed the kick again, but I was a little off-target. Fenn didn't yell at me or anything when I made a mistake, which was a frequent occurrence, but instead, simply pointed out my error and how to correct it for the next attempt.

"Again. Again. Again. Good. Now the right."

And so it went, on and on, until Fenn felt I had sufficiently mastered that day's move. Every morning we spent on strength and stamina training, and every afternoon, Fenn taught me a new move. In the month since my daily lessons first began, I'd learned how to properly form a fist so I wouldn't injure myself, how to throw straight punches and hooks, how to kick from various positions, including from my back on the ground and a number of other fighting moves.

I certainly felt more confident, though I still wasn't sure how well I'd do against one of those mercenaries, let alone a whole group of them. Though maybe...this time around, I wouldn't be alone.

"That's enough of that for today," Fenn announced, relaxing his stiff posture a bit.

"Great! Then let's—," I started.

"I never said we were done though, did I?" Fenn interrupted before I could finish.

I raised an eyebrow, doing my best to look offended and not at all curious about the sudden change in our routine. Fenn had that mischievous look in his eyes again. He always got that look right before...

"Are we trying something new now?" I asked excitedly, completely forgetting my attempt at cool disinterest.

"Weapons training. Starting with this," Fenn grinned, pacing over to a nearby shrub that may have once been trimmed to look like a deer, or maybe a moose. He knelt down and pulled something out, hiding it behind his back as he walked back over to me.

"Oooh! Do I get to learn how to swing a sword? Skewer something with a spear?" I asked, excitedly bouncing on the balls of my feet.

"Since I don't fancy having a limb hacked off by accident, you're going to start with...a dagger," Fenn informed me with a chuckle as he revealed the dagger he had hidden behind his back.

"Oh," I said as the vision of myself masterfully slicing and dicing with a shiny sword went up in smoke.

"Try to contain your excitement," Fenn said drily. He handed me the sheathed weapon, and my fingers brushed his as I carefully took it. The handle was simple and elegant, the soft black leather comfortable in my hand. It was lighter than I expected. I unsheathed it, admiring the keen edge of the blade. Surprisingly, the blade was also black. All of the tools and weapons I'd seen in the town's blacksmith shop had been varying shades of gray. Did that mean this was forged with a different kind of metal?

"I've never seen metal like this before," I mused aloud, examining the blade from different angles.

"That's because it's an elven piece. The dark elves' metal alloys and smithing techniques are their most closely-guarded secret," Fenn explained.

"It's beautiful," I murmured. I supposed it wasn't too surprising that a noble could get his hands on elven work.

"We'll start off on the basics," Fenn told me, gesturing with his hands to demonstrate. "First, practice a forward jab. Use the amount of force you'd use if you intended to actually drive the dagger home. Otherwise, during a real fight, you won't put enough weight behind it to be effective. Like this." He demonstrated the move, his body moving sinuously through the motion. "Go ahead," Fenn encouraged, but still moved a safe distance away.

I tried to mimic Fenn's motion, swiftly striking forward into the empty air. I felt a little ridiculous but gave it my best shot. I looked to Fenn for his reaction and found him shaking his head.

"Like this," he murmured, coming around to stand behind me. He adjusted my stance, then gently wrapped his hand around mine and guided me through the motion. Pink colored my cheeks, and butterflies started fluttering around my stomach. I could hardly concentrate on what I was supposed to be learning with him so close. His scent of pine and warm sunlight wreathed around me, and I silently inhaled.

"Treat the weapon like an extension of your arm," he instructed, seemingly oblivious to my reaction to his proximity. He stepped to the side and said, "Try again."

I took a deep breath and refocused on the exercise. Remembering the feeling of how to do it the right way, and purposefully ignoring any other feelings, I tried again. I could tell I was still a bit off, but I certainly did a better job this time around.

"Better," Fenn said, echoing my thoughts. "Keep focusing like that, and you'll have this move down in no time." He gave me a smirk with that last comment.

I nodded, smiling faintly. Maybe not so oblivious, then.

"About 100 repetitions with each hand should be a good goal for today," he informed me. I almost groaned aloud at that, but steeled myself instead. This was *how I got stronger.* This *was how I could protect myself...and the people I cared about. I could do this. I* had *to do this.* So I moved into the stance Fenn had shown me, and got to work.

I took a much-needed water break after finishing up weapons training for the day. Fenn had offered to hunt some game in the forest for dinner, so he'd likely be gone the rest of the afternoon. It was still pretty early; sunset was at least a couple of hours away, and I wouldn't need too much time to prepare dinner tonight, especially if Fenn's hunt was successful. So far, every time he went hunting, he'd never come back empty-handed.

Well, I knew exactly how to spend the rest of the afternoon. Over the last few weeks, I'd already helped clean and tidy up the parts of the house that Fenn and I used most frequently. Though I hadn't set foot anywhere near *that* room again. I'd also discovered a room that must have once served as the armory, but only a few rusty and broken weapons remained. Instead of more cleaning, and to celebrate my first day of training with a dagger, a nice relaxing ride was in order.

I re-tied my ponytail, which had come loose during training, and stopped in my room to change pants. I was doing my best to take good care of the clothes I'd borrowed from Fenn's sister's room.

I finished changing and headed out back to the stables. I had been so moved when Fenn found the stallion for me. I couldn't help smiling just thinking about it. Of course, I'd thanked him so many times he'd started rolling his eyes at me.

I'd done a thorough deep clean of the stables, washing everything down, putting new straw bedding in the stall I picked out for the stallion, and scrubbing the water troughs and grain bins. After I found the right supplies in the corner of the tack room, I also oiled all the leather tack—not only the saddle and bridle that had been on the stallion when I'd taken him, but also much of the tack that was already in the stables. It was all top quality, and fortunately, the humidity hadn't damaged the leather too much.

All of the brushes, curry combs, and hoof picks had been perfectly fine after some dusting, and true to my word, I'd groomed the stallion until he was ready for a royal parade. I'd even come up with a name for him—Atlas, since his strength had given me a second chance.

Atlas poked his head over the stall door as I walked over to him. I spent a few minutes just rubbing his forehead. The warm scent of hay and the sunlight filtering in through the windows were so comforting and nostalgic. The stables had always been a place of peace for me.

I grabbed his halter from beside the door and put it on him so I could lead him over to the cross-ties. I gave him a quick brush before saddling and bridling him.

After leading him out of the stable, I swung myself up and into the saddle and gathered the reins. The world somehow always looked more beautiful from up here. Or maybe my problems just seemed smaller.

I turned Atlas toward the forest. Normally, I just rode around the estate, racing through the gardens and jumping over small bushes. But earlier, I'd noticed a faint game trail leading into the forest, so I thought I might go on a little trail ride.

Summer was in full swing, and the trees tossed their myriad viridian leaves about in the warm breeze. Atlas walked along fairly calmly, though the occasional rustling of a small animal here and there kept us both on our toes. On either side of the game trail, lush undergrowth grew in a tangled mass, each green tendril desperately reaching for the sunbeams that dappled the forest floor. Every now and then, I had to tug on the reins as Atlas tried to grab a mouthful of some of the thick greenery. Even the birds were out in full force this afternoon, adding their songs to the cadence of the forest.

After winding through the forest for some time, I only became more curious as to where the trail would lead. Pretty soon it would be sunset, and I certainly had no intention of being in the forest at night. So far, nothing good had come out of a night in the forest. Then again, I wouldn't have met Fenn if I hadn't run off into the forest with pursuers on my heels. That, at least, was something to be grateful for.

I was starting to hope that Lester had given up on finding me. As far as I knew, he'd stopped sending men to search for me. Or at least, none of them had made it to the estate looking for me since that one time they'd come too close for comfort.

It would be best if Lester believed I was lost to the forest, or that the beast had eaten me. Hmmm, now that I thought about it, maybe I could just fake my own death-by-beast. Tear up the cloak I'd been wearing that night, scatter a few hairs, splash the blood from a dinner rabbit about, carve some claw marks into nearby trees, and presto! No more Serena to hunt! Surely, Lester would have to give up on me then!

I was so caught up on my scheming that I didn't immediately notice what had caught Atlas' interest. I only realized the problem when Atlas tossed his head, snorting and prancing to the side, his ears pricked forward and to the left of the trail. My heart began to race, and a million thoughts whizzed through my mind. Could there be a large animal nearby? Was it the beast, or perhaps a bear? What if it was Fenn? But what if it wasn't? Oh, why did I think going on a trail ride in the Forgotten Forest was such a good idea?!

We stood stock-still, listening. Now that I was paying attention, I could hear it too—a soft rustling noise. Then, the unmistakable sound of human footfalls.

My heart froze, and I held my breath. So then either that was Fenn, and I was being ridiculous, or, or—. I couldn't risk calling out, just in case. But maybe I hadn't been spotted yet; I could just quietly go back the way I'd come.

I carefully urged Atlas to turn around, praying he would obey and ignore his instinct to identify the threat or just bolt. Atlas started to turn, and I let out a relieved breath.

And that was the exact moment a man burst through the foliage. Our gazes locked, a spark of recognition in his eyes. I recognized him too. He was the mercenary that had suggested "having some fun" with me before turning me over to Lester the Pig.

And naturally, the sudden movement spooked Atlas. I broke eye contact, cursing under my breath as I grappled with the reins to keep Atlas under control. I could hear the man calling out behind him, no doubt to signal the other mercenaries. They never seemed to go anywhere alone.

Atlas danced in place, tossing his head and snorting. I didn't have time for this; I needed to get away! But what if I led them back to the estate? I clearly remembered Fenn's hostility toward me when he thought I'd endangered him and his home purposefully. Maybe I could lose them in the forest, but then I'd be lost too. But then again, once Fenn realized I hadn't returned, he might come looking for me, and he could lead me back.

From the sounds of it, there were other men headed this way, but I still had time. I shortened the length of the reins, turned Atlas to face the part of the trail we hadn't explored yet, and dug my heels into his sides. This time would be different—I was not taking no for an answer.

Under my firm hand, Atlas calmed a little and obediently charged forward along the trail. I just had to hope and pray that wherever this trail led, it was far away from anyone who meant me harm.

As we thundered away, I could hear the man who'd spotted me cursing profusely at my retreating back. He was still tangled up in the brush, and the others hadn't reached him yet. If I could just get out of sight...I could go off trail, maybe find a stream to travel in to disguise my scent to confuse the hunting dogs they likely had with them.

I ducked low in the saddle, Atlas' mane whipping my face with every stride. I kept a sharp eye out for low branches, dodging whenever one came too close. This time, I would not be unseated.

We rounded a turn, taking us fully out of the mercenary's line of sight. My heart was pounding too loudly for me to tell how closely they were pursuing me. So I dug my heels into Atlas' sides again, urging him into another burst of controlled speed. The trees I had been admiring earlier now blurred together, their majesty lost on my panicked eyes.

We followed the trail for what felt like hours but was probably only minutes. After rounding another bend in the trail, I spotted a small stream cutting across the path. I silently gave thanks and checked Atlas' speed. I held my breath, turning my head and listening intently for pursuers. There—after a moment, I could hear them. They were coming, but they weren't too close just yet. A dog bayed, and fear traced an icy finger down my spine.

Fortunately, Atlas didn't balk at walking into the stream, so I pointed him upstream, back in the general direction we'd come from. His hooves splashed down into the water, striking stone, and I slowed him again, fearful a slippery rock could be the end for both of us. A broken leg for a horse was a death sentence.

Mindful of the danger, I pushed Atlas as fast as I dared, desperately needing to be out of sight by the time the men reached the stream. If I was lucky, they'd run right past it and keep going down the trail. But if they were smarter than they looked...then I wouldn't have much time.

As we plodded along, the sun began to set, turning our path into a river of glimmering gold. The further along we went, the wider the stream became. But it was also becoming deeper. I started scanning the banks on either side, searching for a good exit point, not daring to hope for anything familiar. Jagged rocks and thick undergrowth lined each bank, the gaps too thin for a horse to pass through.

After another few minutes, I groaned as I saw a thick tree barring our way forward, its moss-covered trunk stretching from one bank to another. It was small enough that, theoretically, Atlas could've jumped over it, but the landing would be too risky. We'd have to go around.

As I scanned the banks near the fallen tree for an exit point, barking and splashing reached my ears. Atlas' ears flicked back and forward uncertainly, confirming my fear. Not only had the mercenaries followed us, they were close behind. I could only hope they'd split up to search both directions. My heart, which had calmed down a bit, sped back up, and I frantically scanned our surroundings. Then I spotted it, a dirt incline where the roots of the fallen tree now lay, exposed in the fading sunlight.

I urged Atlas toward it, and we scrambled up and over the bank. The splashing was so close now. I couldn't risk re-entering the stream or they'd see me. So I took a deep breath to steel myself and plunged back into the dense trees, my confidence waning with the light.

If only I knew how many of them there were, maybe I could take them on. This was the kind of thing I'd been training for, after all. But I only had the one dagger on me. It wouldn't do me much good if I was surrounded by several of them, especially if they had long-reaching weapons.

Atlas was slowed down by the undergrowth; it was so tall we were practically swimming in it. My only consolation was that it would also slow down our pursuers. I spotted a clearing up ahead. I urged him to go faster, hopeful that I could use Atlas' speed to my advantage over open ground.

Just as we cleared the foliage surrounding the clearing, I was roughly pulled from the saddle and thrown to the ground, my wrenched shoulder screaming in pain. Atlas reared, but didn't run off like last time, since I'd trained him to stay with me.

The man who had grabbed me must have been standing behind a tree, where I couldn't see him. Was it by chance or design that I'd run right past him? As he turned his face toward me, my blood ran cold. How? I was sure he'd been behind me!

That same disgusting look on his face, the pervert leered at me, seemingly taking pleasure in my pain. Even Bruce, the strong leader, would be preferable to this monster. Maybe Lester had rubbed off on him.

"Look'ee what we 'ave here," sneered the man, one startlingly blue eye and one muddy brown eye alight with pleasure. "Lyin' in wait fer ya was the righ' call. Now I 'ave ya all fer meself!"

"So you're not as dumb as you look," I quipped, trying to tamp down on my rising panic. *You've been trained for this,* I reminded myself.

He looked taken aback for a moment, but then his pock-marked face darkened with rage. The instant his grip on my arm loosened, I twisted around and out of his grasp. I swiftly unsheathed my dagger from where it hung from my belt and darted in, the tip of my blade aiming for his neck. He moved at the last second, and my blade pierced his dark eye.

He stumbled back, surprise and pain flitting across his features. He clapped his hands over his eye and howled loud enough to wake the dead. Or draw every hunter and mercenary straight to us. One-on-one I had a chance, but against such a large group...I didn't like my odds.

Before he could recover, I sheathed my blade and sprinted towards where Atlas waited on the other side of the clearing. At the sudden commotion behind me, I glanced over my shoulder and saw the man staggering towards me, blood dripping from his ruined eye, the other promising retribution. Behind him, seven beefy mercenaries were emerging into the clearing.

One axe-carrying man sneered at the one I'd injured. "A little more than you could 'andle, Garrett?" he goaded. "Guess not all the ladies swoon over yer charms, eh?"

"Did ya forget we're to capture 'er alive *and* unharmed?" added a man with a scar through one bushy eyebrow, a short sword strapped to his back.

"Serves ye right," grumbled another.

A few of his fellows snorted at the jabs, telling me that Garrett wasn't particularly popular among them either. Apparently, not all of them were complete monsters after all.

I was halfway to Atlas now. If I could just make it— For a second I thought I saw Fenn's face at the edge of the forest, his face a mask of fury. Hope, relief, and fear coursed through me simultaneously. Hope and relief, that I wasn't lost and alone anymore, and fear that he might get hurt because of me.

I blinked and he was gone. Had I just imagined him? Several of the mercenaries were hot on my tail now. I was almost there; I reached out my hand to grab the dangling reins. I nearly let out a sob when my hand closed over the leather strips.

Everything happened all at once. One of the men caught up to me and grabbed my wrist. A hair-raising growl thundered in the air around us, and my jaw went slack as the massive, dark beast lunged out of the forest and clamped its jaws around the arm that was holding me.

Man and beast tumbled backwards, the mercenary releasing his grip on me in his shock and pain. They grappled on the ground, grunts and growls filling the still air. The beast pinned the mercenary to the ground, and for a brief moment, our eyes locked.

His icy rage-filled eyes softened; he almost seemed to motion with his head for me to flee. I snapped out of my shock, spurred into motion by the all too human intelligence in those eyes.

I vaulted onto Atlas' back and sent him flying into the twilight forest, the sounds of fierce fighting at our backs.

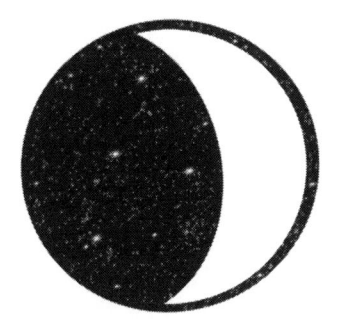

15

My breath came in jagged gasps, the cool night air like daggers in my lungs. I gave Atlas his head, heedless of the direction we were going in now. I was hopelessly lost, and every direction looked the same to me anyways.

As we forged our way through the dense undergrowth, squeezing between trees, the nocturnal critters began to come out. The soothing sound of owls hooting calmed my racing heart, the adrenaline from the fight earlier slowly wearing off. I'd never hurt someone like that before. I shuddered, remembering the horrid feeling of my blade piercing his eye. But even so, if I hadn't defended myself...I didn't even want to think of what might have happened otherwise.

And Fenn! I was sure I had seen him, but then he'd simply vanished into thin air. And then the beast had appeared...right around where Fenn had been. Did that mean the beast had hurt Fenn? For some reason, I couldn't quite believe the beast would do that, despite what I knew it was capable of. It was really as if...as if those blue eyes had been begging me to run.

Was it just luck that the beast somehow appeared every time I was in danger? Before, I'd thought that the beast had gone after the mercenaries while ignoring me because they were clearly the bigger threat. But today, the beast had actually sought out danger when it could have stayed hidden, almost as if it had been protecting me! It seemed the tales about the beast of the Forgotten Forest had not told the whole story.

But the look in those clear blue eyes...Fenn's face appeared in my mind's eye, stunning blue eyes crinkled with laughter, leveled in serious thought, glaring in anger... I gasped as realization hit me like a bolt of lightning. My hands went slack, the reins slipping through numb fingers for a moment before I closed them again.

Fenn was a werewolf.

And not just any werewolf—the supposedly evil beast that prowled this mysterious forest. It was ridiculous, but at the same time, made perfect sense! Why Fenn knew where to find me in the forest that day, how he could always tell what I'd been up to, why he never seemed to tire, why he healed so absurdly fast.

But why hadn't he told me the truth, after he'd saved me? Or even after we started training together? Hurt lanced through me. Was he worried I would be afraid of him, or that maybe I'd try to turn him in or something? Werewolves were uncommon in this country, sure, but it wasn't as if people hated or were especially afraid of them.

Then again, if *I* was the one with that kind of secret, would I be in a hurry to tell it to someone I'd only just met? If I was being honest, probably not. I supposed I couldn't really blame him. Especially since he'd just come to save me, *again*.

Gratitude and worry replaced the brief feeling of hurt. Would Fenn be alright back there? I knew he was strong, but could he take on that many mercenaries alone? I bit my lip, worrying it between my teeth.

Should I try to go back and help him? Even if I could find my way back, wouldn't I only get in his way?

Atlas slowed to a walk, his sides heaving with exertion. I listened intently, but there were no sounds of pursuers behind us. Just then, Atlas stepped out into an open clearing, and I was astonished to find myself back in the beautiful glen with the pond surrounded by lush greenery and moonflowers. The fireflies were just starting to wink into existence around me, illuminating little pockets of space with their warm yellow glow.

I tugged Atlas to a stop in the middle of the glen, and slowly slid off of his back. When my feet hit the ground, a wave of sudden dizziness left me reeling, and I had to cling onto his silken mane to keep from falling over. With my luck today, I'd probably land in some mud puddle. At that wonderful mental image, I laughed out loud. One of Atlas' ears flicked back at the sound as if he was wondering what was wrong with his mistress. That only made me laugh harder.

As the worst of the dizziness subsided, I carefully sank to the ground, keeping the reins in one hand. There was absolutely no way I was repeating what happened last time. This time, I was keeping Atlas close. I would not be horseless and lost in these woods a second time. Especially since Atlas seemed to know his way around better than me.

I put my head in my hands, focusing on taking deep breaths to settle my mind and stomach. I don't know how long I stayed like that, but it was long enough that my limbs started to feel stiff and for Atlas to have recovered his breath and to crop the lush grass around me. The sudden sound of a twig snapping had me whipping my head up and panning our surroundings for more danger. Had I been followed after all? Seeing no movement, I glanced at Atlas and saw that his attention had reverted back to the grass after a brief inspection of our surroundings. I frowned. Did that mean he didn't sense any danger?

Slowly, I got to my feet, still wary of the foreboding forest. My heart couldn't take much more of this.

Movement out of the corner of my eye had me scrambling into the saddle again, before I even registered what I was seeing. Fenn stepped farther into the glen, a smirk hovering on his face.

"You planning on running from me?" he asked with his usual sass, but there was an undercurrent of fear there too.

"Fenn! I'm so glad you're okay! You didn't get caught by the mercenaries, did you?" I rambled, giving a sigh of relief as I dismounted again.

"Let's just say I was the one who did the catching," Fenn quipped with a slight grimace.

As he walked over to me, I realized the reason for his pained expression; Fenn was limping badly, and had a number of cuts along his arms and one nasty one across his chest.

I rushed over to him, all the relief I'd felt at seeing him now turning into anxiety. Atlas gave an indignant snort at the rough tug forward, but I pressed on regardless. Guilt flooded through me, to be overtaken by anger at those wretched men. They'd really done a number on Fenn!

"You're hurt!" I gasped, double-checking for anything life-threatening.

"You should see the other guys," Fenn joked, smirking.

"I'm so sorry, Fenn. This is all my fault!" I exclaimed, guilt and frustration dampening my eyes. "If I hadn't gone into the forest...if I hadn't come here in the first place, then you wouldn't be hurt because of me!" I angrily swiped at my cheeks, furious with myself for feeling so *powerless*.

"Don't say that, Serena," he ordered, the mirth falling from his face, his eyes widening in earnestness.

"You didn't sell yourself to that bastard. You didn't hire mercenaries, or hunters, or send them to hunt a target in the forest." He lifted a hand, placing it softly on my face to make me look him in the eye. "You didn't ask for any of this to happen to you. Despite the odds being stacked against you, you chose to stand up for yourself and your freedom," he said, his thumb wiping away a tear.

"You're far braver than I. And I'm glad to have met you. I may be loath to admit it, but I didn't realize how lonely I'd been until you came along."

"Besides," he murmured, that sparkle of mischief returning to his clear blue eyes, "those guys are no match for me."

His words felt like a soothing balm on the absolutely raw holes in my heart, that my own mother and that pompous noble had left. In my head, I knew that circumstances I had no control over were not my fault. But that knowledge hadn't dulled the pain. To hear him say that I wasn't at fault, that I was doing what was right...it soothed my soul.

"Thank you," I whispered shakily.

Coming back to reality, I gently took Fenn's large, calloused hand in my smaller one, and started toward the pond.

"Let's get you cleaned up before those wounds get infected. I should have enough bandages in my saddle bags, even for someone as reckless as you," I said with a faint smile.

After grabbing everything I'd need from my bags, and giving Atlas a mollifying pat, I knelt down next to Fenn at the edge of the water. I handed Atlas' reins to Fenn, so I could get to work. However, I could only see part of the gash that was on his chest, since his shirt was now a ragged mess.

"I'm going to need to take your shirt off, so I can take care of your injuries," I told him, biting my lip, my cheeks warming.

Fenn hesitated, seeming surprised and a little uncomfortable. "I'm fine. I'll heal soon anyways," he muttered, glancing away.

"What's wrong, Fenn?" I questioned, worry lining my brow.

"It's nothing," he mumbled. At my glare, he fidgeted for a minute before huffing in frustration. "Fine. I...I have many scars."

"Is that what you were worried about? Fenn, I could care less. I have scars too, you know," I informed him, my hand automatically tracing the nearly invisible lines on my cheek and chin where broken glass had cut me. "Scars from my mother's drunken rages, scars from accidents while working with the horses." I showed him a mark just beyond my elbow. "A mare bit me right here when I tightened the saddle's girth. That was an important lesson in reading horse body language," I said ruefully.

"At least let me treat those injuries properly so you won't have to add another scar to your collection," I finished gently.

Fenn's eyes searched mine. Satisfied with what he found, he conceded, saying, "Alright then."

Feeling his blue eyes boring into me, I hesitantly lifted his shirt up and over his head. I couldn't quite conceal the concern in my expression at what I saw. His chiseled torso was criss-crossed with old scars, some of which looked to have been far worse than his current wounds. I looked up and met Fenn's level gaze, but he threw me off when he quipped, "Like what you see?"

I huffed indignantly and flicked his nose, my cheeks achieving a new shade of scarlet. Regardless, I reached out a hand and traced one of his scars. He shivered under my touch.

"How did you get all of these?" I questioned quietly.

"A lifetime of disagreements," he answered, his sly smile flickering a little.

"Will you...tell me about them, sometime?" I asked hesitantly.

For a moment, I thought he wouldn't answer. But then he took my hand and moved it over to a thinner scar on his left bicep.

"I got this one while practicing sword fighting with my little brother," he said, a sad smile tightening his features. "He was a few years younger than me, so I was going easy on him. We were using dulled blades for the first time, so he could get a feel for how different the weight distribution is compared to our wooden practice ones. Suddenly, he noticed that this girl he liked was watching us spar, and he wanted to show off for her. He started swinging all over the place. When he tried to do a flourish, he lost his grip on his sword and it went flying past my arm. It was a shallow wound, but he apologized for months afterward," Fenn finished, a wistful look in his eyes.

"A few of these nicks are actually from him," he chuckled, the corners of his eyes crinkling.

"It sounds like you two were pretty close," I commented.

"We were," Fenn answered ruefully. "We got into loads of trouble together."

"Somehow that doesn't surprise me," I said wryly, with a smirk of my own. "Is that why you're so familiar with this forest, since you explored it with your brother growing up?"

"Yes," he answered but didn't offer anything further.

"So since you grew up here...have you seen that big black wolf before? The townspeople tell all kinds of tales about it" I asked as I dipped a clean cloth into the clear water of the pond, wringing out the excess. I watched for his reaction out of the corner of my eye. *Should I tell him I knew his secret?*

Fenn stiffened imperceptibly, his clear blue eyes shuttering. "Are you...afraid of it?" he asked.

I paused, considering. "The first time I saw it, I was terrified," I recalled, reflecting on that first meeting at this very pond. Fenn's eyes skittered away from mine.

"...I'd heard tales in town about a black beast in these woods. They said it was a monster, that it ate anyone who entered the forest, or that it stole little children from their beds if they misbehaved. But I'd never heard of it harming anyone from town, or even venturing out of the woods. And after last time, and today...no, I'm not afraid of it. If anything, that noble is more of a monster than any beast in this forest could ever be. Besides," I added as I began to carefully wipe away the blood and dirt from Fenn's wounds, "the wolf that protected me today is definitely not a monster. It seems more like my own guardian spirit."

While I was talking, Fenn had turned his head to gaze at me in surprise. Some deeper emotion I couldn't name flitted across his features for a moment before it was gone again, leaving me wondering if I'd even seen it at all. He relaxed again at my words. Maybe that talk about the whole werewolf thing could wait, for now.

I proceeded to carefully dab at his worst injuries. Miraculously, or maybe thanks to the enhanced healing of a werewolf, most of them had already stopped bleeding, though the gash on his chest worried me. It was deeper than the others and blood still leaked from it. Selecting a fresh pad of gauze, I applied some cleansing ointment to it.

"Press this against the center of that gash," I instructed Fenn, who nodded mutely, obediently doing as he was told.

Becoming mildly unnerved by his prolonged silence, I decided to see if I could get him talking again while I wrapped some cloth bandages over the worst of his wounds.

"You had a little sister too, right? What was she like?" I asked.

After a pause, Fenn said, "She always tried to keep up with her brothers. She'd wear breeches and tromp through the forest with us. Mother would always scold her, since we always came back covered in dirt and scrapes. But I think she also secretly liked dressing up to attend parties."

"It sounds like you had so much of fun together," I said with a smile. Tying off a solid knot on the bandages for the last of his serious wounds, I set about applying healing ointment to the various cuts and scratches on his arms. His biceps flexed at the slight sting of the ointment.

"We sure did," he murmured, a distant look clouding his eyes.

I wondered if either of his siblings had escaped that dreadful night when their parents had been attacked. Had they died in that room too? It would be too cruel to voice these questions aloud, even though Fenn had likely already considered such a possibility. I didn't want to see the light go out in his eyes again.

After working in comfortable silence for a few minutes, I rocked back on my heels to survey my work. Fenn was practically wrapped up like a very sexy mummy at this point. But at least the bandages would keep his wounds clean.

When I stilled, the clouds cleared from Fenn's blue eyes, and he took a moment to appraise my nursing skills. Satisfied, he leaned back, bracing his arms behind him.

"As enjoyable as this has been, we should probably be getting back," he suggested with a wry smile. "I'd rather not undo all your hard work by pummeling those trespassers a second time tonight. Especially that one-eyed bastard, Garrett. He won't be a problem anymore."

"Don't you dare," I scolded, trying and failing to keep from grinning as I mockingly shook my finger at him. Though that last line sent a chill down my spine.

Fenn stood up as gracefully, as if he had no injuries, and offered a hand to help me up. Grinning to myself, I took it, letting him pull me to my feet.

"Why don't you ride with me on the way back?" I suggested, hoping the darkness would hide the slight tinge in my cheeks.

He raised an eyebrow, eyeing Atlas skeptically. "He's so spindly. Could he handle my weight too?"

Atlas tossed his head and snorted, seemingly taking offense at the rude suggestion. I laughed, giving Atlas a pat to mollify him.

"Don't worry, he's plenty strong enough, and he's had a nice long break and watering since earlier." I slid the reins back over his head and hopped into the saddle.

"Come on up! Put your left foot in the stirrup so you can swing up behind me," I instructed.

After another snort from Atlas, Fenn swung himself up with little difficulty, settling in behind the saddle.

"You might want to hold onto me," I said with a secretive smile.

"What do you—" Fenn started.

"Atlas, let's go!" I called out, before giving his sides a firm squeeze, sending us rocketing forward, and leaving Fenn scrambling to grab me around the waist before he could fall off.

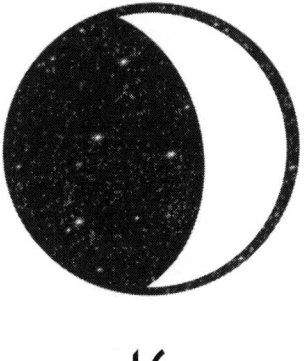

16

Lord Lester Lindora, of the Glorious Lindora Duchy, who was sprawled on the ornate, velvet-cushioned chair he had brought with him on this irksome journey, scratched angrily at the blistering rashes spreading across his protruding belly. He huffed in irritation. His multiple butlers and various servants were proving less and less competent as the days dragged on.

Was it really so difficult to track down one cursed girl?! His stiff, richly dyed attire chafed him, and even his normal pursuits to pass the time, such as punishing servants, feasting on meat and delicacies, and perusing the *goods* on display at brothels could not divert his attention for long.

If *only* he hadn't made a public announcement to every noble in the country before even departing on this trip that he would return with the rarest, most stunning bride in the land. And what could be rarer in a country of blondes and brunettes, than a redhead? Especially one with such vivid green eyes? Upon hearing her description from the information guild's report, he'd set out immediately to lay claim upon her.

His father was becoming impatient for his return, and other nobles had begun to whisper about his apparently foolhardy quest. He needed to put those pompous court ladies in their places! They would all regret turning down his offers of courtship when he returned with this girl...

Lester began impatiently tapping his polished leather boot on the wooden floor. His thick thigh wobbled with the motion, but the sharp, resounding *tap, tap, tap* only slightly lessened his anxiety. What could possibly be taking so long? Surely he was paying enough coin for better service than *this!*

A series of three smart raps sounded on the door to the room, and at once Lester ceased his fidgeting. At last!

"Enter," he barked, his nasally voice reverberating around the rather empty room. How peasants could stand to live in such filth was beyond him.

The door creaked open on loose hinges, and his current head butler ushered in a cloaked stranger, grandly announcing, "You stand before my lord, Lester Lindora, son of Duke Lindora, and heir apparent to the Lindora Duchy. Pay your respects, ruffian," the butler ordered the stranger, glaring at the newcomer.

"My lord, what an—" here the hooded man paused, giving a noticeable sniff at the odor permeating the room, courtesy of Lester's perspiration from the warm day, "indubitable honor it is to stand in your presence." The greeting was accompanied by a graceful bow, but Lester had the unsettling feeling that the eyes beneath that hood did not leave his face for even a moment.

"Took you long enough to get here," Lester sniffed, disdain dripping off every word like wine off his rather patchy mustache.

"My...deepest apologies, my lord," murmured the cloaked figure.

Lester's left eyebrow twitched in irritation at that pause. Was the man slow?

"So you're the best the Keir Guild could offer, hmm?" Lester hummed, his searching eyes unable to locate even a single weapon on the man.

"At your service, my lord," he replied, with a small flourish, which caused his cloak to flutter about his dark leather boots.

If Lester didn't know better, he could have sworn he could hear the man smirking underneath that hood. The audacity!

"Hmph. We'll see about that. I have a job for you. Partial payment upfront," Lester said, nodding to the butler. The butler then produced a small coin purse, which he rather unceremoniously dumped at the feet of the cloaked man, causing several gold coins to spill out.

In one fluid motion, the man bent down and scooped up the bag of coins, which then disappeared soundlessly within the folds of the cloak.

"And the rest of it," Lester smiled grimly, steepling his hands, "upon proof of completion."

Wordlessly, the man spun on his heel, his cloak moving about him like living darkness, and faded into the shadows.

"Are you sure you can keep up with me?" I called to Fenn, grinning.

We had just finished weapons training for the day, and I had just been saddling Atlas when Fenn strolled into the stables with a cocky tilt to his head and that mischievous gleam in his eye.

He'd then essentially challenged me to a race—three times around the extensive front yard of the house, him on foot and me on Atlas. He teased me, saying, "We both know you couldn't catch me on foot." Can't catch him, my ass! We'd just see about that. There was no way I would lose on horseback!

"I'm faster than I look," Fenn smirked up at me. He was currently stretching out his legs in preparation for this little contest.

I tried not to think about the last time I had been racing on horseback, with Fenn holding onto me. That whole experience was just a tangled mess of emotions. Being afraid for my life *again* and being rescued like a damsel in distress by Fenn *again*. At least a little good had come out of—I got to learn a little more about Fenn. Even if the sensation of his strong arms wrapped around my midsection made me all kinds of confused and happy and nervous. And his hot breath on my neck had sent shivers down my spine and had my stomach doing little flips. It was a miracle we'd made it back to the estate at all, considering the state I'd been in by that point. It had been dawn by the time we finally got back.

Atlas must have picked up on the tension in my spine because he started prancing to one side, his hooves striking the grassy earth impatiently.

"Someone's excited," Fenn commented. I assumed he was talking about the horse, but for some reason he was looking at me instead.

"Atlas wants to get this show on the road!" I said, averting my eyes as butterflies took flight in my stomach. I looked out over our "racecourse."

Acres of rolling green lawn spread out before me, split in half by the cobbled road leading to the front entrance of the mansion. Whomever completed three laps around the perimeter of the green would be the winner.

"Loser cooks *and* cleans tonight!" I called over my shoulder with a grin, digging my heels into Atlas' sides.

Atlas took off like a shot, and I leaned forward in the saddle to keep my weight balanced. A quick glance over my shoulder revealed that Fenn was hot on our heels and grinning like a fox in a hen house.

"What happened to 'On your mark, get set, go'?" Fenn called.

"What happened to that confidence of yours?" I quipped back, giggling. I could practically hear Fenn rolling his eyes at me.

Atlas' hooves beat a steady staccato rhythm as we flew across the grass, his long, silky mane flowing in the wind. In no time at all, we were done with our first lap. As we started on the second, I glanced back, prepared to do a little gloating.

To my surprise, Fenn was right behind us, his long legs eating up the distance. When he caught me looking, he gave me a wink and somehow started picking up the pace! I tried not to show my surprise, and instead shifted into racing position. Atlas' ears flicked back at the change, and I urged him on, loosening the reins.

Atlas picked up the slack, and we barreled through the second lap. By this point in the race, a light sheen of sweat had his coat gleaming like polished ebony.

As we began our final lap, I refused to look back. Instead, I gave Atlas his head and asked him for more speed. My long red hair worked its way free of its tie and streamed out behind me like a banner. I closed my eyes for a moment, enjoying the sensation of the wind on my face and the rocking motion of Atlas' smooth stride. It was moments like these that made me happy to be alive—memories of joy and peace I could tuck away for a darker time, when that light would sustain me.

The swift pattering of feet had me opening my eyes, and I gazed in shock at Fenn, who was running beside a galloping horse and actually keeping pace. My jaw dropped in utter surprise. And, naturally, Fenn was smirking at me.

"See you at the finish line!" Fenn called out as he actually *sped up and passed me!*

"Sheesh, are you even human?" I said without thinking. He stumbled for a second but kept on increasing the distance without replying. *Oops. poor choice of words.*

Despite me digging in my heels and sending Atlas flying over the finish line, Fenn still managed to get there first, much to my continued shock and amazement. He hardly even looked winded!

I opened my mouth to tease him a bit but closed it when Fenn's head suddenly snapped toward the forest. His shoulders tensed, and he stared intensely at an especially dark patch between the trees. Even following his gaze, I couldn't detect any sort of movement.

Atlas' ears had also swiveled in the same direction, and he flared his nostrils, scenting for danger. I strained, listening for any sound that would tell me what was out there. It couldn't possibly be the mercenaries; they weren't particularly stealthy.

But then Fenn relaxed, turning to face me. Atlas apparently reached the same conclusion and tried to take a swipe at the grass.

"Was someone there?" I asked, a little shaken by the thought of danger coming so close.

"I thought…I thought I felt eyes on us. The dangerous kind," Fenn replied.

"Was it a mercenary?" I asked nervously.

"No, definitely not," Fenn dismissed my concern. "Whomever it was is gone, at least for now."

"But more importantly, I won!" Fenn exclaimed, grinning from ear to ear.

"How is it possible that—" I started.

"That I enjoy eating your cooking so much? I really couldn't tell ya. However, subjecting you to my cooking would be an offense to all chefs," Fenn interrupted glibly. "Don't worry though, I promise I'll still help out with the clean up afterwards."

"You'd better!" I laughed, deciding not to push the subject. I trusted Fenn's judgment. We hadn't known each other for very long, but since I'd met him, he'd earned my trust thrice over.

"Why don't you prep that rabbit you caught while I give Atlas a quick rub-down?" I asked as I turned Atlas back toward the stable. "I'll be there in a bit!"

"Alright, see you at the house," Fenn said as he started walking back.

"And don't forget to wash your hands first this time!" I taunted over my shoulder, smirking.

I couldn't make out a reply, but I was pretty sure Fenn was grumbling all the way back to the kitchens.

17

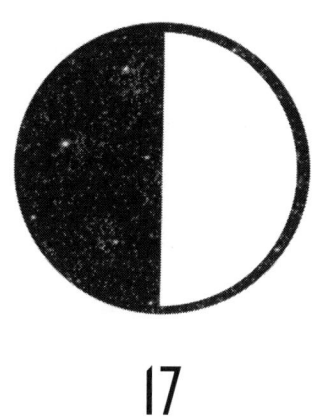

Since I had found some old recipe books while cleaning out the kitchen, I decided to surprise Fenn with some fresh cookies. I was particularly excited to find a recipe for cinnamon rolls, but I couldn't find all the ingredients I needed in the pantry, so that treat would have to wait.

We'd rarely had the ingredients or the equipment to make sweets at home. Though, I no longer truly considered the hut where I'd grown up home. Chris' family and the warm Ranger household had felt safer and more welcoming than my own had since I was little. I hoped they were all doing well. Knowing them, they'd hold onto Soren for me, and I could go back and get him sometime in the future, once the noble had forgotten all about the unruly peasant girl with red hair.

Shaking my head to clear it of such melancholy thoughts, I tied my ruby red locks up in a high ponytail to keep it out of my face. I rolled up my sleeves, donned a fresh apron, and set out all of the ingredients on the table. Consulting the recipe, I measured out flour, sugar, and butter into a big wooden mixing bowl. It was fortunate the butter had been kept in a sealed jar in the cellar. It still amazed me how long the stuff could last when stored properly. Next, I cracked a couple of the eggs Fenn had found on one of his hunting trips into the bowl as well.

Grabbing a curious metal contraption that was apparently called a whisk, according to the recipe book, I began to mix the ingredients together. Then I dumped a little bowl full of huckleberries I'd picked into the mix. I wanted to make sure all the huckleberries were evenly distributed throughout the batter.

Just when I was almost done mixing, I heard the sound of metal on metal. I froze mid-stir, listening. My heart began racing, fear and adrenaline rushing through me. Was that just Fenn practicing with his sword outside?

The sound came again and again, faster and louder than before. I heard Fenn yelling—something he rarely ever did—and then an answering voice that made my hair stand on end. Someone else was here—and he was attacking Fenn!

As silently and swiftly as I could, I put down the bowl and set the apron beside it. I knew Fenn could handle himself, and getting in his way or distracting him at the wrong moment could be disastrous. Maybe I could sneak up and give Fenn an opening to strike. I reached for my dagger but found only empty air.

I cursed silently at my own foolishness. How many times had Fenn told me to carry it with me at all times? I must have left it in my room after our last training session.

But Fenn had also told me to use whatever was around me to gain an advantage. I scanned the kitchen, looking for something I could use as a weapon. I didn't want to waste time hunting for a knife when Fenn might need help, so I quickly grabbed a couple of nearby items I could use, and silently crept out of the kitchen.

Peeking through the window to the gardens, I saw Fenn fighting a stranger who was wearing a pitch-black cloak. The fighting was ferocious; Fenn's dark sword flashing through the air like lightning, only to be met by twin daggers that clashed against it with a sound like thunder. They were moving so quickly I could hardly follow them with my eyes!

But that also meant they were both so focused on battling each other that they wouldn't notice me. As silently as I could, I exited the house, ducking behind an overgrown hedge that lined the pathway. The two fighters were on the other side of the hedge, closer to the forest than the house.

I crept along, keeping an eye on the ground in front of me so that I wouldn't snap a twig, or worse, trip on a rock or a root and make a commotion on the way down. *Now* that *would be embarrassing.*

As I got closer to the end of the hedgerow, I realized they were actually having a conversation—if you could call it that—in between blows and grunts. I started to pick out a few individual words here and there, but what I was hearing didn't make much sense to me.

Something about a job...a dog...and of course many of the typical insults that go along with almost every fight. I stopped, coming to the end of the hedge. I crouched low to the ground and peered through the straggling leaves on the side of the hedge. I set the heavier impromptu weapon down softly in grass so I could grip the other with both hands.

While I was making my way towards them, the ferocious battle had moved closer to my position. Now the cloaked man's back was towards me, Fenn facing off against him with a determined scowl on his face.

A slight breeze blew past me, setting the dark cloak aflutter. Two things happened at once; Fenn's eyes widened, and he glanced directly at my hiding place, and I realized that the movement I had mistaken as fabric moving in the breeze was actually what looked like living shadow detaching itself from the cloak and arrowing straight for Fenn!

The shadows moved like smoke, layers of darkness unfurling, twisting constantly in a dizzying dance. I opened my mouth to shout a warning to Fenn, but it was too late. The shadows wrapped around Fenn's sword while he was distracted, flinging it far out of reach, before surging forward and wrapping around Fenn's throat, pinning him to the ground.

"Oh, how the mighty have fallen!" came the rasping voice from beneath the hood. "To think, the once revered hunting dog of the kingdom could be brought low by a simple shadow technique. When I bring your head back to that pretentious pig of a noble, even the Guildmaster of Keir will have to recognize my talent!"

Keir?! I stifled a gasp. That was the name of the most feared dark guild in the land! The cursed guild had a hand in just about every illegal activity you could think of—but their specialty was assassination. It was rumored that was the reason the emperor turned a seemingly blind eye to them, while exterminating every other dark guild they could find. The crown supposedly had enemies, both foreign and domestic, that the Keir Guild had conveniently "taken care of" for them.

Why on Earth was Lester desperate enough to send an elite Keir assassin after me? He must have realized Fenn was protecting me after our last run-in with that band of mercenaries in the forest.

"What makes you think you're getting out of here alive?" growled Fenn in a guttural voice, lower than I'd ever heard it. The shadow writhed around his neck like a collar, forcing him to bite out the words.

"Ooh, I'm so scared," mocked the assassin. "The orphaned pup thinks it has fangs." Suddenly, the mocking tone was replaced by one that was deadly serious. "Today is the day you die like a dog!"

Fenn snarled at the assassin looming over him, his eyes glowing a bright, icy-blue. The assassin clenched his fist, commanding the shadows to constrict.

Without thinking, I lunged out from behind the hedge, raising my improvised weapon high. The assassin began to whirl around at the sudden movement, his fist loosening, but he wasn't fast enough.

I brought my flour-coated rolling pin smashing down on the back of his head with all the force I could muster. The rolling pin gave a satisfying *crack* as it met his head, though his hood seemed to cushion the blow a bit. He reeled back, stunned by the unexpected blow, and I took my chance to grab the iron skillet I'd left in the grass. Before he could recover, I swung it straight into the back of his neck, and he crumpled to the ground.

The shadows that had been pinning Fenn down rapidly dissipated in the sunlight, leaving no trace that they'd ever even existed. Fenn lay there, staring at me for a few seconds, before climbing to his feet. His eyes were back to their normal blue hue.

Rubbing his neck, he walked over to me, a tad unsteadily at first. He glanced down at my hand, which was still firmly clutching the skillet, before he burst out laughing.

I grinned, all the tension in my body melting away in relief as I sank to my knees. I could hardly believe I'd just done that—and it had actually worked!

"That," Fenn said, wiping away tears, "was the most amazing attack I have ever seen. I can't believe you took out a Shadow Assassin with some cookware."

"Me neither," I exhaled, looking at my hand holding the skillet like it had a mind of its own. "I just grabbed what I had lying around." I let the skillet fall, joining the rolling pin in the grass.

"You made for a pretty good distraction there," I told Fenn, smiling slyly at him. "You kept him monologuing there for a good long while, with your scary face and everything," I laughed a little breathlessly, gesturing towards Fenn.

His eyes shuttered a bit at that last comment, making me regret saying it instantly. But actually, no. I'd told Fenn everything about myself, and no matter what, I could never be anything but accepting of the person who'd saved my life. Several times, in fact.

"I guess I did, huh?" Fenn said, relaxing a bit and running a hand through his hair self-consciously.

"I'm glad I was actually able to be helpful to you this time. Though I guess...you wouldn't have needed help if I wasn't here in the first place," I said, looking down at my clenched hands in my lap. The gravity of the situation hit me as the adrenaline began to fade.

The grass rustled as Fenn bent down in front of me. He covered my trembling hands with one of his own but I didn't look up.

"If I hadn't distracted you while you were fighting, he wouldn't have caught you with his shadows," I said, my voice trembling. "You knew I was there, didn't you?" I accused softly, my vision misting as I finally looked at Fenn.

He opened his mouth, looking like he was about to deny it, then closed it again. Sighing in frustration, he said, "Yes, I could tell you were there. And yes, I was worried for your safety. But, Serena," he said softly, reaching out a hand to gently wipe away the tears spilling down my cheeks, "I had faith in you too. After all, what have you been training for? I don't think those swings would have been nearly as powerful a couple of weeks ago."

Looking at his concerned expression, I realized something didn't quite add up. I'd thought Fenn had been struggling, but...was that really the case? His expression during the fight had been the one he usually wore during...training. I stilled, a sneaking suspicion worming its way into my head. Surely, he wasn't *that* reckless.

"Please tell me you didn't just let yourself get pinned *on purpose* because you wanted me to put into practice what you've been teaching me," I accused flatly, glaring at him. And here I'd been feeling all guilty about getting this conniving guy into a tight spot!

He shifted uncomfortably, and I knew I'd hit the bullseye. I gasped in outrage, clenching my hands into fists.

"You jerk! I was so worried about you! I thought you were in real trouble there!" I shouted, standing up abruptly.

"I thought it would be a good opportunity," Fenn said rather sheepishly, rubbing his neck.

"Mmph," mumbled the assassin. He twitched a bit, letting me know he was starting to come to. I'd been so anxious, I hadn't even thought about disarming him and tying him up. Then again, how did one disarm *shadows?!*

"Perfect timing," I ground out. I picked my skillet back up, stepped over to the assassin, and pulled his hood off. His face was pale and scarred, his puggish nose looking like it'd been broken one too many times and had forgotten how to heal properly.

Now that I had a clear shot and nothing to lessen the blow, I let him have it with the skillet. I swiped roughly at my eyes with my arm. I needed to let out my anger, and at least the stupid assassin was out cold again.

Huffing, I turned to look at Fenn, who was now watching me with some mild concern.

"Well, since apparently you can totally handle this guy yourself, I'll leave you to it. I call dibs on any nice daggers he has though." I hefted the rolling pin in my free hand, resting it over my shoulder like the weapon it had become.

"I *was* baking some cookies for you, but now I'm thinking I'll just eat them all myself. So have fun tying him up," I sniffed indignantly, sashaying back to the kitchen. Now I'd have to clean the blood off the rolling pin.

"Wait—cookies? Oh come on, Serena! It was just a little training exercise!" Fenn whined at my retreating back.

I smiled to myself.

In the end, I brought some cookies to Fenn, and was rewarded with his radiant smile. He'd tied the assassin to a chair in a room filled with daylight, since apparently strong light reduced the power and range of his shadows, though it couldn't entirely prevent him from using them.

After searching him, Fenn had found five daggers, one of which had a curious silver blade, three vials of poison, and six throwing knives concealed on his person. Surprisingly, the man had been hiding a bald head beneath his dark hood. Fenn had left the cloak in a pile on the floor, and I couldn't resist putting it around my shoulders and striding around the room, the cloak billowing out behind me.

I turned towards Fenn in time to catch him watching me and trying not to laugh. I raised one eyebrow. That did it—he burst out laughing, trying and failing not to spew cookie crumbs everywhere.

"You're cleaning that up later," I informed him with a smirk.

"Fine, I will. Just don't hurt me, O Scary Assassin," Fenn teased, laughter lighting up his eyes.

I strutted around for added effect, then pretended to use my shadow powers to snatch another huckleberry cookie for myself. I pulled a chair up next to Fenn's and sat down, the cloak pooling around me like liquid night.

"So, Fenn, how do you know this pasty toad?" I asked casually, gesturing at the still unconscious man across from us.

"I don't know him personally," Fenn stated, his eyes taking on a faraway look as he recalled something. "My family had some unpleasant run-ins with the Keir Guild, so we developed a bit of a reputation among its members. Looks like Lester has taken advantage of that."

"What should we do with him? After we question him, I mean," I clarified.

Fenn regarded me shrewdly, his gaze assessing. "The Keir are known to follow the orders of the highest bidder," he stated slowly, as if considering. "We might not have to kill him, if that's what's worrying you. But if it does come to that, I'll take care of it," Fenn reassured me, his eyes flashing with a steely resolve.

"But first..." Fenn trailed off, glancing at our prisoner. He grabbed the glass of water I'd brought with the cookies and doused the assassin with it. The pale man woke with a start, sputtering as the water dripped off his beaky nose.

He looked around frantically and began tugging at the ropes that bound him. He tried to summon his shadows, but before he'd managed to gather more than a few wisps, Fenn growled, "Don't even try it."

The man glared at Fenn before his baleful black eyes settled on me. "It would seem the hunter has become the hunted," he rasped. His eyes flicked to the cloak on my shoulders.

"We have a few questions for you," I declared more confidently than I felt. "And you'd better answer them if you value your life."

The assassin's laugh sounded like a crow with pneumonia. "We of the Keir do not fear death, little rose."

Fenn stood, stepping slowly but purposefully forward. He twirled one of the assassin's own knives in his hand, brandishing it in front of him. "There may be other things more valuable than your life," Fenn insinuated, glancing down pointedly and angling the knife.

The man went pale, glaring at Fenn with hatred and a hint of grudging respect. He nodded shallowly.

Fenn glanced at me. I took the hint and began with, "We already know who sent you and why." The assassin blinked. "But what's your name?"

For a moment, the man just stared at me. Then he cackled. Now I was the one staring. "What an odd pair you two make," he croaked out, one corner of his mouth twitching up. "I go by Dorent."

"Alright, Dorent," Fenn said as he returned to his chair. He sat down on his chair as if it were a throne, his voice taking on a commanding tone. "First, I want information. Lester's movements, his personnel, his secrets. Second, I want you to report the success of your mission to him. And finally, I want to commission you to obtain a very specific piece of information for me."

"Commission me? How much are we talking?" Dorent asked, narrowing his eyes.

"Oh, I think something appropriate can be arranged," Fenn stated with a wicked grin.

18

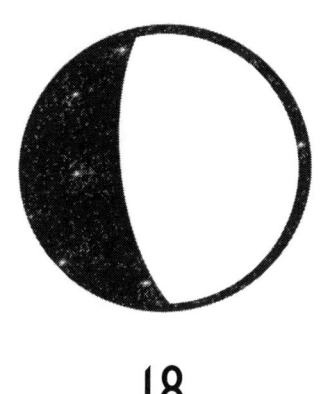

The setting sun cast warm rays of light through the windows in the kitchen, particles of flour dancing in the golden light. But I was much too sore to appreciate the sight. Muscles I hadn't even known I *possessed* ached with a fierce vengeance. Even simply assembling the ingredients for tonight's dinner felt ridiculously difficult.

I did smile at the simple note Fenn had left me in the kitchen. We'd taken to leaving each other little notes in the areas we spent the most time in for the other to find. This afternoon's note simply read, "See you tonight, O Master Chef."

Fenn's conditioning sessions were only getting longer and harder, though. I partially had Dorent to thank for that. I think having a shadow assassin pop up on the lawn had been a bit of a shock for both of us. At least I always had combat and weapons training to look forward to after—and time with Atlas if all else failed. A nice canter across the lawn always helped me relax and clear my mind.

But as tired and achy as I was, it was a good kind of pain. My sore muscles were proof that I was making progress towards my goals, towards becoming someone capable of defending herself, and perhaps, someone else as well, eventually. I could hold my head higher, knowing that I wasn't the same timid girl who was worried about offending one of the town gossips or my own mother. What good had it done me to tiptoe around my mother if she was going to sell me off anyways?

And so I sighed happily, relishing the sensation of stretching my sore muscles as I went about making a hearty meat and vegetable stew for the two of us. I was looking forward to our day of rest tomorrow. The last week had flown by and I was not going to pass up the glorious opportunity to sleep in. If Fenn slept in, it wasn't very late, since he always managed to be up before me. That was one contest I could very happily let him win.

Though this time, I had something special in mind, so I wouldn't be able to sleep in as much as I would've liked.

I yawned, stretching my arms above my head and tucking a stray piece of hair behind my ear. No matter how tightly I wound my bun, a lock or two of hair always managed to slip out and fall around my face.

I was just pouring the aromatic stew into a pair of bowls when Fenn just magically materialized in the doorway. Funny how he always managed to appear at just the right moment, especially when food was involved.

"Do my ears deceive me, or is there a moaning cat in here?" Fenn asked impishly, reaching for the closest bowl.

"You're hilarious," I intoned, giving him the stink eye. "My muscles feel like they've been massaged with a bag of rocks," I grumbled, plopping a spoon in his bowl so strategically that a couple of drops splattered onto his hand.

"But your cooking gets more delicious every day," Fenn complimented me, licking the errants drops off his hand.

Feeling slightly mollified, I responded, "You better believe it," with a slight smile.

We talked a little about training during dinner, but mostly we ate in comfortable silence, our spoons making the only sounds. Fenn washed up after we were done eating, and my eyes kept drooping in the flickering candlelight. Being safe, warm, and full at the same time still felt like a luxury to me.

"Serena," Fenn whispered, placing his warm hand over mine. "Come with me. I want to show you something."

"Hmm? Where are we going?" I mumbled sleepily, rubbing my tired eyes and trying to suppress a yawn.

"It's a surprise," Fenn said, with that mischievous twinkle in his eyes.

"Oh goody, my favorite," I grumbled, but smiled anyway.

Fenn offered his hand, so I took it, letting him pull me to my feet and lead me out of the kitchen and onto the terrace. When he showed no sign of stopping or turning, my steps slowed, worry crowding my mind.

"This surprise isn't in the forest, is it?" I asked apprehensively.

"It is," Fenn replied, giving my hand a little tug.

"Are you sure this is such a good idea?" I asked, biting my lip. "Nothing good ever seems to happen to me at night in that forest. Or any other time, for that matter."

The Forgotten Forest loomed menacingly in the darkness. Even the light of the nearly full moon wasn't strong enough to penetrate the gloom beneath the treetops. I knew it was silly to be so scared of a simple forest. I'd never been afraid of it before. It was just that...between the beasts that guarded its depths and my frequent run-ins with hunters and mercenaries, these days I never left the forest unscathed, or even the same person as when I went in. What if something terrible happened this time as well?

"Don't worry," Fenn told me, his eyes softening. "You're safe with me."

I nodded, letting Fenn pull me forward into the trees. I released the breath I hadn't realized I'd been holding as we stepped under the canopy and into the darkness. I let Fenn guide me, knowing he was much more familiar with this forest than I was. For someone who had been ready to fall asleep on the kitchen table, I sure was wide awake now.

The deeper we ventured into the forest, the harder it became to see. Fenn would point out logs we'd have to hop over and low-hanging branches to avoid. Still, I managed to trip over unseen roots and rocks periodically. The darkness hid my pink cheeks, but I could still hear Fenn chuckle at me.

He led us along a path known only to him, making sudden turns in one direction or another. He moved so silently and stealthily through the trees that he seemed like another denizen of the forest. I supposed he was, in a way. After a while, my eyes adjusted to the gloom, and I was able to avoid most of the obstacles and only tripped on the most well-hidden roots. To Fenn's immense amusement, of course.

Just as I was beginning to wonder if we were going in circles, Fenn came to a halt so abruptly that I nearly ran into him. The area up ahead looked lighter, but Fenn's broad shoulders blocked most of the view.

"We're here," Fenn said quietly, turning to look at me. His face was unreadable, and I shifted nervously. What did he want to show me all the way out here?

He tugged me forward, so I was standing beside him. The hanging branches of a weeping willow tree created a lush curtain in front of us, through which dappled moonlight spilled. Fenn squeezed my hand reassuringly, then reached out his other hand to draw back the living curtain.

I gasped in amazement and delight as I released Fenn's hand and stepped past the curtain, my eyes widening at the beautiful sight before me. A lush, rolling bed of moonflowers blanketed a wide-open clearing. Some of the light I had seen from the forest was thanks to the faint glow each moonflower blossom emitted. Collectively, the field of moonflowers bathed the whole area in soft, silvery light, and fireflies added their own glimmer to the air.

In the center of the clearing, atop a small hill, stood a massive cherry blossom tree, its delicate pink flowers perfuming the air with their sweet fragrance. A small pond lay between two of its roots, purple lilies gracing the edge of the water.

"What are those?" I whispered softly, my gaze riveted on several creatures I'd never seen before. Some lay among the moonflowers, while others lapped at the crystalline water in the pond. They resembled foxes, but their silver fur glowed in the moonlight, and ethereal wings adorned their backs.

"They're called Vulclaria," Fenn whispered back, stepping up next to me. "They live in this forest too, though they're shy of humans. Legend has it that those who manage to catch a glimpse of them will have fortune follow them for the rest of their days."

"I sure could use some of that," I murmured. I noted to myself the way Fenn referred to humans. Did werewolves not consider themselves part human?

Fenn smiled in answer. "You and me both."

"Come on," Fenn said before he began walking away in the direction of the cherry blossom tree. After so long following Fenn hand-in-hand through the forest, mine felt oddly empty now.

I noticed that he managed to find a path through the moonflowers, so he could move forward without crushing any of them. That seemed like the wise thing to do, so I followed suit.

The moment I began walking, every Vulclaria in the clearing turned its gaze on me, ears pricked forward. I was intrigued to note that each fox-like creature had different colored eyes.

I froze, afraid they would all run away, or that they considered me a trespasser. The seconds ticked by like hours, as each crystalline gaze met mine. It almost felt like those eyes were peering into my soul, intent on discerning my essence.

I blinked, and the Vulclaria went back to what they were doing. I let out a little sigh, relieved to have passed whatever kind of test that was. I glanced in Fenn's direction, realizing he had stopped to watch the spectacle. He stood smiling at me from halfway up the hill.

Picking my way carefully through the moonflowers, I made my way over to Fenn, passing a Vulclaria grooming itself. It flicked an ear in my direction, fluffing its feathers as I neared, but gave no other indication that it knew I was there.

"Sorry about that," Fenn said as he ran a hand through his hair. "They're pretty used to me coming here, so I forgot they might be a little surprised by you."

"Heck of a thing to forget," I hissed at him. "It felt like they were peering into my soul or something."

"They were," Fenn said simply. "They won't tolerate being near someone whose soul is clouded by malice."

Without giving me any time to process *that* little tidbit of information, Fenn took my hand again, sending a little thrill through me, and led me the rest of the way up the hill, until we were standing beneath the branches of the cherry blossom tree.

A sudden breeze sprang up, causing loose cherry blossom petals to fall around us like snow. The petals danced and swirled in the air, and a pair of Vulclaria lifted their wings and took to the air. They chased each other among the floating blossoms, spiraling, diving, and rising in their own ethereal dance.

"Wow," I breathed, mesmerized by the display.

When I turned to see Fenn's reaction to the dancing Vulclaria, I found him watching me instead, with the strangest expression on his face. His eyes, normally a light blue, had deepened to bottomless pools of sapphire. Butterflies took flight in my stomach, rivaling the twists and twirls of the two flying Vulclaria.

"This way," Fenn said huskily, showing me to a soft patch of grass under the tree that was relatively flat.

Releasing my hand, Fenn lay back in the patch of grass and patted the spot next to him. Lying down in the damp grass didn't seem particularly appealing to me, but I bit back a small sigh and lay down anyways.

"If you look through the gap between these two branches, you can see the stars," Fenn told me, while pointing out the gap.

It took me a few seconds to find it. Framed by the delicate pink blooms, a tapestry of stars filled the heavens, each one arrayed seamlessly in a never-ending pattern. Constellations both familiar and strange winked at me.

"I never knew such a beautiful place was hidden away in this forest," I said. "Somehow this place makes the darkness seem a little less foreboding."

"Mhmm. This place has always been special to me," Fenn murmured. "I used to come here with my siblings."

"Did you come here with them often?" I asked tentatively.

Fenn didn't answer, but his eyes took on a misty, far-away look, as if he was seeing something, or someone, that wasn't here anymore. Seeing such a pained expression on his face, I immediately regretted asking.

"Nevermind, I shouldn't have asked," I said softly, shifting my gaze back to the stars above us.

Silence stretched between us, interrupted only by the soft rustling of the branches in the wind. Except, only the branches above me were rustling. I felt a spike of alarm until I noticed the pair of curious emerald eyes peering down at me, barely visible amongst all the flowers.

I smiled up at the beautiful little Vulclaria. It cocked its head to one side, then it sort of smiled back at me, its pink tongue lolling out of its mouth like a dog's.

Suddenly, the fox-like creature dove off its branch, aiming straight for my face. Startled, I sat up, planning on dodging the little furball. Fenn looked over at the movement, his gaze refocusing. But he just chuckled as we both watched the ethereal creature extend its wings and glide down into my lap.

Tentatively, I reached out my hand to pet it, pausing to make sure I wasn't about to be bitten. The Vulclaria made a little humming noise, which I took to be a sound of encouragement. I delicately ran my fingers through its soft, silvery fur.

When I lifted my hand again, it closed its eyes and pushed its head into my hand, making that melodic humming noise. I continued stroking it, a smile lighting up my face. I ran my hand through the downy feathers of one wing, feeling like I was touching air given form.

The winged fox gave my hand a lick, before twisting around and swiftly pulling out a small feather from its wing. It nudged my hand until I opened it, then placed the feather on my palm.

"Is this a gift for me?" I asked, touched by the gesture.

"That's its way of saying thanks. I've been told that if a Vulclaria gives you one of its feathers, you can call on it once for aid," Fenn explained, with respect shining in his eyes. "I've never actually seen it happen before, though."

The Vulclaria yipped at Fenn, as if agreeing with him, before curling up in my lap and promptly going to sleep. The gentle rise and fall of its chest felt comforting, and I placed a hand on its back, stroking it absently.

"What amazing creatures," I murmured, gazing at the furry little beastie.

"This is where we would come to get away from all of our responsibilities and all of our parents' expectations," Fenn said quietly, answering my earlier question. "When I was little, I wasn't quite living up to my father's expectations. As the oldest, I needed to be the strongest and fastest, the most intelligent and well-versed, not just of my siblings but of all the children. So, he sent me off to be trained."

Fenn closed his eyes, his lips thinning as he recalled painful memories. "I wasn't allowed to come home until I was top of the class. It took me years to get there, but when I finally returned, after my sister's letters stopped coming..." he trailed off. "Everyone was already gone." He paused for a moment. "I have no way of knowing whether my brother and sister were in that room too," Fenn said forlornly.

"Oh Fenn, I'm so sorry," I said, my hand on my heart. My relationship with my mother was complicated, but at least I knew she was alive.

"Maybe Dorent will be able to find something out," I said, thoughts and plans swirling around in my mind. "We could also see what we could find out ourselves. It's not like we have a reason to stay here. It would be a grand adventure! And who knows, maybe I'll even spot a nice area for a ranch along the way."

Fenn looked surprised, then thoughtful as he mulled over my abrupt proposition. "I...guess I don't see why not. I was hoping I'd be here if either of my siblings returned, assuming they survived that night, but it's been around a year since I came back, and it doesn't seem like that's going to happen."

"Will you go on this adventure with me Serena?" Fenn asked, looking me in the eye.

"Of course!" I replied confidently, smiling in excitement. Traveling around, seeing the country with Fenn... There was nothing I'd like more!

Fenn's eyes dropped to my lips, and heat rose in my belly. I leaned forward imperceptibly, my hand stilling in the Vulclaria's feathers.

Fenn tenderly cupped my face in his hand, his thumb caressing my cheek. His eyes searched mine, questioning.

I leaned into him in answer and closed my eyes as our lips met, and the stars sang.

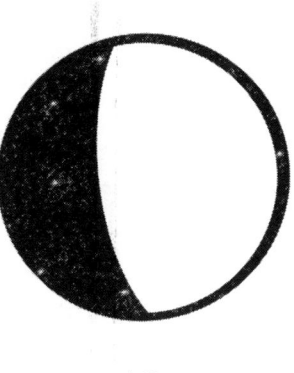

19

I pulled the hood of my cloak down low, casting my face in deeper shadow as I stepped out from beneath the protective canopy of the Forgotten Forest. The pre-dawn light barely illuminated the deserted dirt road into town, and not even the farmers and ranchers were up yet. Which was exactly why I'd picked this time for my little trip into town.

I just needed to pick up a few ingredients we were running low on. Fenn hadn't exactly been excited about the idea, and I could hardly blame him. Going into town, especially when that ridiculous noble was still looking for me, was foolhardy. But the pantry was dangerously low, and although I supposed we could've survived on whatever Fenn could catch in the forest, our cooking sessions together were special to me.

As long as I kept the hood of my cloak up to hide my face and hair, all anyone would see was a traveler passing through. I squared my shoulders and set off down the dirt road, towards the edge of town, Fenn right beside me.

Fenn's shoulder playfully bumped into mine, his own face shrouded in shadow from his hood. He hadn't been to town very frequently, especially not dressed as a commoner, but it was still better to be cautious. Fenn twined his fingers through mine and gave my hand a little reassuring squeeze.

Happiness bubbled up through me at his thoughtfulness. Last night had been so magical, I'd wished it would never end. That memory I tucked away, close to my heart. The feather the emerald-eyed Vulclaria had gifted me was safely hidden beneath my shirt. I'd used a bit of wire to securely attach it to my crescent moon pendant. I'd also strapped my dagger to my thigh. After that surprise visit from the shadow assassin, I'd taken to carrying it with me wherever I went. We were just lucky that Dorent could be bought off and redirected with a bag of gold. Well, more like several bags of gold.

My breath formed a misty cloud in front of me and the chill in the air nipped through my cloak with ease. It only took us a few minutes to reach the edge of town.

We slipped through a narrow alley between two houses, cautiously winding our way through alleyways and side paths. We managed to avoid the main street, where there was a much higher chance of running into someone who might recognize one of us.

By the time we reached the market, my nerves were a frayed mess. Once he'd made sure the area was safe, Fenn went over to the blacksmith's shop alone to acquire a whetstone and some polish, since two hooded figures would garner unwanted attention. The first rays of dawn cast my figure in deeper shadow as I opened the front door, the bell ringing to alert the clerk to my entrance.

A groggy woman shuffled out from the back, where she'd undoubtedly been organizing the day's fresh deliveries for sale. At least she didn't look askance at my outfit; it was fairly common garb for travelers, and Verdain saw enough of them passing through that my disguise wasn't overly suspicious, as long as I didn't draw attention to myself.

"What'll it be?" asked the woman grumpily.

"One scoop of salt and sugar, two crocks of butter, three scoops of flour, and a bag of your freshest vegetables," I requested in a low tone of voice.

"That'll be one silver for all of it," intoned the clerk.

She did not move to begin collecting the items until I had produced the coin and a cloth bag. And even then, she moved about as speedily as a sloth in the sun. I did my best not to fidget.

After what felt like an eternity, the clerk returned my bag with all of my purchases in it. I gave her a polite nod, before turning and hurrying back out through the door.

Making my way onto the main street, I tensed at the sight of the handful of people now occupying it. Most were either local women or maidservants going about their early morning chores and errands.

I began walking behind one such group of maids, far enough away that they wouldn't notice me, but close enough that I could still faintly hear their conversation.

"I have so much extra work to do today," groaned one girl, sighing dramatically.

"Why is that?" questioned another.

"Because Lord Lindora has hired just about every free hand in town. Apparently, he's preparing to leave, to go back to the Duke's estate. Which means I have to do all the tasks that Esther and Rebecca normally take care of."

"He's leaving? Why so suddenly?" wondered the third girl.

"It is rather tragic. I'd been hoping I could get a position at the Lindora estate. I bet the maids there are paid handsomely! Plus, they don't have to put up with 'Do this, Lina, do that, Lina, you're doing it wrong, Lina, don't be stupid, Lina!'" whined the girl whose name was apparently Lina.

"At least you don't have to care for your mistress' newborn!" lamented the other girl.

I fell back as the girls began a contest to determine who had it the worst. *If what they were saying was true, then did that mean Lester had given up on trying to find me?* A thrill of hope ran through me at the thought. Perhaps he had been recalled by his father or had some business matter to attend to elsewhere.

I grinned, overjoyed at the thought that soon, I would no longer have to hide. With the lordling gone, perhaps I could return, finish paying for Soren, and have a proper goodbye with Chris before going on that adventure with Fenn!

I paused for just a few moments to peer into the window of the supply shop, admiring the decorated bridle and soft leather riding gloves that were on display. Maybe, once I had my own stable, I could afford such niceties.

But for now, I just had a couple more errands to run before I could meet back up with Fenn. I continued guardedly along the main street, popping into a shop here and there, and leaving with an additional package or bundle in my arms. One last stop, and then I could make my escape.

The sun was well above the horizon now; most families had finished their breakfasts and were beginning the day's work. Hurriedly, I followed my nose to my final destination.

The bell tinkled as I stepped through the door of the bakery, warmth and the rich aroma of baking bread enveloping me. I tugged on my hood again, just to ensure it was still securely covering my face and approached the counter.

"What can I get for you today, traveler?" asked Mrs. Thompson as she wiped some excess flour onto her apron.

Hearing her familiar, soothing voice again filled me with the kind of happiness that was tinged with sorrow. I would have loved to speak to her as myself, instead of as a traveling stranger. But that was a risk I just wasn't willing to take.

"Four of your cinnamon buns, please," I said, trying to disguise my voice with a lower tone.

Mrs. Thompson paused, cutting a searching glance my way, before resuming her bustling activities with a wide smile.

"Coming right up, dear." She carefully wrapped four steaming buns in some paper and placed them gently on the counter. I handed over the copper coins and was about to leave when she began speaking again.

"Best stay clear of the inn down the road, traveler. A visiting noble has taken over the entire building, so you won't be able to find any lodging there."

I stiffened slightly, clutching my packages a little tighter to my chest. What suspiciously helpful advice. I glanced at my disguise, wondering what gave me away. Sheepishly, I tucked an errant strand of hair back inside my hood. I smiled to myself, relaxing a little, and nodded in thanks.

"And since you're likely unfamiliar with the area, I should also warn you about the dense forest that borders the edge of town. It became known as the Forbidden Forest after a tragedy took place there to a special family some time ago, and fearsome beasts are said to roam its depths, encased in darkness. Even the locals won't go near it now." The spark of an idea ignited, and I stepped closer, hoping to finally find some more clues.

"Do you know what exactly happened to that family?" I asked, trying not to sound overly excited.

"The rumors about that incident have become more distorted as time has passed, I'm afraid. Some say that they were attacked by hired mercenaries." A chill ran down my spine at her words. "Others claim a dark wizard cast a curse upon them. And still others say the family was forced into slavery by a rival family, who was holding one of their children hostage."

"A sad tale, to be sure," I murmured, unnerved by the gruesome possibilities.

"Though perhaps this tale is still unfolding, and may yet have a happy ending, my dear. Chin up," she told me kindly, her dimples flashing.

"Thank you, ma'am," I replied, my smile warming my voice.

"You're welcome, dear. Be safe out there," she told me as I turned and made my exit.

As I stepped out into the warm mid-morning light, a spike of alarm shot through me at the sight of a group of mercenaries loitering outside of the tavern across the street. They were busy chattering amongst themselves and eyeing any female within eyesight, each one clutching at least one tankard of ale. I cautiously scanned their ranks; their leader, Bruce, wasn't among them. If I kept my hood up and didn't attract their attention, I would be fine.

I turned and walked at a leisurely pace down the street and away from the tavern. Just before I was about to slink into a quiet side street, I caught a snippet of the conversation passing between a group of local housewives outside of the nearby apothecary that piqued my interest.

I paused by the windows, pretending to examine the herbs on display while eavesdropping.

"It will be such a relief when those barbarians are gone," whispered one of the ladies, glancing sidelong at the men outside the tavern down the street.

"The sooner the better, if you ask me," grumbled her neighbor, her grip on her basket tightening. "I've had to be extra careful to keep my daughter as far away from them as possible."

"I almost pity the poor beast," chuckled a voice I suddenly recognized as Mrs. Smith.

A chill dripped down my spine at her words. *The beast? Were they planning on raiding the forest to find me?!*

Before I could think better of it, I abandoned my attempt to feign interest in the apothecary windows and walked over to the small circle of gossiping ladies.

"Did you say the beast?" I asked, keeping my voice an octave lower than usual.

Mrs. Smith sneered at me as she raked her gaze up and down my cloaked frame. "What a rude and unsightly traveler we have here. Didn't your mother ever teach you any manners?"

"None that I can recall," I replied with a little more edge than I meant.

"Clearly," stated Mrs. Smith with a sniff, though her eyes softened. The other ladies did not attempt to hide their disdain though. I tightened my grip on my packages, wondering if I'd made a mistake and was just wasting my time.

"Well, traveler, I suppose there's no harm in enlightening you as to the current state of affairs," Mrs. Smith continued, surprising me. "Apparently you haven't heard, but the little lordling that took up residence in the inn is organizing a large party of mercenaries, hunters, and adventurers. Evidently, he is gearing up to hunt the legendary black beast that is rumored to reside in the forest that borders this town. His true aim, though, is to "rescue" the girl from this town who was taken by the beast some time ago."

"Though if you ask me," Mrs. Smith continued, leaning forward and dropping her voice to a whisper, "From what I've seen of his lordship, the poor girl may be better off in that forsaken forest with a beast." Mrs. Smith scoffed. The ring of ladies had tightened, but one or two still glanced out warily to ensure no one had overhead Mrs. Smith's commentary on a noble.

"I guess that explains all of those men loitering about," I murmured, tilting my head the slightest fraction in the direction of the tavern. Out of the corner of my eye, I realized one of the men was blatantly staring in my direction, his tankard all but forgotten on the table. My hooded appearance and whispered conversation were drawing too much attention. I needed to find Fenn and to get back to the safety of the estate.

"When is this hunt taking place?" I asked a little too hurriedly.

Mrs. Smith eyed me for a moment, sensing my nervousness. Her gaze flicked in the direction of the tavern before returning to my shrouded features.

"Tonight, under the light of the full moon. The fool's archers will likely be shooting at shadows all night," Mrs. Smith confided quietly.

My face went pale, and fear traced its icy finger down my spine. Fenn and I were in serious danger! Rage followed in its wake; that arrogant aristocrat was using me as justification to go after the supposedly evil beast!

If they were going tonight, that didn't leave us much time. I had to find Fenn to warn him. There was no way we could fend off such a massive group, even with a terrain advantage. It looked like we would have to leave on our adventure a little earlier than planned.

"Thank you for informing me, ma'am," I nodded in thanks to Mrs. Smith. "I must be going now. Good day, ladies."

I clutched my packages to my chest, my knuckles going white. I could still feel the gaze of the mercenary boring into my back, so I continued on past the apothecary, taking even, measured steps, before ducking into the deserted alleyway beside it. I couldn't afford to draw any more attention, especially now.

I knew all the side streets and back alleys of this place like the back of my hand. Newcomers would be hard-pressed to keep up with me here. Hopefully, that man had lost interest, but just in case, I picked up the pace, striding purposefully through the streets, winding this way and that.

We had to get out of here before it was too late!

20

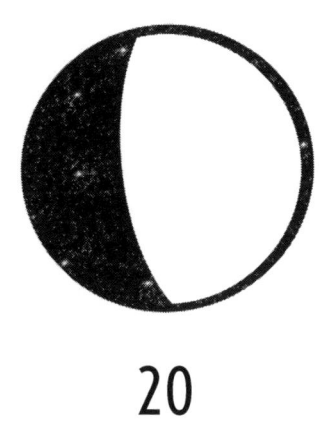

My heart beat a steady rhythm as I focused on taking even, measured breaths. I kept my head slightly tilted to the side, so I could listen for the telltale sound of footsteps echoing on the rather uneven cobblestones that made up the network of streets.

So far, I had only passed a few souls, but they were wholly disinterested in me, much to my relief. I constantly scanned the path ahead for any situation that could lead to trouble.

This early in the day, the womenfolk were about the business of running the household, and the children were playing together in the streets, their laughter ringing through the warm air.

After a few minutes of wending my way through town, I could see the tops of the trees peeking over the last few rows of houses. Just a little farther and I could reunite with Fenn. We'd agreed to meet in the forest by noon at the latest.

Some of the tension fled from my shoulders, and I let out a breath I hadn't realized I'd been holding. I was looking forward to seeing Fenn's reaction when he tried one of Mrs. Thompson's cinnamon buns. Maybe we could stop in a clearing on the way back so that he could try them while they were still warm. A small smile tugged at my lips.

I turned a corner, my gaze passing over a cloaked street woman who appeared to be daydreaming, slouched on a doorstep, with a half-empty bottle of ale clutched in her gnarled hand. I gave her a wide berth as I passed, attempting to keep my footsteps light, so as not to disturb her.

Suddenly, the woman leapt to her feet and dashed towards me, latching onto the crook of my arm with a surprisingly strong grip. Shocked, I staggered back, attempting to regain my balance and jerk free of her grasp without losing any of my packages in the process.

"Help me," croaked the woman from beneath her hood. Her foul breath stank of alcohol; bile rose in my throat at the stench, and at the horrid memories it conjured.

"Release me!" I commanded, shaking my arm for emphasis.

"Coins! Give me coins!" the hag wailed, waving her free arm, and the liquid in her bottle sloshed from the motion.

Realizing there was only one way out of this situation without injuring the woman or drawing additional attention, I sighed, irritation sparking at the delay.

"Fine, fine, I'll give you some coins," I gritted out, carefully extracting a few copper coins from my pocket. As I peered down at the woman to hand her the coins, my breath caught, and horror raced through me.

Before me groveled my own mother.

Her hair hung in greasy strings, dirt and errant leaves intertwined with the once rosy, luscious strands. Her face seemed to have aged decades since I'd been away, deep lines etched into her forehead and around her mouth. Deep bags hung under her eyes, which were clouded with the need for the drink. Every part of her was coated in a thick layer of dirt and dust, and even the threadbare cloak she wore was riddled with holes and jagged tears.

All of the emotions I'd worked so hard to repress when it came to my mother came roaring through me like a tidal wave. Hurt and resentment warred within me, no doubt reflected starkly on my face, which was thankfully still hidden by my loose hood. A small part of me found satisfaction and justification in the fact that this woman who had relied on me, but betrayed me, had fallen so low. It served her right, after all the abuse I'd suffered at her hand.

And yet, at the same time, the little girl in me, who'd yearned for her mother's love more than all the food and comfort in the world, felt only sadness for the sight before her.

Too late, I realized that my hood had slipped back an inch, and my staring had invited an examination in turn. A spark of recognition lit up my mother's hazy eyes, which widened in surprise.

"My baby," she whispered, a smile creeping across her haggard face. She tenderly raised a hand to my face.

My breath hitched at the pang two simple words could elicit. My mind was a whirl of possibilities, bouncing from one thought to the next. Had she missed me at all? What on Earth had happened to her after I ran that night? Why was she here, instead of in our little house by the woods?

"How dare you, you ungrateful wretch!" she suddenly spat, her reddening face contorting into the enraged mask I had come to expect from her after a bottle or two. The hand that she had raised so tenderly now became a claw that dug into the folds of my cloak.

"After I went to the trouble of acquiring a filthy rich husband for you, this is how you repay me?! All you had to do was stand there quietly and look pretty, and we both would have been set for life! A life of luxury for you, and you never would have had to deal with all the shame and scorn that I did!" she ranted and railed, shaking me vehemently.

I bit my lip to keep it from quivering. I understood how difficult it had been for her, constantly being mocked and ridiculed for having a child but no husband. I'd been the one to comfort her when she lay sobbing in bed, the insults spreading like poison under her skin. She'd held onto me, and we'd cried together.

But at some point, I'd come to the realization that feeling sorry for myself wouldn't put food in my belly. And I'd decided that I wouldn't care enough about others to let their opinions and words destroy me like my mother had let them destroy her.

Maybe that was why I had always been drawn to horses—they didn't care about my status or pedigree. I could be myself with them. We could work together towards a common goal, with no need for words.

Where I had turned to work and horses, my mother had turned to alcohol and violence. Sure, I got bruises from working with horses, but those never hurt nearly as much as the ones my own mother gave me. She would apologize when she was sober, but as the years went by, those words sounded more and more hollow to my ears. I had endured it all, right up until...

My mother had begun tugging me back in the direction of the main street, keeping up her constant litany of complaints about me.

"He'll be so happy to see that I brought you to him, so happy. He might give me another reward! It goes so fast, you see—I'm already out. But with more gold coins, coins, coins, I could buy another dozen barrels of that good wine, a whole dozen...all for me," she rambled, stumbling forward with me in her vise-like grip.

She'd already drank all the wine and spent all the gold Lester had paid for me? She could have lived the rest of her life in comfort if she'd only used it sparingly! I stiffened, then let my packages slip from my arms and scatter on the rough ground. I grabbed my mother's arm and twisted, wrenching it quickly around and behind her back. The surprise caused her to lose her grip on her bottle; it spun out of her reach before shattering on the cobblestones, shards of glass and drops of alcohol scattering around us in an array of glimmering color.

"How dare you—" my mother screeched, no doubt more upset at the waste of alcohol than at the discomfort of her immobilized arm.

Her now wordless shrieking was unbearably loud. The wrist I held felt so fragile to me now, like I could break it with the slightest pressure. *Why had I ever been so afraid of her?* I gazed at her sadly. I supposed it was her soul that was really the most fragile, though.

A window shutter two houses down the street shifted, and I realized what a racket we, well, my mother was making. I was attracting way too much attention. I needed to leave, and quickly.

"Mother," I said in my most commanding tone, "I am sorry you suffered because of me. Every day I did my best to provide for us. All I ever wanted was for you to love me, like you used to when I was little." A lump rose in my throat. At the emotion in my voice, her screeching cut off, and she stilled.

"But I am not an object to be bought or sold. I am my own person, with my own plans and dreams. I am grateful for what you've done for me, but I will no longer allow you to hurt me. You often told me I was a burden to you," I said, tears pricking the back of my eyes, "so I'll make this easier for the both of us and declare myself an orphan. You have no claim on me any longer."

I swallowed down the lump in my throat as I finished, pain and relief filling my heart. I slowly released my hold on her arm, allowing her to turn and look back at me. Her mouth slightly open in shock; she gaped at me, dumbfounded. The sheen of unshed tears turned her eyes glassy as she slowly sank to her knees, irreverent of the sharp glass splinters littering the cobblestones.

As I swiftly turned to gather up all the things I had dropped, I said thickly to my mother, who still hadn't moved, "Keep all the coins I dropped. Consider them my final farewell."

My hand trembled as I picked up the last package. I didn't know whether I should laugh or cry. It felt good to finally stand up for myself and be honest with my mother. It felt like a vast weight had been lifted off my chest, and I could finally take a deep breath.

I was almost surprised to realize I had completely forgiven her for selling me off, even for all of the insults and beatings she'd doled out as I was growing up. Given the opportunity, I wouldn't change a thing.

Because this path in life, thorny though it may have been, had led me to Fenn.

Wordlessly, I took out one of the steaming cinnamon buns I'd purchased and placed it on my mother's lap. My happiest memory of her was of the first time she took me into town. We had split one cinnamon bun as a special treat, laughing and licking our sticky fingers.

I walked away from my mother then, leaving her behind in more ways than one. I had a bright future with ice-blue eyes waiting for me. I picked up the pace, my boots clicking as I headed for home.

But as I turned the corner onto the next street, a heavy hand clamped down on my shoulder.

21

Adrenaline shot through me, and the grueling training drills I'd undergone in the last few weeks kicked in.

I immediately dropped into a crouch, surprising the armed man that had tried to grab me. Quickly, I swept one leg out, hooked the heavily muscled man behind the knees, and yanked.

He fell backwards onto the rough cobblestones, cursing like a sailor all the way down. Before he could recover, I hopped up and delivered a swift kick to his groin, eliciting even more colorful language, though this time an octave higher than the last string of curses.

Still clutching my packages to my chest, I darted around and past the downed man, the slightest hint of a smile tugging at my lips. All that training had come in handy!

Any amusement I'd felt fled when I realized there were nine burly mercenaries blocking the way forward. The shortest route to the forest was now cut off. Fenn had taught me the basics of fighting, but I wasn't arrogant enough to think I could take out nine armed mercenaries alone, without the element of surprise.

My heart pounding in my ears, I whirled, hoping I could dart into a side street and lose them in the warren-like maze that made up this part of the neighborhood. The man I'd already dealt with was clambering to his feet, grumbling under his breath about how he was, "not getting paid enough for this."

I dashed forward, skirting around him and aiming back the way I'd come. If I could just reach one of the narrow alleys in between houses, then I might be able to lose them, or maybe climb up onto a rooftop and travel cross-country.

But just as I was almost clear of him, his calloused hand shot out and snagged the loose fabric of my hood, choking me. I gasped for breath, dropping my items for the second time, and grabbed the fabric at my throat to lessen the pressure.

Too late, I realized my mistake. I should have stepped backward or unfastened it, but instead I gave the mercenary the few precious seconds he needed to wrap an arm around me, pinning my arms to my sides.

"Let's see what we've caught, boys," my captor said in a gravelly voice, though I noted with some small satisfaction that his tone was still a little higher than it should have been.

Roughly, he yanked my hood back, exposing my fiery locks to the bright morning light. Instead of the surprise I expected, I was met with expressions of grim satisfaction or cold indifference. That could only mean one thing.

"Finally, our hunt is successful," grinned my captor as he grabbed a fistful of my hair, jerking my head around so he could clearly display it to his approaching comrades. I'm pretty sure he pulled hard enough to tear at least a few strands out. "Who would'a thunk we'd catch the little red hare not in the forest, but in the town?" he guffawed.

"We'll be eatin' good tonight!" exclaimed one.

"Good catch, Mal!" congratulated another to the man holding me.

"Let go of me!" I screamed, flailing about. I kicked out backwards, hoping to distract him long enough for me to get away, or at least grab my weapon. If I could just reach my dagger!

"Not this time," he growled, catching my leg mid-swing. "There's no escape for you, little hare. No big bad wolf to protect you anymore."

He barked out orders to his men, who so conveniently happened to have several lengths of rope on them for just such an occasion. The big one who held me pinned me to the ground so that the others could easily tie my wrists and ankles together.

When my captor went to search me for weapons, he seemed to be having the time of his life feeling me up. To my dismay, he quickly found my dagger, but continued his "exploration." Tears of rage and humiliation pricked my eyes, but I refused to let them fall, to give him the satisfaction. When his eager hands got to my chest, I lunged forward, sinking my teeth into one of his wrists and biting down as hard as I could.

"Arrrgh! Get 'er off me!" he hollered.

The man tying my wrists together behind my back jumped to help, trying to pry my jaws apart. I held on, glaring my defiance at him. *I would not submit to these monsters.*

A hard slap to the side of my face stunned me, and stars danced in my vision. My grip loosened, and Mal wasted no time in jerking his arm out of my reach.

His face livid, he leaned closer, though well out of my range, to scream profanities at me, spittle flying. A vein throbbed in his forehead. I spat his disgusting blood in his face, sending him into absolute hysterics, and I noticed a second vein had joined the first.

Taking a quick breath, I screamed, "Murderer! Kidnapper! Fire! Fire! Fi–" My cries were cut off by a rough hand covering my mouth. Desperately, I glanced around us, hoping against hope that someone had heard, that someone would come. Not a single door hinge squeaked, despite the shadows that lurked in a few nearby windows.

No one was coming.

"Gag her," ordered Mal, still nursing his wound.

I tried to bite the hand covering my mouth, but thick, coarse rope quickly took its place.

"What that lordling sees in this one is beyond me," muttered Mal, sneering in my direction while rubbing his injury.

"At least we're gettin' some nice coin outta' it," chimed in a mercenary with a few missing teeth.

"Most of this is worthless, but these might be nice," smirked one of them as he opened the bag containing my three remaining cinnamon buns.

"Hey, hey, gimme some!" crowed one man.

"I'll take those!" exclaimed another.

In the end, the men wound up in a tussle, with three of them coming out victorious and stuffing the still-steaming buns into their faces. For some reason, watching these barbarians devour the treats I was going to share with Fenn hurt so much more than the insults and the ropes chafing at my wrists and ankles.

Of course Fenn had been right. It was foolish of me to think that coming into town was feasible. Dimly, I wondered how long he would wait for me before he realized I wasn't coming. Would he think I'd run away, that I'd abandoned him? Or would he race in here to rescue me?

Here I was, a damsel in distress yet again, in need of saving. Was this some sort of cruel, twisted destiny I couldn't escape? To be treated no differently than an apple, sold to the highest bidder? And all because of the color of my hair? Was being the author of my own destiny really such an impossible dream?

I didn't want to be the reason Fenn got hurt yet again. My heart shook at the thought. This time, I would just have to get myself out of this mess...somehow. If I bided my time, surely an opportunity would present itself for a quick escape. I had to find a way out of this situation, so I could find my way back to Fenn. I had to warn him about what was coming. At the very least, I had hope that the party going to hunt down the beast would pass by Fenn on the outskirts of the forest, and continue in deeper, none the wiser.

Had any of them bothered to look, they might have noticed the fire burning in my eyes. But they were all too preoccupied with divvying up my things amongst themselves.

Now that they'd finished that up, Mal heaved a sigh, glaring at me with distaste. I returned the sentiment. He lumbered over to me, and keeping his hands well away from my face, he grabbed me around the waist. Then with a grunt, he swung me up and over one of his broad shoulders like a sack of apples.

"Alright, boys, let's go," barked Mal as he swung around and started walking briskly back towards the center of town.

Windows shuttered as we passed, and each step away from the forest felt like a punch in the gut. Since I was hanging backwards over Mal's shoulder, I got to watch as his men arrayed themselves in formation behind him without a word. They must have been so accustomed to working together that they no longer needed words to communicate.

It was only once I'd been unceremoniously tossed into a large, opulently decorated room in the inn, the door shut and locked, that I allowed the first tear to fall.

Back on an unassuming cobblestone street, not far from the borders of the forest, a single ruby strand of hair glinted in the blazing sunlight.

22

I don't know how long I waited in that room. Certainly long enough for a good cry and to notice the expensive-looking rugs covering the rough wooden floor, the polished gold candelabras, the gilded chests stuffed with fine silk garments, and the ludicrous amount of fresh fruit and wine crowding every available surface. A massive four-poster bed dominated the center of the room, thick blankets and multiple pillows adorning it.

I had been deposited near the foot of the bed, where the gilded trunk sat, some of its contents spilling down the side. I'd never seen such extravagant clothes before. Every item was covered with ruffles and encrusted with gemstones.

I used my shoulder to brush away some of the tears still blurring my vision. That didn't quite do the job, so instead I focused on curling my body into a tight ball and bringing my tied wrists from behind my back under my legs and in front of me.

After clearing my eyes, I leaned forward and brushed my hand along the silken sleeve spilling out of the trunk. But when it moved, I caught a glimpse of the crest that was emblazoned on the side of the trunk. Dread settled into the pit of my stomach.

The crest depicted a coat of arms featuring red and gold colors, with a snake coiling around a sword. The symbol of the Lindora Duchy.

For this crest to be here could only mean one thing. I had been locked up in Lester Lindora's bedroom.

Well, that was just *great*.

He may have captured me, but I wouldn't let him take me without a fight. I probably didn't have much time until he came back. I pushed myself to my knees, then carefully stood up, waiting a few moments for my legs to stop tingling.

Surely, I could find something in this room that I could use to cut the ties binding me. I rifled through a few drawers, finding nothing sharp enough for my purposes. Until I looked up and noticed that on the fruit platter in front of me lay a knife. Now that, I could use!

Quickly, I grabbed the knife and wedged it into a crack so I could begin sawing at the bindings on my wrists. It took longer than I'd hoped, and I was jumping at every noise from the other side of the door. But finally, I sawed through the last fiber.

I grabbed the rope gagging me and removed it, then set to work sawing away at the ropes on my ankles. Scanning the walls, I noticed heavy draperies on one side. I went over to investigate and was elated to discover a window! Peering out, I could see over the rooftops of neighboring buildings, which meant I was on the second story of the inn. At least the window wasn't facing the main street, where the entrance to the inn and most of guards were. It was too high to jump without some sort of problematic injury. Those cobblestones could be quite unforgiving.

I turned around and scanned the room, trying to think of something I could use. What would Fenn tell me to do? My gaze settled on the bed and the chest at its foot. Quickly, I strode over and stripped the sheets off the bed, tying two together with a thick knot. Next, I added a few more lengths by knotting a couple of those soft silk shirts to one side. I triple knotted one end to the bedpost closest to the window.

Just as I finished, heavy footsteps sounded outside the door; I could hear a key rattling as it was inserted into the keyhole. I froze, my heart stuck in my throat. It had to be Lester!

I sprang into action, sprinting to the window with my makeshift rope trailing behind me, grabbing a candelabra as I went. There was a distinctive *click* as the key unlocked the door. The hinges squealed as it swung open, revealing one very large Lester standing in the doorway, two guards at his back.

His mouth fell open as I swung the candelabra with all my might, shattering the window. I dropped it and scrambled onto the windowsill, keeping a firm grip on the sheets. Heavy footsteps sounded behind me, and just before I climbed out of the window, one meaty hand snaked out and grabbed my hair, pulling me back into the foul-smelling room.

"Well, well, well," whined that despicable nasally voice. "Look what we have here." His breath clouded the air with the pungent scent of alcohol. My stomach roiled at the familiar stench.

He dragged me back into the center of the room by my hair, sending thousands of tiny daggers into my scalp. Through half-closed eyes, I watched him stumble twice. His balance was clearly compromised by the poison running through his system. At the slightest hint of a mistake or an opening, I could strike and make a run for it.

He leaned in closer, yanking my head up so he could clearly see my face. I glared at him, trying to think of any moves I could use to get out of his hold.

"It's the worthless whore that ran away after I'd already paid for her!" he shrieked, spittle flying from his swollen lips.

Stars exploded across my vision, and the tang of iron flooded my mouth. I slowly turned my head back towards my tormentor, my cheek stinging where he'd slapped me. He'd packed a surprising amount of force; this clearly was not the first time he'd struck a woman.

I glanced at the two guards, who'd taken up position on either side of the door, to see if they'd display any kind of reaction. Neither so much as blinked.

I breathed in deeply through my nose, deciding not to give him the satisfaction of seeing me in pain. Clenching my hands into fists, I spat a glob of blood straight into Lester's face, where it landed on his cheek.

"Well, well, well, look what we have here," I retorted in an even, placid tone, while my eyes glared daggers. "It's the fat pig that had to buy a wife because no sane woman would stoop so low."

He rocked backwards, shocked enough to release his hold on my hair. Lester's jaw had dropped, his mouth opening and closing like a fish out of water. The blood slowly slid down his cheek, and his face rapidly took on a reddish-purple hue.

With a wordless scream of pure fury, Lester launched himself at me, his hands forming claws. I moved, sensing an opportunity. As one of his fingernails scored a trail along my cheek, I whipped the silken bedsheets I still clutched in one hand up and looped them around his neck.

I twisted the sheets, tightening the noose, and pulled with all my might. But then the two guards were there, one wrenching the sheets out of my hands, the other frantically loosening the cloth choking his master.

"Get off me, you imbeciles!" yelled Lester as he scrambled to remove the last lengths of fabric from around his neck. He had the guard holding me bind my wrists once more, the coarse rope digging into my already tender flesh.

At a gesture from Lester, the guards returned to their positions by the door, their faces returning to a mask of cool indifference. Still panting to get some air back into his lungs, he took a moment to compose himself, straightening his gold-threaded jacket and running a hand through his greasy locks.

Lester walked forward with more composure than I'd seen him display since he first stumbled through the door. A sickening grin crept across his piggish face as he gripped my chin in one meaty hand, forcing me to meet his gaze.

"We'll see how long that feistiness lasts once I have your protector clapped in chains and begging for death," he spat, eyes narrowing in glee.

I blinked, taken aback. What on Earth did Fenn have to do with any of this, especially now that Lester had what he wanted? Was going after Fenn an act of revenge, or did he simply want me feeling even more useless than I already was?

"What do you mean?" I asked quietly, swallowing my pride in hopes of coaxing more details out of him. Perhaps if I appealed to his sense of pride...though after what I'd already said, I doubted that would work. But even so, I had to try.

"I can't just let him go after his defiance of me. Besides, I have a score to settle with him," Lester replied with a smirk, seemingly pleased with the trace of fear on my face.

"You'll never be able to find him in that forest," I protested, hoping for more information.

"Once that dog gets the present we send him," Lester explained with a sneer, unsheathing a small, ornamental dagger at his voluptuous waist, "he'll come running right to me."

With that, Lester grabbed a lock of my hair, slicing off several inches with his sparkly little dagger. I paled, knowing Lester actually had a valid plan this time. Fenn would come running to save me and end up caught in a trap!

"And I'll be ready to properly 'greet' him when he does," Lester chuckled grimly, trying and failing to sheathe the dagger two times before getting it right.

"You leave him out of this!" I exclaimed. "He has nothing to do with this!"

"Oh, he has *everything* to do with this!" snarled Lester, his face distorting in rage. "But I'm not an unreasonable man," he continued in a calmer voice, once again grabbing my chin. "So perhaps I'll throw the dog some scraps and let him watch as I make you mine!"

Pure, unadulterated rage surged through me, red dying the edges of my vision. I jerked my head out of his grip and viciously bit down on his hand, clenching my jaw as hard as I could.

The guards rushed forward once more, though this time it took them quite a bit longer to wrench Lester's fat hand out of my teeth. Once freed, he fell back to the floor, and I spit his disgusting blood out of my mouth, landing it on his expensive tunic this time.

"You can try!" I growled at him. "But you should know I won't just submit without a fight."

This time, when he got up, Lester kept well out of my range, and ordered both guards to hold me. Unsurprisingly, Lester could dish it out, but he couldn't take it.

"Put her in a cage, where she belongs," he instructed the guards. "And dump this just inside the treeline of that stupid forest." He handed the lock of my hair to one of the guards, who tucked it into a pouch at his waist. Naturally, I promptly sat down, forcing both of the guards to haul me up by my armpits and drag me from the room.

After exiting the inn, the two men dragged me all the way to where the mercenaries had camped out in the town square, ragged tents and garbage filling the once-pristine area. There would be no more market days here for a while.

But as they started heading towards a wagon in the middle of the tents that had an iron cage instead of a covered wagon bed, I tried to make a break for it. They only tightened their grips, hauling me towards the cage as quickly as they could.

My little parade had gathered the attention of the mercenaries who were idling about camp. Groups of them came to watch as I was carried up the steps and deposited into the cage. Both desirous and pitying stares followed me, the mercenaries watching from every angle. The guards quickly locked the door, and I shrank back from the bars, feeling very much like a hunted animal watching its hunters stoke the cooking fire.

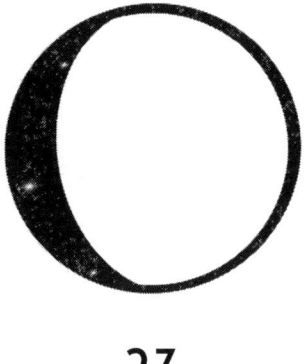

23

The shabby houses in Verdain soon gave way to wide-open fields where young wheat and corn grew tall, waving gently in the warm summer breeze. The bars of my cage rattled around me with every rut and furrow of the hard dirt road. The inside of my cheek still ached where I'd accidentally bitten it, courtesy of an especially large pothole.

A mercenary who looked a solid year younger than me sidled up next to my cage. He glanced around warily at Lester's men before slipping a piece of jerky in between the bars.

"Here," he whispered so quietly I could barely hear him.

"Tim, over here," one of his fellows called out to him, gesturing for Tim to join him. With one last glance at me, he complied, joining his comrade. I'd been so surprised I hadn't even managed to thank him.

I gratefully chewed on the jerky. At least it took the edge off my hunger. After I was done, I slowly worked my hands back and forth, rubbing my wrists raw but also loosening the ropes binding them.

I moved slowly enough that any movement could be blamed on the bumpy ride.

Most of the guards had stopped blatantly staring or salivating at me after a few hours, as mid-afternoon soon turned to sunset. They had been watching me, but I'd also been watching them. Despite the rude gestures sent my way by some, the majority of the men around didn't look particularly…excited about my presence. In fact, a few looked rather uncomfortable and muttered amongst themselves, shifting uneasily. Others looked downright disgusted. Those were the men that complained the loudest, and the most boldly, about "going against the code," "dishonorable tactics," and "taking orders from the pampered pig." Tim appeared to be a part of the latter group.

Hearing the dissent voiced by so many of the mercenaries gave me some small measure of hope. If they were this dissatisfied with working under the thumb of an arrogant noble, perhaps there was some room there for some sort of bribe, or maybe even assistance escaping. I even received a few apologetic looks and whispered words. Those were the men that volunteered to guard my cage and glared at the handful of men that looked about ready to torment me further in one way or another. I also noticed that Lester's soldiers kept well away from the mercenaries.

Another jolt from a bump in the road set my teeth on edge, bringing me back to the present as the road took us past the last outskirts of the farms and into the Forgotten Forest. The moment we passed beneath the first branch, a chill settled over us, the blood-red light of the setting sun casting tortured shadows around us.

Where before the men had been talking and joking amongst themselves, they now fell silent, as if on alert and straining to detect the slightest sound. Knowing how swiftly and silently Fenn and the other denizens of this forest could move, I didn't expect them to catch so much as the snap of a twig.

I subtly scanned the forest anyway, seeing if I could spot some trace of Fenn the mercenaries could not. Fenn must have been worried when I hadn't come back this morning, but since I also hadn't heard any sort of commotion, Fenn must not have tried to follow me into the inn or the mercenaries' camp, thankfully. He would have definitely stuck out like a sore thumb, not to mention being vastly outnumbered.

There was only one individual that hadn't fallen silent and watchful once we entered the darkening forest: Lester. I could hear him up ahead, chattering on about his amazing plans and making snide comments about the mercenaries' lack of horses. Though to be fair, I had also found it rather odd that this particular group of mercenaries didn't keep their own horses. Normally, a mercenary would have his own horse, so he could travel and complete jobs more easily. Even most adventurers had one or two horses these days.

I bit back a groan as Lester slowed his Arabian stallion, clearly aiming for my cage. Apparently, it hadn't taken him long to find a replacement for the one I'd stolen. Fleetingly, I wondered if Fenn had fed Atlas dinner yet. The new horse Lester was riding was a dappled gray, outfitted in golden, tasseled tack, just as Atlas had been.

I shuffled to the side of my cage farthest from him, hoping the extra effort would redirect his attention to easier prey. Unfortunately for me, Lester maneuvered with some difficulty and no small amount of whipping his poor mount alongside the bars of my cage. I sighed, not exactly looking forward to whatever poison he wanted to whisper in my ear this time.

"Quit wriggling around so much," Lester whined once he finally drew alongside me.

Not deigning to respond to that one, I instead opened with, "Come to gloat some more? That cost you blood last time." I kept my tone level, with just the hint of an edge, and examined my ragged and torn nails.

My words had the desired effect, and Lester moved a little farther away from my cage, absent-mindedly rubbing the hand I'd bitten. His face still turned a rather horrid shade of magenta at my lack of honorifics. I smiled in grim satisfaction.

Lester cleared his throat, regaining his composure. And here I'd hoped that little jab would be enough to get him to leave me alone.

"I just thought you might like to know..." he trailed off, looking at me gleefully out of the corner of his eye. He curled his lip in what I was sure he believed was a winning smile.

This man was as transparent as glass and about as deep. I hated to play his little game, but any information I could get from him could be useful later.

"Know what?" I asked tersely, wishing I could land one solid punch on his piggish face.

"Well, I didn't get the opportunity to tell you before, due to your depraved behavior earlier," he paused, looking to see my reaction to his little barb.

I gave none, keeping my face carefully blank. Depraved behavior... rather ironic coming from the man-boy that thought buying a wife and then hunting her down like an animal when she ran away was in any way respectable behavior.

Lester huffed, obviously disappointed at my lack of reaction. "Well, I have several very good reasons for you to cooperate with my plans," he continued, that horrid smirk returning.

A feeling of trepidation spread through me at his words. I had the sneaking suspicion that I really wasn't going to like whatever Lester had to say next. "What reasons are those?" I asked, already dreading the answer.

"I have recently had the pleasure of entertaining some very special guests, who are now enjoying their stay in my finest dungeon. They may actually be acquaintances of yours. Your mother, and some little family...What were their names again? I think the boy's name was Curt? Or maybe Colin?" he mused, grinning down at me.

All the blood drained from my face. "Chris?" I whispered, hoping, praying, I was wrong, that this noble wouldn't go so far as to—

"Chris! That's his name! It's so easy to forget peasant names, isn't it?" Lester prattled on, not even attempting to hide his glee. "And I can't tell you how excited I was to acquire a new stable for myself. Most of the shoddy horses there will have to go. After all, I can't have my purebloods tainted, now can I?"

My stomach dropped, horror lancing through every part of me. The only people who'd ever cared for me, their livelihood, their precious *home*... The truth settled on my shoulders like a boulder. If I hadn't run away, then Chris and his family would've still been fine, living happily and peacefully on their little slice of paradise.

And my mother...I didn't want to waste any time on her, but I didn't exactly want her imprisoned or dead, either! Apparently, Lester was not as stupid as I had first believed.

I numbly stared wide-eyed at my bound hands, unblinking. How had it come to this? All I'd ever wanted was the freedom to create my own path, and chase my own dreams! How could something so simple and innocent turn into the garish nightmare in which I found myself?

"You wouldn't want anything else happening to those peasants, would you? All it takes is one word from me..." Lester cackled, grinning devilishly. I glanced back at him as he made a slashing motion across his throat.

In that moment, I truly felt that I beheld the face of evil. Rage and despair stormed through me, but not a sliver of emotion made it through my numb mask. I refused to give him the satisfaction. Was there truly no way out of this mess?

The monster dressed in gilded clothes was giving me a clear ultimatum. Obey him, help him destroy the black beast of the forest, and meekly let him have his way with me, or witness the murder of my friends and family. Unless I could somehow find a third option, he had me in checkmate.

I hung my head, refusing to look at the monster beside me for one moment longer. He laughed at me then, satisfied he had broken me, before retiring to his gilded carriage now that he was exhausted from sitting on his fancy horse and tormenting me.

24

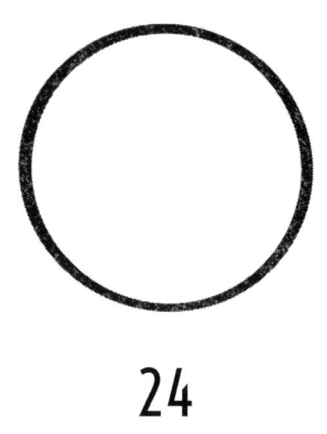

After twilight had fully blanketed the forest, I realized dimly that the constant rattling had ceased. My prison on wheels had finally come to a stop, though the ache in my bones persisted.

Mercenaries and servants alike bustled around me, busily preparing in the wide clearing I found myself in. The top of the full moon was just clearing the treetops, but all of the normal sounds of the forest coming alive were drowned out by the racket of shouting men and the pattering of feet as the servants scurried about.

I didn't mind being ignored, despite the persistent pang of hunger in my belly. It gave me time to think. My hands were tied—literally and figuratively. I was stuck in an iron cage, surrounded by mercenaries and Lester's people. My chances of escape were slim, though not completely impossible, based on the pitying looks some of them kept throwing my way, and Tim's act of bravery and kindness. But how could I try to escape, if the cost of my freedom was the death of my chosen family? It seemed someone would be dying either way—my family, or my protector. Was there no third option I could find? One where no one had to die?

A loud commotion drew me from my spiraling thoughts, and I glanced over to where Lester was emerging from his carriage, now that all the set-up had been completed. The leader of the mercenaries, Bruce, and his second, Mal, hurried over to Lester and began talking animatedly to him.

Lester and his entourage toured the clearing, so he could examine his underlings' handiwork. A massive cage, forged with gleaming silver, stood in the center of the clearing. A silver collar and four silver manacles were attached to the bars. The glint of silver in the moonlight from a different location caught my eye, and I realized Lester was holding what looked like a silver collar.

Apparently, both girls and beasts were to be kept in cages, though for some reason I found it funny that it was the beast that would be wearing a silver necklace. I nearly laughed aloud at the absurdity of it all. Somehow, I doubted feigning insanity would get me out of this cage, though it might be entertaining to try.

As Lester finished going over his plans with his people, their little group turned and began heading towards my cage. My stomach twisted itself into knots at their approach, fear lifting a portion of the haze of numbness that had fallen over me. Fear not for myself, but for the dark wolf that cage had been built for.

As they drew near, Lester gestured to Bruce, who nodded and ordered two of his men to enter my prison. Two of the rougher-looking men who'd helped capture me earlier came forward and unlocked the door to my cage, swinging it open on rusty, squealing hinges.

Grabbing me roughly by the arms, they hauled me closer to the front of the cage, where Lester stood watching. They unbound my wrists, but kept a firm hold on each arm.

"You'll never be able to catch him," I stated matter-of-factly. "So you may as well give up now."

"Normally, I'd be inclined to agree," Lester said with a smug look on his face. "But that's what you're here for." He gave a sharp nod to the men holding me, causing his extra chins to wobble.

My eyes widened as one of the men swiftly unsheathed a dagger, slicing it along my arm in one clean motion.

"What are you doing?" I shrieked, my arm throbbing in time with my heartbeat.

Lester stepped forward and produced a spotless white handkerchief from his coat pocket, signaling to the other man to hold my bleeding arm out towards him. Reaching through the bars, he held it to my wound, letting my blood soak into the fabric.

"That stupid beast is oddly protective of you," Lester mused, his gaze locking with mine. "So, the simplest way to fulfill my end of the deal and properly destroy that bastard, is to use you as bait."

My eyes widened as understanding dawned on me, Lester's narrowing in triumph. After another few moments, Lester removed the now crimson handkerchief and handed it to Bruce, who tied it to the end of a long spear.

Lester turned to walk away, but paused and said to his servants, "Bind up that wound. I can't have a wife with such an unsightly scar. Oh, and do try and enjoy the show, Serena. Don't forget, all of this is for you, my love. Consider it my wedding present."

And with that, Lester left, giving instructions to Bruce to wave the bloodied fabric high in the air all around our little encampment to ensure the scent was carried by the breeze to every corner of the forest.

The two men held me while one of Lester's servants put a healing salve on my arm before proceeding to wrap it tightly in a clean bandage. Once that was done, the men retied my hands, locked my cage, and left to join their brothers in preparation for the arrival of the wolf.

I did my best to ignore the fading sting in my arm, hoping against hope that he wouldn't be drawn into such an obvious trap. The clamor of weapons being readied filled the cool night air, and barely contained excitement seemed to ripple through the men like a living creature.

Night was fully upon us, and there was a chill in the air that set my teeth on edge. The hubbub quieted as the full moon rose higher in the sky. The earlier clamor had turned to anxious fidgeting as each person wondered when the beast would appear.

As the moon reached its zenith, the mercenaries began to shift from foot to foot, and whispers filled the silence.

A bone-chilling howl pierced the air, echoing seemingly from every direction and none at all. The mercenaries snapped to attention, scanning the dark edges of the forest with wary eyes. The slithering sound of swords and daggers being unsheathed rang out, and silver flashed in the moonlight.

The absolute silence after the unearthly howl was nearly as intimidating, and goosebumps rose on my arms. The whole place seemed to be holding its breath in anticipation.

I started scanning the periphery of the forest as well. No movement caught my eye, but I did notice that Lester was hanging back, surrounded by beefy mercenaries and his own personal guards. Seeing Lester all nervous and twitchy for a change was rather nice.

As I looked back at the forest, something out of place snagged my attention. A pair of icy-blue eyes gazed back at me from the deep shadows. I drew in a sharp breath. I shook my head the tiniest amount, begging with my eyes for him to flee before anyone else noticed him. The eyes narrowed, and I darted mine towards the silver cage and back again. Blue eyes flicked to look at it, before returning to mine and narrowing with rage.

Again, I shook my head. *Run!* I mouthed silently. His eyes shifted, taking in the group of at least thirty armed men, as well as the little group surrounding Lester. His pupils turned to slits, and he bared his fangs in the direction of the noble, hackles rising.

The black wolf that was Fenn leaped out of the shadowy forest, aiming straight for Lester. At the last second, Bruce managed to bring his round buckler up, deflecting the sharp fangs. The wolf jumped backwards to avoid Bruce's follow-up slash, and the two stared each other down, a low growl rumbling from the wolf's throat.

"Arrgh!" shrieked Lester, clearly shocked by the sudden attack.

The guards surrounding him looked just as shocked, and several jaws dropped at the size of the beast. He stood as tall as most of the horses, with fangs the size of daggers. I gave an involuntary gasp myself. I'd only ever seen glimpses of him in the shadows, so I'd never realized how truly massive he was. I could see why anyone who caught a glimpse of his wolf form would call him a beast.

The mercenaries quickly formed a horseshoe-shaped ring around the wolf, weapons at the ready. Unlike the guards, the mercenaries didn't seem overly surprised by the size of the wolf. On the contrary, most of them wore expressions of extreme anger. Was it just that last skirmish with the beast they were angry about? No, it seemed far more...*personal*, than that.

The wolf kept his gaze locked on Bruce, though his ears swiveled, taking note of the other men tightening the circle around him. A minor commotion came from Lester's general direction. Apparently, he had recovered from his shock.

"Fenn, how nice of you to accept my invitation," Lester sneered, gesturing vaguely in my direction.

Blue eyes met mine, holding me for a heartbeat in their icy depths, before returning to Lester and the threat of the mercenaries, a menacing growl emanating from deep in his chest. I could've sworn I saw uncertainty flicker in the blue depths for just a moment.

After everything, was Fenn still afraid I'd reject him once I'd learned the truth? I yearned to reassure him, to tell him I'd known his secret for a while now, that it changed nothing. He'd been afraid of me finding out and yet he'd come anyway, knowing the truth would come to light.

Warmth bloomed in my chest, gratitude and love swirling together in a maelstrom of emotion. Fenn had selflessly saved me the first time we met, first from the men chasing me, but more importantly, from my own sorrow and insecurities. Despite his own fear, he'd come for me. I don't think I'd ever met anyone so courageous.

"You managed to evade or get rid of every single hunter and assassin I sent your way, so I had to get a little more...*creative*. Who would have thought, all it took to bring down the big bad wolf was a certain sweet little redhead," Lester boasted as he strolled over to my cage, Fenn's gaze tracking his every move.

Fenn's eyes widened at Lester's words, uncertainty flashing through them before they shuttered. With a small gasp, I realized what Lester was trying to do. If he couldn't beat Fenn when he was at his best—confident and fearless—then the only way to take him on and win was to break his fighting spirit.

I opened my mouth to vehemently deny what Lester was implying, that I'd been working for him all along, when Lester wrapped a hand around one of the bars of my cage and leaned closer.

"Play along, or the boy dies," he whispered imperceptibly, lips barely moving.

The words died in my throat, and I swallowed down a scream of frustration. Lester had every advantage here; he and I both knew it. I hadn't given Lester enough credit. He was far more cruel and cunning than I could have imagined.

Fenn's ears flickered back and forth uncertainly. I ached to run my hands through his thick fur and tell him it was all lies, that he knew me, that I'd never do something like this, that all the time we'd spent together hadn't been a lie. Instead, I held my tongue as tears pricked my eyes and my heart cracked.

"Get him," Lester ordered the mercenaries triumphantly, glee filling his voice. The circle closed around Fenn. Several of the mercenaries closest to him dropped their weapons, steel and silver blades thudding softly into the rich earth.

Suddenly, I recalled a detail from my first encounter with Bruce all those weeks ago. Of exactly what I saw the moment my silver pendant touched his skin. Dread crept along my limbs like poison. If Fenn could be hurt by silver, then that meant the mercenaries were also...

I watched the scene unfold before me as if in a trance. The men that had released their weapons all dropped to a crouch. They rapidly swelled in size, fur sprouting all over their bodies and faces elongating into savage jaws. Their shredded clothes lay on the ground, and wicked claws and sharp fangs took the place of their discarded weapons.

Bruce's coat was a salt and pepper mix of black and white, and he stood just a few hands shorter than Fenn. His second, Mal, had a tawny coat with dark brown markings. The others were a range of grays and browns, though none stood quite as tall or were as massive as Fenn.

Fenn stood tall, glaring down at the wolves facing him. He snarled, snapping his fangs, almost as if he was goading the others on. Bruce answered with a snarl of his own, and at that signal, all of the wolves leaped at Fenn, jaws open, fangs gleaming in the light of the full moon.

25

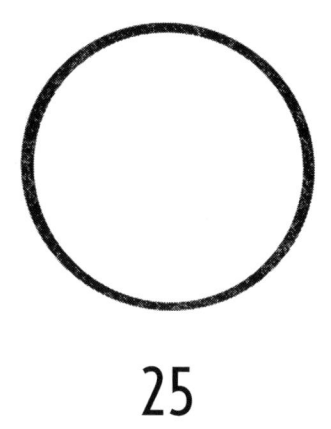

I watched in numb disbelief as Fenn ferociously fought off the dozen wolves attacking him from every side. He'd dodged those first lunges, dipping and weaving among the wolves, delivering a bite here and a swipe from his claws there. But there were too many of them for him to take on alone.

Fenn grabbed a lunging gray wolf's throat in his powerful jaws, clamping down before flinging the wolf at two others coming for him, knocking them back. Before Fenn could recover his balance, Bruce lunged for Fenn's throat. Fenn shifted a fraction, so Bruce's fangs sank into his shoulder instead, missing his jugular. Fenn roared in pain, and two other wolves took their chance to clamp onto his side and a hind leg.

His eyes narrowed against the pain, Fenn reared up and swung Bruce and the other wolf off of him, his blood still dripping from their fangs. Twisting, he bit the neck of the wolf still crushing his leg and flung him nearly to the edge of the clearing, where he struck a tree. That wolf did not get up.

It looked like Bruce had twisted one of his paws on the landing, so he stayed back. With a growl and a flick of his ears, he ordered three wolves to rush Fenn. Fenn crouched, and sprang over the oncoming wolves, leaving them to plow straight into their circling brothers.

Fenn landed lightly, though he was favoring his injured leg. To my surprise, I realized that the wound was already closing. My mind flashed back to the wounds I'd bandaged for Fenn and how quickly he'd removed them, with hardly any evidence of a wound remaining. Apparently, werewolves healed even faster when in wolf form.

Fenn went after Bruce, likely hoping that eliminating the leader would throw the rest of the pack into disarray. I held my breath as Fenn lunged at Bruce, jaws agape. Instead of fleeing or engaging, Bruce gave a wolfish grin, and I noticed too late the trap he had set up.

While Fenn and I had been so focused on the wolves, the mercs still in human form had stayed back, weapons readied for the opportune moment. Before Fenn could reach Bruce, two armed mercs scored Fenn's flanks with silver knives that had leather grips, leaving long gashes.

Fenn whirled, snarling in pain and rage, and with a swipe of his paws, he sent those men flying. They landed in the dirt with loud thuds, weapons flying from stunned hands, only to be taken up by others.

The wolves charged at Fenn again, having had time to recover and heal. Seven of them leaped at him, sinking their fangs deep into his hide, claws furiously opening more wounds.

Roaring, Fenn spun, shaking off a wolf or two before more lunged at him again. They fought so ferociously that Fenn and all the other wolves became a blur of fur and claws and fangs, howls of rage and grunts of pain echoing all around us. The tang of blood filled the air, and clumps of fur of all shades of brown, gray, and black drifted slowly to the ground.

Although the wounds Fenn sustained from the other wolves quickly began to heal, the gashes from the silver knives did not. The edges of the wounds appeared charred, as if the silver had burned whatever it touched.

As the whirlwind of snarling wolves stormed through the clearing, the human mercs held the perimeter, silver weapons glinting in the moonlight. Every time Fenn was distracted, one of them would quickly stab him with a silver weapon. Fenn's beautiful black fur was now covered in grime and blood, marred by dozens of smaller wounds that weren't healing.

Fenn was reacting more slowly to each new attack, and his breathing was coming in short gasps. I wasn't the only one who noticed, either. The wolves sensed it too, redoubling their efforts. Even the mercs seemed to be getting excited; they were all gesturing animatedly to one another.

Fenn's howl of anguish drew my attention back to the wolf fight. Fenn was reeling from a particularly deep cut from a silver blade. It was then I noticed that Bruce was back in human form, and he was talking animatedly with one of Lester's guards, who was holding something in his hands. With a quick gesture from Bruce, four wolves latched their jaws around each of Fenn's legs, immobilizing him. Fenn turned his massive head to bite at the nearest werewolf, leaving his neck exposed.

That one moment was all the guard needed to quickly fasten a massive silver collar around Fenn's neck. The instant the collar was fastened in a complete circle, the metal flared, a blinding white light filling the clearing, accompanied by a howl of agony so visceral I could feel it in my bones.

I blinked rapidly to clear my vision after the flash. My eyes were watering, whether from the sudden light or my own pain, I couldn't quite tell. I gripped the bars of my cage, my knuckles turning white against the dark metal. The indistinct shapes slowly came into focus.

Blurry mercenaries rubbed their eyes, their wolf counterparts whining in the backs of their throats. My eyes narrowed in on the dark shape in front of me. As my eyes focused, the dark shape that was Fenn fell to the ground. I released the breath I'd been holding when I saw his sides rise and fall in nearly imperceptible breaths.

The collar around his neck still glowed dimly, casting the scorch marks around it into high relief. Fenn lay panting on his side, eyes closed against the pain of the silver collar.

The clearing was eerily silent now that all the fighting had come to a halt. Only ragged breathing and the occasional whimper could be heard. It looked like several of the wolves and a few of the still-human mercs were either dead or severely wounded.

Loud, slow clapping shattered the stillness as Lester emerged from his protective entourage. He casually strolled over to where Fenn lay, blood dripping from dozens of wounds.

"Oh, how the mighty have fallen," Lester jeered, prodding Fenn's still form with the toe of his shiny brown boot. "Now you will obey me like the dog that you are!"

At that, Fenn's eyes snapped open, and he lunged at Lester, jaws snapping shut near his neck. Lester stumbled and fell backwards, clapping a hand to his rotund neck. His pudgy hand shook as he drew his hand away, and Lester started trembling uncontrollably when he spied the blood on it. Fenn growled in frustration at the near miss, collapsing back to the ground, energy spent.

"Restrain that beast!" shrieked Lester.

His servants swarmed around him to clean and bandage the scratch on his blubbery neck, while his guards cautiously began attaching silver manacles to Fenn's legs. The moment each ring of silver was closed around a leg, it flared brightly for a moment, just as the collar had done. With each one, Fenn's cries of pain grew weaker, until he could hardly move at all.

Rage coloring his face a horrid shade of burgundy, Lester barked orders to one of his attendants, who scurried off towards Lester's carriage and came back a few moments later, reverently carrying an ornate chest. The attendant knelt before the lordling, lifting the chest up with shaking hands.

A hideous smile crawled up Lester's face as he removed a golden key from one of his pockets and excitedly inserted it into the chest. A sharp *click* rang out as he turned the key.

Lester opened the lid and carefully retrieved the object within. I squinted, trying to make out the details. It looked like a sculpture of a wolf's head, made entirely from the same kind of silver that had been used to forge the collar and manacles. Except...

My eyes widened in horror, and I desperately hoped my guess was wrong. Lester sauntered over towards Fenn, the silver in his hands glinting ominously. The wolves he passed shuddered and moved away from him.

He had only gone halfway towards Fenn when he paused and half turned in my direction. I went absolutely still at the malevolence I saw in those eyes.

"Bring me the girl," he ordered a pair of his guards.

They came over to my cage, unlocking the door so they could roughly grab me under the arms and haul me out of the cage and over the blood-spattered grass. My ankles were still bound, so the guards actually had to drag me the entire way. Naturally, I made sure to be as unhelpful as possible.

Once we reached Lester, he nodded and continued his progress towards Fenn. The guards carried me a step behind him. As we drew closer, I couldn't tear my gaze away from Fenn. His breathing was shallow, and the closer we came, the worse his many wounds appeared. Especially the ones caused by silver blades.

We came to a halt right by his head. I scanned him frantically, feeling my heart break a little more for each new scratch and cut I discovered. In one of the deeper, still oozing wounds, silver glinted. Pieces of those silver weapons had broken off, embedded into the wounds they'd made. The silver was still burning him, sapping his strength with each passing breath.

One gesture from Lester and the guards holding me up swiftly set me on my feet. One cut the ropes tying my ankles; the other freed my hands. I staggered, my legs wobbling as feeling slowly returned to them. My freed hands itched to plunge something sharp straight through Lester's black heart, and I eyed the decorative sword strapped to his side.

Lester embraced me, his foul lips tickling my ear. "Try it, and your mother dies, as slowly as my executioner can manage. If you want her, that boy, and his family to see the sun rise, you will do exactly as I say."

Lester dripped his poison in my ear, so softly I could hardly make out the words. I closed my eyes, fighting back my horror at what I was about to do. I opened them in time to see one of Fenn's ears flick towards us. Could he make out what Lester was saying?

"Here you are, my love," Lester said loudly, so everyone could hear. He handed the silver object he carried to me, and planted a wet kiss on my cheek. The silver felt like ice in my hands. Lester stayed a safe distance away from Fenn, likely still shaken from earlier. He gestured me forward.

I stepped forward on numb legs and crouched in front of Fenn. His beautiful blue eyes were slitted against the agony of his wounds and the silver binding him. But he raised his head, looking only at me.

"I..." I began, voice breaking. I swallowed. Tried again. "I was only tricking you...for my dear...fiancé. I..." I trailed off, glancing at Lester, begging him with my eyes. His glare cut me to the bone. But what I had to say next in his script would destroy my soul.

"I could never...actually love...an inhuman...monster," I finished in a whisper, my lower lip trembling. I held his gaze, begging him to play along. I knew Fenn would be able to scent the lies on my breath, the fear in my racing heart.

He nodded so imperceptibly that I could've imagined it. Silently, he let his head fall back to the ground. A single tear traced through the fur on his face.

I shakily sat down beside Fenn, trying to push back the sobs that threatened to be my undoing. I reached forward and placed the silver wolf head mask on Fenn, my hands brushing against his silky fur. The moment the silver was secured in place, the werewolf mask flared brightly, the acrid scent of scorched fur filling the air. Fenn's jaws opened in a silent scream, his eyes going wide before rolling back in his head. Fenn went limp, silver chains clanking as they settled on the bloodied earth.

26

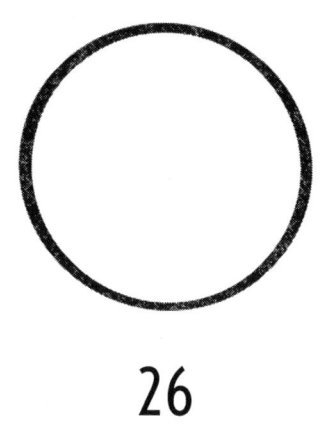

Panic gripped my chest like a vise, the seconds ticking by as a roaring sound filled my ears. The slightest rise of Fenn's chest had me exhaling shakily. *He's still alive.*

I crumpled to the blood-soaked earth, tears streaming freely down my cheeks.

"What a marvelous show!" Lester laughed gleefully, his half-crazed eyes hungrily drinking in the sight of Fenn's prone form.

Even the mercenaries and guards had the good sense to look disturbed by Lester's outburst. Many even cast me sympathetic looks. I did not deign to acknowledge them.

"If only I had brought a painter with me, so he could forever capture this moment. I suppose my description will have to do as a substitute," Lester muttered, rubbing his hands together.

"This concludes our deal," Bruce asserted, stepping forward from where he had been speaking with his men. He held his left wrist close to his chest, the skin bruised and swollen.

The smile dropped from Lester's face as he abruptly turned to Bruce. "And what gave you that impression?"

Bruce appeared taken aback. After a lengthy pause, he growled, "Release our families," he jerked his chin towards me. "You have what you wanted."

At their leader's change in tone, a group of mercenaries padded closer, taking up position behind him. A gesture from Lester had his group of guards scurrying around him, silver weapons on full display.

"Our deal isn't complete until I am escorted safely back to my estate," Lester drawled, lips curving slightly. "Unless you think you can free your loved ones yourselves…? That is, before my executioner can carry out his orders should I be even an hour late?"

He fished around in his coat pocket, producing an ornate key that no doubt went to his dungeons—a key made entirely of silver. Bruce's lips peeled back in a wolfish snarl, his one good eye flashing dangerously.

"You underhanded—" Bruce started, stepping forward menacingly. He towered over Lester, muscles straining with tension.

"Now, now, no need to behave like," Lester smirked, "animals. I simply needed some leverage, to ensure myself a safe return home following the conclusion of tonight's events." He waved the key in the air, tauntingly close to Bruce's scarred face. He didn't so much as blink.

"Once the girl and I are secure at my father's estate, I will provide you with this key and several pairs of gloves for your convenience," Lester continued smugly.

"Fine," Bruce grunted. A muscle feathered in his jaw. "But I will remember this, human." With that, he turned on his heel and stormed off, his men following right behind.

"Damn dog," Lester muttered once they were out of earshot. Though one of the wolves glanced towards him, eyes narrowed. Lester didn't notice. "Put that animal in the cage where it belongs," he ordered his guards. "The rest of you, prepare to leave immediately."

Six guards hurried towards Fenn. They proceeded to roughly drag him towards the huge silver cage, heedless of his injuries.

"Hurry it up," barked Lester, irritated by the slow pace. "You, and you there, help them," he ordered, gesturing to two more guards. "And clean him up just enough for him to survive the journey."

With the additional help, they made much quicker progress towards the cage, though they were still clearly struggling under Fenn's immense weight. Once they reached the silver monstrosity, they hauled Fenn up and deposited him on the cold iron floor of the cage. Nervously, they attached his shackles to the silver chains built into the cage, glancing frequently at his eyes to reassure themselves he was still unconscious. Several servants hurried into the cage as well, and pulled shards of silver from his wounds with shaking hands. Fenn exhaled perceptively as the last shard was taken out.

They finished swiftly, though on their way out of the cage, a guard with a ridiculously twirled mustache gave Fenn a sharp kick to the side, the toe of his boot digging into an open wound. He sneered in satisfaction before following the others. I marked him in my memory.

"Oh, and put her in there too," Lester called as he turned towards his opulent carriage. "No need to tie her up again. She is well aware of her place."

With that, I was hauled to my feet. The two guards shoved me ahead of them, and we followed the trail of blood to the silver cage. This much silver surely could have fed the entire town of Verdain for at least five years. Instead, it was being used to torture one person. But for some reason, I couldn't quite find it in me to care.

I was shoved into the cage, and I stumbled, tripping on the silver chains. I fell on top of Fenn, grateful he wasn't awake to add another bit of pain to his load. The guard then slammed the door and locked us in with another accursed silver key.

I crawled around to Fenn's head, the sight of the cruel mask sending a bolt of agony through my heart. Carefully, I lifted his head and put it on my lap. It was a small mercy that the floor of the cage wasn't made of silver as well.

The hustle and bustle of servants and mercenaries alike dashing around to pack up and ready to leave became a blur of sound and motion. I tuned them all out. At some point, a team of four horses were hitched to the silver cage, and this circus we were in began to move back through the forest.

"I'm sorry," I whispered to Fenn as I absently stroked his soft fur, my tears falling on his onyx fur, on the silver. "I'm so sorry."

The ride was long, and it was painful. It took us two whole weeks of teeth-jarring ruts in the road and snide comments from Lester before we finally, inevitably, reached the sprawling estate of the Lindora Duchy.

After that first night, I'd been taken from Fenn's cage and put into a different sort of bondage. I'd been stuffed into a suffocating corset, and smothered by layers upon layers of the finest silken skirts. My hair had been neatly piled atop my head, and tiny, useless shoes pinched my toes. The carriage I rode in was Lester's, though whenever he fancied a ride on his stallion, the doors were locked and guards posted.

The only reason I didn't completely go insane was the fact that I spotted Tim and a few of the other werewolves cleaning Fenn's wounds every day. It was slow going, since they had to be obscenely careful not to graze the silver bars of the cage. With the strips of jerky Tim was slipping him, Fenn was strong enough for his wounds to start healing.

Lester took every chance he could to parade me by Fenn's cage, so at least I could check on his wounds up close. Lester seemed to me a sort of demon, that drew sustenance from the misery in Fenn's eyes from these little "diversions," as he liked to call them.

A few short words about the fate of my chosen family should I falter in the act had me whispering lovely nothings into Lester's ear and tittering at every so-called joke he made. I felt my soul dying a little more with every false smile. The thought that Fenn could hear my racing heartbeat every time I lied gave me little comfort.

Though I was forced to eat, I began to lose weight, and my skin seemed pale and sallow, despite my tan and freckles. It seemed my body was reflecting the withering of my soul.

The mercenaries acted as guards, surrounding our little caravan, though none of them looked especially happy about it. I made sure to store away any mutterings or tidbits of information I overheard from them. When he wasn't tending to Fenn, Tim would chat with me during the long hours when Lester was riding around on his horse. I'm afraid I made a poor conversationalist, but I was grateful for the company.

I noticed that several of the men wore wedding bands on their fingers, but they only looked at them with sadness, and longing. Maybe the families of these werewolves were being held in the same cells as my mother and the Rangers.

The gilded carriage had become my new cage, and there was no escaping it. It, or the monster clothed in silks and velvet that frequently dwelled within.

I did my best to ignore every insipid promise Lester made to me. Even his detailed descriptions of exactly how he would take me by force, every night, starting on our wedding night, could not pierce the numb void into which I had fallen.

After a time, he grew bored by my vacant expression and lack of response to his taunts. Several times, he raised his hand to strike me, but knowing prominent bruises would ruin his charade with me, he restrained himself.

It was almost a relief when the extensive gardens of the Lindora Duchy first came into view. Almost, but not quite. Dread stirred faintly in my stomach briefly before the numbness took hold once more. Soon, I would be trading the cramped carriage cage for a luxurious cage of misery.

How wonderful.

The gardens of the estate were admittedly quite beautiful. Marble fountains were surrounded by vibrant flower beds, and hedges had been trimmed into the shapes of horses, lions, and swans. As the carriage passed by, I even glimpsed a greenhouse off to one side.

What a beautiful cage it was. All my life, I'd wondered what it would be like to not worry about where my next meal was coming from, to sleep in a warm, soft bed, instead of a straw-stuffed pallet. But would I still have wanted all the fairy-tale luxuries if I had known precisely what it would cost? Were any jewels or fine foods worth the cost of my freedom and joy, the lives of my chosen family?

On the contrary, I would trade away the entire view before me in a heartbeat if it meant freedom for me and mine. Fenn's expression right before I placed that accursed mask on his face...it haunted me. Echoes of guilt and pain reverberated in the vacant numbness where my heart had once been.

The carriage rocked, coming to a stop in front of the grandly carved double doors of the castle. The carriage door swung open silently on oiled hinges, warm sunlight filling the tiny space. Liveried footmen lined the steps to the door, uniforms immaculate, posture as stiff as a board. I noted their nervousness. So, Lester likely behaved even worse at home than in public. Not that that was news to me.

"Welcome to your new home, Serena," Lester said smugly, gesturing grandiosely to the massive estate.

He waddled out of the carriage, which I could've sworn rose an inch or two once he was off of it. He turned and offered me his hand. And so the performance was to continue.

In that moment, I came to a decision. I steeled myself, knowing the road ahead would be a difficult and painful one. I resolved to do whatever it took to free myself and my loved ones, without submitting to Lester's depravity. The fog of numbness started to lift, just a little.

I placed my hand in his and delicately exited the carriage, stepping down lightly onto the stone pathway. I smiled demurely, allowing my hair to cascade over my shoulder, catching the sunlight and blazing like ruby fire.

Lester grinned widely, his palm damp and clammy. But the servants and footmen, they paused, eyeing me with a combination of contempt and curiosity.

As I allowed Lester to lead me up the steps, I did not permit one spark of my fiery determination to show in my emerald eyes. The charade had ended, but the game had only just begun.

27

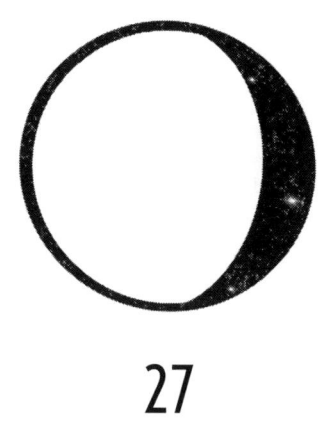

"This blue sapphire would look wonderfully elegant with this white lace," commented Lily as she held up the sparkling stone to the neckline of my dress, her delicate nose wrinkling in concentration. Her short black bob shifted with the slight tilting of her head. She had to rise onto her toes to reach the jewelry box resting on the shelf.

"But an emerald would really bring out the color of her eyes," argued Sophia. Her thick black hair was elegantly pinned to the top of her head, and her movements reminded me of those of a dancer. Her dark, almond-shaped eyes examined mine before flitting over the rest of me once more.

"Miss, would you *please* stop slouching?" demanded Wendy, needle and thread in hand. "At this rate, the hemline will be in a zig-zag pattern instead of a straight line."

Wendy sighed through her nose at me, but I could see the corners of her mouth twitching upwards. Her slight figure belied her inner strength, and her silky chestnut hair was plaited in a braid that kept falling over one shoulder as she worked, the needle flying between her fingers.

"Sorry," I murmured, straightening my spine once again. You wouldn't think simply standing still would be more difficult than baling hay for hours. But somehow, it was. I'd first stepped up onto the little stool several hours ago, but my wedding dress was nowhere near complete.

Wendy sighed again, and I realized I had shifted again without noticing. I squared my shoulders sheepishly so she could continue adjusting my hem. It was tedious work, since a simple slip-up could damage the lace border, setting her up for more work. The golden thread Lester had ordered was very sparkly, but also very fine and slippery.

"Enough bickering about the jewels, and get back to adjusting her sleeves," Wendy instructed Lily and Sophia, who put down the precious stones with no small amount of grumbling.

Lily and Sophia were the ladies in waiting that had been assigned to me upon my arrival at the estate two weeks ago, and Wendy was the head seamstress for the Lindoras. Apparently, the noble family had enough work to employ a full-time seamstress and designer, in addition to a team of younger seamstresses. Wendy was actually only a few years older than me, but her talent and work ethic had gotten her a prestigious appointment as the lead seamstress.

"The sketches you showed me last time were gorgeous, Wendy," I complimented, glancing at her from the corner of my eye.

Sophia and Lily murmured their agreement, absorbed in the task of taking in the delicate lace sleeves of the dress.

"Thank you, Lady Serena," Wendy replied, her long fingers swiftly pulling the threaded needle through the lace. "I do prefer designing elegant dresses for you to sewing simple men's attire. In fact, I have heard that we have some very *special guests* staying with us, though I have been informed that they will not be requiring any *special accommodations*." Her warm brown eyes met mine and held for a beat, before returning to the hem.

I glanced sidelong at Lily and Sophia. No notable reaction.

"Your talents should never be wasted on men's tunics," sniffed Lily, Sophia nodding her agreement.

During my many dress fittings, I had gotten to know Wendy fairly well. Her story was not so different from mine, so we had been able to bond over our shared difficulties. She had started off much as I had, born into a poor family, yearning for some parental love, and doggedly working towards the sort of "pipe dream" that others had deemed either impossible or improper for a woman.

To Sophia and Lily, Wendy's last statement would be seen as an opinion, perhaps a complaint. But to me, I heard the priceless tip layered in her words.

Over several days of careful back-and-forth, Wendy and I had developed a set of key words and code phrases, so we could communicate important information even when we weren't alone. Besides, you could never be sure someone wasn't listening in a castle with so many people in it.

The phrase "special guests" referred to my mother, Chris and his family, and the families of the werewolves. "Special accommodations" referred to the dungeons that lay beneath the castle. I'd needed confirmation that they were all being kept here, and not in some remote location, before I could put my plan into motion.

This was the first good news I'd had since I arrived. I hadn't been certain if Lester would keep his hostages close, since that was much riskier, especially with all of the important aristocrats who would be attending the wedding. At least this made things easier.

Now, all I needed to do was find them, free them, free Fenn, and free myself, all without getting killed or anyone in the castle noticing. Simple.

I inhaled deeply, slowly exhaling. Breathe. I just had to breathe. *I could do this.* One step at a time.

"How is the dress coming along?" I asked Wendy pointedly.

She hummed, surveying the layers of silk, tulle, and lace making up my bridal gown.

"Lace can be...very tricky, my lady," she replied with a wry smile. "I'd say it will take at least another two weeks, perhaps even longer. Especially if there are any more unexpected...additions."

I nodded. Lester had demanded nothing less than perfection in a dress, but also wanted a say in the materials, the beading, and the embroidery. After all, he needed to show off the Ducal wealth at this extravagant wedding, down to the smallest details, from having the finest invitations to the largest cake and the most bejeweled bride. Hence the golden thread, and the pearls on the bodice, and the excessively intricate lace.

"That is understandable. And so long as the lace isn't torn," I smiled faintly, "then it sounds like everything will proceed smoothly."

"Of course. That would be a shame, were the lace to tear again," Wendy replied demurely. But the corners of her mouth curved upwards, and a spark of amusement lit her eyes.

In order to buy more time, we had been strategically causing issues with the dress alterations. And Wendy was so skilled that even the head butler didn't notice the changes. One of our favorite tactics had been "accidentally" ripping holes in the lace.

"Not to worry, miss," Lily said reassuringly, "we're being extra careful with it."

"Wonderful. I know I can count on you," I said, looking at Wendy while I said the last part. She inclined her head ever so slightly.

A knock at the door prompted Sophia to set down her needle and rush over to open it. The head butler stood in the doorway, twirling his greasy mustache. His gaze slithered over me, lingering a little too long on the plunging neckline of the dress.

"Mr. Stevens, do you have a message for me?" I asked coldly, face carefully blank.

He hastily dragged his eyes back up to my face, fumbling for a moment for his reason for finding me.

"My Lord Lester has had tea prepared. You are to join him in the parlor immediately," he blustered, before turning on his heel and marching off.

Wendy and the girls frowned at his tone and for leaving without being dismissed. I was used to it by now, though. What else could I expect from the Lindora's longest-serving butler?

"Thank you, ladies," I said, stepping down from the raised platform. "If you would be so kind as to help me change, that would be appreciated. It seems I am needed elsewhere."

The three got right to work, helping me carefully out of the partially finished gown and into the simpler dress I had been wearing earlier.

"Please, take your time, though, ladies. I must be looking my best for my betrothed, mustn't I?" I added, smiling at the thought of Lester's face turning that peculiar shade of purple at my tardiness.

To my mild disappointment, Lester's face only appeared slightly flushed at my tardiness. Though I supposed I couldn't rule out lustful thoughts as a primary cause, either.

The parlor would have ordinarily been a room in which I'd delight in spending most of my time. The walls were painted a soft buttercup yellow, and floral oil paintings lined the walls in gilded frames. The richly-upholstered chairs and couches were very comfortable, and fresh flowers were always placed at the center of the quaint white table. Large windows looked out over the flower gardens, and warm afternoon light filtered through, illuminating the entire room in its cheerful embrace. Servants, including Lily, who had accompanied me, stood silently along the walls, ready to refill a teacup at the slightest gesture. Sophia and Wendy had stayed behind to continue work on the dress.

Without the monstrosity currently occupying it, this room would have been perfect for reading, tucked away from the hustle and bustle of the rest of the castle.

"How kind of you to finally grace me with your presence," Lester whined, a harsh edge to his voice.

He brought a delicate porcelain teacup to his lips, slurping up some amber tea before placing it back in its saucer with a loud *clink*. "Sit. The tea is getting cold."

I gritted my teeth at the order but plastered a docile smile on my face and sank down into the other chair, the skirts of my dress whispering around me. Today, I wore a muslin pink dress, with an embroidered bodice and a square neckline. Naturally, Lester had been the one to select each and every dress in my wardrobe.

Nevertheless, I managed to get out, "You called for me?" I eyed the selection of miniature pastries arrayed before me, the delicate teacup filled with the same amber liquid. His favorite.

"Yes. I thought it only prudent to inform you," he began, picking up his teacup and swirling it around, the way one does with wine. I would not be surprised if he had added a little something extra to his tea. "That our wedding will take place exactly two weeks from today."

It was all I could do to keep from squeaking in shock. To hide my surprise and buy some time to think, I quickly popped the pastry I'd been eyeing into my mouth. The berry tart tasted like ashes in my mouth.

I swallowed dryly, his gaze boring into mine. "But my dress is nowhere near ready! And what about the guests? Won't they need more time to arrive?" I shifted in my seat, Lester's heated stare tracking the fluttering fabric. *I needed more time!*

"The seamstresses will just have to work harder, and most of the guests should arrive by then," he waved off my concerns impatiently.

I knew I was grasping at straws here, but I had to stall for time. "Didn't the Duke and Duchess specifically request that the royal family bear witness to our union?"

"Those royal do-gooders are always late anyways," Lester harrumphed, irritation entering his voice.

Oh? Did that mean the royal family and the Duke of Lindora were not on good terms? I filed away that little golden nugget for later.

"Nevertheless, would not the ceremony be illegitimate without their blessing?" I pressed. "Surely you can handle an additional week or two of waiting, my lord." Bile rose in my throat at using his title, but if that's what it took...

A satisfied grin lit up his face at my reference to his title, and he leaned back in his chair, the wood groaning in protest under his weight. "I suppose I could wait an additional week, to ensure things proceed smoothly. After all, what is a week compared to the lifetime we'll have together?"

A dark promise shone in his eyes, and I suppressed my shudder. I let out a silent sigh of relief. It would be tight, but I could work with that.

"If that is all, then I shall take my leave," I said, rising. He said nothing as I walked to the door, Lily falling in step behind me.

"You can't put it off forever," he stated matter-of-factly. I paused at the door, without turning around. "It's only a matter of time, now." I continued through the door, not deigning to respond. The only sound was the sharp *rap* of my heels hitting the polished marble floor.

Later that night, after an equally uncomfortable dinner, I reclined in a spotless claw-footed tub. I sighed. Even scrubbing at my skin until it was raw couldn't entirely cleanse me of Lester's dirty gaze.

Three more weeks, I reminded myself. Just three more weeks of this, and then it would all be over, one way or another.

Two weeks. It had already been two weeks since I had first set foot here. Two weeks of condescending maids gossiping about the gold-digging commoner masquerading as a noble.

Two weeks of Lester's thinly veiled threats, of his arrogant attitude.

At least I had been able to find some allies. It had come as no surprise that Lester had made plenty of enemies, even among his own household—maids, butlers, stable hands. Especially stable hands, with the way he treated them and the poor horses. Horse or human, he spared none the whip. I supposed the only reason he had yet to turn a whip on me was that little issue of visible bruising during the wedding ceremony.

I had spent the last two weeks feeling out the staff, making allies, and observing how the household was run. I needed as much information as I could get before I made my move.

My first encounter with Wendy had been rough, since the only information she'd had on me was the rumors that had been circulating among the staff. She'd been so cold at first. But after she saw the way Lester treated me, and the way I treated the maids, she'd changed her mind about me. She'd said she could sympathize with another young commoner who'd been unfortunate enough to catch the eye of this particular noble.

Wendy had agreed to gather information for me after I'd shared my story with her and promised her some compensation for the risk she was taking. I think money was a part of it, but what she really wanted was revenge.

But now I would have to speed up the timeline. I only had three weeks left. Fenn's face flashed through my mind, accompanied by that familiar twinge of pain. Lester never hesitated to taunt me about what he was doing, or rather, having done to Fenn.

Hang on, just a little longer, Fenn, I thought. I fingered the precious Vulclaria feather and silver pendant I always kept with me, safely tucked out of sight. *Just a little longer.*

28

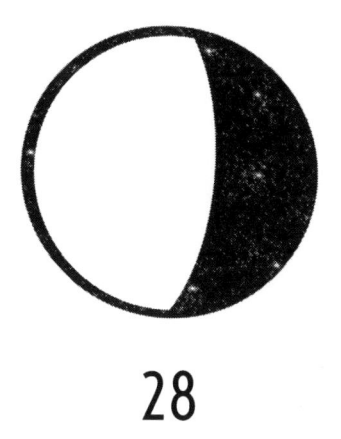

"Your pastries really are the best, Aly," I said around a mouthful of heavenly, sugary perfection. "What are these ones called again?"

"Those are macarons, my lady," Aly replied, smiling broadly. "These were originally created in a neighboring land, but we managed to exchange some recipes with them at the trade summit years ago."

Aly and I had quickly become fast friends after she'd discovered me creeping around the kitchens late one night during my first week here. Naturally, we'd bonded over our shared love of baking, and sweets. I had been surprised to learn I was a year older than the brunette, though she'd been working in the kitchens for several years.

I chewed thoughtfully, savoring the sweetness. "Years ago? Have there been no additional meetings since then?"

"No," Aly sighed, a wistful expression on her face. She crossed her arms, heedless of the stains on her apron, before she glanced around at a few chefs working busily on the other side of the kitchen and lowered her voice so only I could hear. "Duke Verdania was the one who organized the summits, so one hasn't been held since his...disappearance."

I swallowed, eyes narrowing slightly in excitement. "Not even the Verdainians are sure of what happened," I whispered, adding as casually as I could, "Are there any particularly interesting or outrageous rumors about it in this territory?"

Again, Aly glanced at the others out of the corner of her eye, before turning her steely gray eyes on me. I selected a pink macaron this time, and bit down to discover a lovely raspberry flavor. "I'm sure at the next summit, we'd be able to learn even more from them," I said with quiet meaning.

Aly stared at me, eyes searching. Whatever she found there seemed to satisfy her because she replied, "There have always been outlandish rumors about the events of that day, and they've only grown more outlandish with each passing week. There are, however, a few stories that seem almost ridiculous enough to be true."

I nodded my head, encouraging her to continue. "One rumor claims that the duke angered a powerful sorceress, who cast a curse upon the entire family, turning them all into monstrous beasts. Another claims that the entire household was beset upon by vicious assassins, either leaving none alive or forcing them all to flee to a neighboring kingdom. However, one thing that is for sure is that the Lindoras rushed over to aid the Verdanias in their time of need, but arrived too late to save them."

"Quite the range of tales, then," I commented, tucking away those tidbits for later. I watched as a scullery maid picked up a tray laden with what appeared to be kitchen scraps and headed for the door leading to the servants' hall.

"My lady, if you keep going like that, you won't be able to fit into your wedding dress," Aly scolded as I popped yet another macaron into my mouth. Vanilla this time.

I smiled and winked at her. "My, what an absolute tragedy *that* would be. The poor seamstresses would have to adjust it yet again."

"Honestly, my lady," she scolded, though her lips curled slightly.

"Besides, how could I possibly resist all of this sugary goodness when the head pastry chef is so skilled and generous?" I asked in mock outrage.

Aly laughed aloud at that, shaking her head. "What a strange mistress you are. The nobles never even set foot in the kitchen, yet here you are, every day. The current lady of the house would never be caught dead in a kitchen."

"Well, I suppose I mustn't be caught then," I said jovially to Aly, grabbing one last macaron—a purple one this time—before sliding off the kitchen stool in a decidedly un-lady-like manner. "Thanks for the treats, Aly!"

"For Tim," I murmured, my lips barely moving as I pressed a tiny piece of rolled-up parchment into her hands as I pretended to give her a hug. Her nod was nearly imperceptible.

I made my way over to the servants' hall, enjoying the flavor of the vaguely lavender macaron cookie. The others in the kitchen hardly batted an eye at my departure, though I had no doubt that at least one or two of them would be reporting my visit to their masters shortly.

I strode purposefully down the hall, my footfalls soundless on the carpeting designed to reduce noise. After all, servants must not be seen or heard, unless they're being useful, of course.

The other benefit to the soft carpet was that shoes made a deep impression in it, for a short while at least. I quickly followed the most recent set of footsteps, which continued straight past the doors lining either side of the hall. Most of those doors led to rooms where the nobles needed attendants, such as the ballroom, banquet hall, and parlors. They served essentially as shortcuts and screens, so that the noble masters had no need to bump into servants scurrying about their chores.

I would be the exception, since I had already become familiar with the layout of both the noble and servant areas within this giant mansion. I believed Lester and his family were under the impression that it was only natural for a lowly commoner such as myself to be more comfortable among the servants, though Lester's parents had both made their displeasure at my presence quite obvious. A noble's idea of an insult was pretty weak compared to what I'd heard from other stablehands, so I hadn't particularly cared what they called me. It had been entertaining to see their faces become more and more confused as I smiled in response to their best insults.

The footsteps eventually led me to a shabby-looking door that I had never noticed before. I slowed my pace, nodding to a maid as she passed. She bobbed a quick curtsey in my direction before hurrying on, the fresh laundry in her basket wobbling with each step.

Once she was out of sight, I slowly turned the handle and pushed the door open, wincing at the slight creaking of the hinges. I stepped through and quickly closed the door behind me. It took a moment for my eyes to adjust to the sudden gloom of this hallway; there were no windows, and the candles lining the wall were few and far between.

Motion caught my eye. The bright white of the maid uniform skirt flashed through the darkness as the wearer turned the corner up ahead of me. I padded down the worn wood floor as silently as I could, ears straining for the fading sound of the maid's footsteps.

Cautiously, I peeked around the corner and continued on when I didn't see anyone else. After another minute or two of the same dingy hallway, a stone staircase led down into a cramped stone hallway. The damp, uneven stones lining the walls and floors of this tunnel told me I was in the right place.

After taking a deep, steadying breath, I followed the faint sound of the maid's footsteps down the foreboding stairs. Shadows seemed to writhe and slither across the stones, brought to life by the weak, flickering candlelight that lined the walls sporadically.

My fingertips brushed the cold, damp walls as I descended into the darkness. Falling down these steps and making a huge ruckus would be highly undesirable.

At the bottom of the stairs, another stone tunnel led straight ahead, but no doors lined the sides of it. Now I could see the maid ahead of me; I must have caught up to her a little more quickly than I intended. The glow from the candle she carried cast her in a bubble of light that was easy to track in the dim corridor.

I hung back a little, stepping softly as I trailed her. A soft murmuring met my ears, so quiet that at first, I wasn't entirely sure I was hearing it at all. The maid gave no reaction to the sounds, which told me she was either expecting it or already familiar with it.

The farther down the corridor I walked, the louder the voices became, until what had started out as whispers became screams and wails. A shiver ran down my spine, but the maid kept going, so I did as well.

"Let me out! Let me go!" screamed one of the voices.

"Help me," begged another.

"Mama! Where's my mama?" wailed a third.

The maid turned a corner, and I picked up the pace so I wouldn't lose her. I paused, peeking around the corner, and that one look turned my bones to ice. I froze, horrified and unbearably mesmerized at the same time.

I had found the Lindora Dukedom's dungeons... and torture chambers.

The voices that I'd heard had been coming from the cells that lined either side of the dank tunnel. But the screams, the screams echoed off the cold stone from the end of the hallway, where a large circular chamber opened up. It was easily the size of the grand entrance hall, but the only light came from the torches on the walls.

People dressed in rags and covered in bloody wounds were chained to the walls. Most hung limply, defeat etched into every line of their battered and bruised bodies.

Horrible contraptions filled the rest of the space; tables on which people were strapped down, with wicked metal tools nearby, chains that hung people by their wrists from the ceiling, metal racks and chairs, even foreboding, human-shaped coffins made of what looked like iron.

And then there were the monsters in human skin, wielding tools that glinted metallic in the torchlight, but were swiftly bathed in red.

I squinted in the dim light, trying to make out more details. My eyes widened when I realized that apart from a few men along the walls, most of those in the large chamber and filling the cells in the corridor were women and children! They were filthy, though most of them seemed unharmed, other than some bruising. But what really made my heart ache was the sight of a silver cage and the black form it contained.

The eerie cries I'd heard must have been coming from the children. It looked like they'd been in here long enough for their ribs to start showing. But they weren't being tortured, not like the others. *Could all of these people be hostages? Just how many people was Lester blackmailing?* I wondered, horrified.

The maid I had been following didn't so much as glance at the end chamber. Instead, she walked about halfway down the hallway and stopped in front of one of the cell doors. She bent down and placed the tray she'd been carrying on the dingy floor.

"Here," she grunted, shoving the tray of scraps through a little slot in the bottom of the door.

"Please, when can we go home?" rasped a familiar voice. A voice that was much more suited for telling jokes in golden fields and for soothing anxious horses.

"Whenever the lord decides you are no longer valuable as hostages. Though, since you're in here, he's just as likely to decide you've seen too much to let live." She snickered. "Perhaps he'll feel generous after his wedding night and send you a few scraps from the banquet."

She turned to head back towards me, causing a jolt of fear to flash through me. There was no place to hide in this barren corridor! She would surely see me, and then Lester would likely have me locked in my room. The only reason I was permitted to roam about was to keep up appearances and because Lester knew I could never forsake my loved ones.

"Wait!" Chris called out to her, causing her to pause and half-turn towards his cell.

Silently thanking Chris, I turned on my heel and silently but hurriedly scurried back down the corridor. Once the stone steps came into view, I raced for them, taking the steps two at a time. I just had to pray that no one else would be coming down to the dungeon.

At the top of the steps, I bolted, my feet flying across the floor. My breaths came in soft gasps, and my heart pounded in my ears. The hall seemed to stretch endlessly before me. When the door to the servant's hall finally came into view, I picked up the pace, hurtling towards it like a shooting star.

I abruptly came to a halt in front of it, straightening my dress and taking a moment to try and get my breathing under control. I kept an eye and an ear on the hall behind me, making sure the servant wasn't about to suddenly appear.

When my breathing was closer to normal, I straightened and turned the door handle carefully. Checking to make sure the hall was deserted, I slipped out and softly closed the door behind me.

I strode down the hallway purposefully, though my heartbeat was still loud in my ears. I breathed deeply, trying to sort through everything I'd just witnessed and learned. At least now, I knew where Lester kept his prisoners.

29

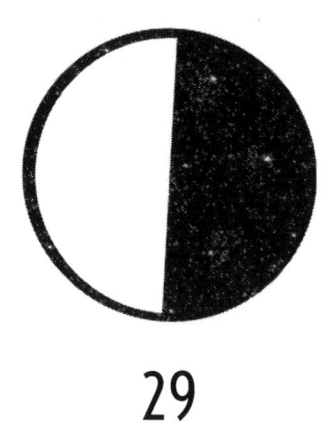

At the all-clear signal from Aly, who had been scouting ahead while on her way to deliver a tray of freshly baked pastries to the duchess, I slipped around the corner and made my way along the hallway. Fortunately for me, polished suits of armor were the only guards present.

I'd planned it all out perfectly. At this time of day, the duke and duchess were both taking their afternoon tea in this wing of the castle, so the servants, unless they were helping with it, normally made themselves scarce, attending to other duties.

Once I turned another corner, the carved oak door to Lester's personal study came into view. The hall was deserted; only my own footsteps disturbed the silence.

I slipped my hand into the hidden pocket of my dress and retrieved the ornate key. My heart pounding in my ears, I inserted it and nearly jumped for joy when the key caught the tumblers, opening the door with a muted *click*.

Quickly I opened the door, darted inside, and shut it securely behind me. I made sure to lock it from the inside, just in case a maid or butler checked the door.

A large, mahogany desk took up the center of the room, with an extra-padded, extra-wide chair behind it. Large glass windows filled the wall behind the desk, and bookshelves and cabinets lined the walls. Though, I noted with some amusement, a large oil painting of Lester hung prominently next to the door, presumably so Lester himself could gaze upon it. Normally, those kinds of portraits would be hung in hallways, or at least behind the desk, so that those entering could view it and feel appropriately humbled.

Mounted on either side of the portrait were three stuffed, snarling wolf heads. Two of the heads were huge, though the third was smaller, more...juvenile. The blood drained from my face and I brought my trembling hand to my mouth, choking back the scream rising in my throat. The image of a dark, empty room filled with rusty bloodstains appeared in my mind's eye. I reached one hand towards the smallest head, stopping just shy of its ebony fur. Not even the craftsman who had stuffed this head had been able to completely erase the fear in its —his— eyes.

Fenn's little brother hadn't escaped that night after all.

I took a deep breath, and then another. *What sort of sick, twisted monster would do something like this?!* I let the horror wash over me, let it settle deep in my heart. Let it fan the flames of fury that now lived there. I simply had one more reason to bring Lester to his knees.

It took some effort to pull my eyes away from the wolf heads and back towards the middle of the study.

Papers were piled high on every available surface, and not in orderly stacks. More paperwork lay scattered across the floor, and some loose leaves were even shoved into the bookshelves that lined the walls.

The mess was likely a result of Lester's paranoia and natural disorderliness, since he did not allow any servants in here for cleaning and couldn't be bothered to do it himself.

I carefully moved through the obstacle course of items on the floor to get to the desk. I sank down into Lester's cushioned chair and began sorting through the documents on his desk. I shouldn't have to worry about being missed for at least a few hours, though I hoped my search wouldn't take that long.

Footsteps echoed down the richly carpeted hallway, and I held my breath as they approached, my hand hovering over the next pile of papers. As they drew closer, I tensed, preparing to dive for cover should I hear a key turn in the lock.

The footsteps reached the door...and passed it, fading down the hallway. I exhaled shakily, my eyes returning to the next stack of papers. I grabbed them, leafing through quickly. I skimmed the documents as swiftly as I could, searching for specific words and ignoring all the rest.

Finding nothing, I carefully returned the stack to the desk, exactly the way I'd found it. I scanned the luxurious office, trying to puzzle out where Lester would keep the things he didn't want found.

It was such a relief that Lester wasn't at the castle today; I'm not sure if I would have found the courage to sneak in here if I'd been worried he could pop in at any moment. Because Wendy had informed me that Lester would be away from the estate for most of the day today at a horse racing competition, I had been able to put a plan together to get into his office.

Yesterday's daily ghastly "tea time" Lester insisted we have, during which he'd taunted and leered at me, had presented the perfect opportunity. First, I got him to brag about his official duties, which basically amounted to lofty-sounding titles in charge of nothing in particular, except dealing with prisoners, of course. I got him to wave around the brass key to his office, so I could note exactly to which pocket he returned it.

After that, as I made my exit, I made sure to gracefully trip and fall all over him. Which he enjoyed immensely, as evidenced by the gleam in his beady eyes.

But I'd gritted my teeth and plastered an embarrassed smile on my face as I discreetly slipped the key out of his pocket and tucked it into a pocket in my skirts as I pretended to readjust them.

Naturally, I'd spent quite a while in the tub that night, to rid myself of the feeling. Hopefully, it would be worth it if I could find something useful in this office, though it was proving difficult.

The papers weren't exactly grouped according to importance or even relevance. After shuffling through the top layers, I'd come to the conclusion that Lester just dumped papers on his desk or the floor as they came in, and never looked at them again. Most of the documents I'd been searching through on his desk pertained to horse breeding and racing, which was apparently Lester's favorite hobby. He was also a rather unsuccessful gambler when it came to these horse races.

According to some betting tickets I found, Lester had gambled away quite a substantial portion of the Duchy's finances. Perhaps that explained the almost obsessive amount of notes on breeding and lineage that lay scribbled across every spare scrap of paper.

I moved to the papers on the floor, only to discover an even more extensive timeline of losing bets, with only a handful of winners among them.

I tucked a few of the more impressive losing tickets into one of the pockets of my skirts as an insurance policy. Considering what I knew of Lester's character, or lack thereof, his parents likely didn't know exactly how much of their estate their son was losing.

These tidbits were great and all, but I needed something substantial— and quickly. I rose from the floor and walked behind the desk, careful not to disturb any of the paper piles. One touch and I'd likely cause an avalanche if I wasn't careful.

The top drawers revealed quills, ink, ribbons, wax, and Lester's personal seal. The middle drawers held stacks of blank paper and plenty of envelopes. I opened the bottom drawers, hoping for something more useful. I let out a sigh at the copious amount of betting cards, most of them losses. I closed the drawers, letting my eyes wander around the room. If I were Lester, where would I hide the truly important documents?

My gaze wandered along the dusty bookshelves, noting tomes on history, military strategy, and finances that had likely never been opened, if the sheer number of cobwebs on them was any indication. My eyes skittered over the painting and the wolf heads. I'd seen enough of *that* to last several lifetimes.

My gaze snagged on an especially tall and thick volume on a bookshelf to the right of the desk. At first, I couldn't figure out why it had caught my attention. What was different? And then I realized—Lester didn't read, so why was there no dust on this book?

I stepped closer, noticing that the shelf in front of the book was also free from dust, as if the book was frequently taken out and returned. I walked over to it, noticing that there was actually a clear path between the piles of papers straight to that section of the bookshelf.

I walked over and carefully pulled out the tome. It was oddly lighter than I expected. I quickly realized why. I opened the cover and saw that a rectangle had been cut into the pages so that only the very edges of each page remained, to give the impression of a regular book.

Inside the hollow that remained were several official-looking documents, as well as notes that had clearly been written by Lester. As I began skimming over them, I smiled grimly.

Here were the answers to my questions, damning evidence, and my salvation. Sure, I had known Lester wasn't exactly an honorable man, especially after coming in here...but his crimes were beyond my expectations.

I tamped down on the fury rising in me. I needed to act swiftly. Carefully, I rolled up the precious documents and put them in my pockets. Replacing the book, I backtracked to the door and paused, listening intently for any activity on the other side.

Hearing nothing nearby, I carefully unlocked and opened the heavy door, wincing at the loud groan of the hinges. I peeked around the door, and seeing no one except a maid walking away from me at the other end of the hall, I quickly exited and closed the door softly behind me.

I fumbled around in my pockets for the key, feeling relieved when my fingers closed around the cold metal. I locked the door and slipped the key back into my pocket. I turned around and came face-to-face with Lady Lindora, Lester's mother. Two of her ladies-in-waiting stood a few paces behind her.

Lady Lindora, unlike her son and husband, was surprisingly quite trim and usually wore extravagant gowns that accentuated her tiny waist. Her auburn locks were pulled back in a severe bun. The wrinkles etched around her angular face could not be called laugh lines, as I rarely ever saw her smile, let alone laugh. Though I supposed her pinched expression may have had more to do with her dislike of me than the suffocating tightness of her corset.

She had made her disgust crystal clear from the moment I was brought to this den of gilded cruelty. In her eyes, I was the dirty peasant girl with whom her son was currently soiling her family's good name and pure bloodline. As if it could get any dirtier.

"Your Grace," I greeted, dropping into a swift curtsey, praying she didn't notice the slight sound of rustling paper that accompanied the motion. My heart raced at her sudden appearance. How had she snuck up on me so silently?

"Serena," she sniffed, her cold gray eyes peering down at me from behind her gold bejeweled fan. "What brings you to this part of the manor?"

Translation: How dare you turn up underfoot in my pristine section of the estate, forcing me to gaze upon your putrid face.

I had no idea how long she'd been watching me. It couldn't have been too long, or she would be demanding why I'd been in her son's private study. Or just outright slapping me for my brazen disobedience.

"Your Grace, I had come to ask a question of Les-of my betrothed, but it would seem he is not currently in his study, as there was no answer to my knock," I said demurely, keeping my eyes downcast and my tone meek.

"My son is away at the races being held at the Windsom Estate today," she stated, eyeing me disapprovingly. "I suppose I should not be surprised that a mere commoner is incapable of remembering even the most important of events. It would seem a pretty face can only get one so far."

"Ah yes, I had forgotten he was away. Thank you for graciously reminding me," I said, fighting to keep my tone even and indifferent. I refused to give her the satisfaction of seeing me upset.

"Perhaps your time would be better spent with additional etiquette lessons," she sneered at me, snapping her fan closed in one sharp motion. "Come, ladies," she said to her ladies-in-waiting, who dutifully took up position behind her as she strode down the hallway, presumably towards her personal tea parlor.

Once she was out of sight, I sighed, letting the tension out of my shoulders. I certainly preferred being thought of as idiotic rather than suspicious or threatening. At least that meant she'd have her guard down. After all, what could a dirty peasant girl like me possibly do?

Before I could be waylaid by anyone else, I set off for my chambers. I had much work to do and very little time in which to do it. Including finding a way to slip the key back into Lester's pocket tomorrow afternoon, once he returned from the tournament. I couldn't say I was looking forward to *that*.

I pulled the roughspun cloak over my head and straightened the apron of my maid uniform, glancing around to make sure the courtyard was deserted. I quickly scurried across, aiming for the encampment a little ways away from the main house, where the mercenaries had been allowed to settle. Dusk was falling, casting the grounds into misty shadow.

After another torturous dinner with Lester and his parents, I had finally been allowed to retire to my rooms. After all, a bride needed her beauty sleep.

All of the servants had been buzzing about like bees to prepare for the upcoming wedding, which would take place tomorrow. Guests had been arriving over the last week, though only the most prestigious ones were offered rooms in the estate. The rest had found accommodations in the city nearby.

Having all those additional eyes had only made me even more grateful for the aid of Aly, Wendy, and a few of the more sympathetic maids and kitchen staff.

It was actually Aly who'd been able to help me coordinate tonight's meeting. Under the pretense of enquiring about how many of the mercenaries would be attending the wedding as guards, and therefore how many of them would require food, she was able to go to their encampment without arousing suspicion. There, she'd been able to pass my note to Tim, who'd been able to deliver it to Bruce and help convince him to give me a chance.

Everything was riding on tonight's meeting. No matter what it took, I absolutely needed the mercenaries' help tomorrow. I closed my hand around the papers I'd brought with me, reassuring myself they were still there for the tenth time since I'd left my room.

I entered the outskirts of the camp, drawing a few curious gazes from idle men, but no one came to question me, as it was common for servants to come here as messengers. Aiming for the large tent in the middle, I strode purposefully, trying to calm my racing heart and not let fear get the better of me. Since even in human form, they could probably still smell it.

True to form, Lester had postponed the release of his werewolf captives, citing the need for their services until the end of the wedding ceremony. That only made the mercenaries even less fond of Lester.

Off to one side, a flash of silver caught my eye. Another giant silver cage had been placed in the mercenary camp as both a promise and a warning. A promise that obedience would get them the keys they needed to free their families. And a warning, that any defiance could land themselves and their families in a similar cage forever.

The sight reminded me of the last time I'd seen Fenn. His back towards me, his chest rising ever so slightly with each breath. My heart ached at the memory of him, of the wounds he'd suffered because of me.

I resisted the urge to go to his cage in the dungeons, to cry my heart out, to explain everything and beg for forgiveness. I turned my cheek and clenched my hands into fists. I had a deal to make. Hopefully, I'd be able to beg for forgiveness soon, if everything went according to plan.

I paused outside the flaps of the large tent, the indistinct sounds of deep male voices reaching me. A sharp bark sounded, startling me. A wolf I hadn't noticed lay in the shadows by the tent. A sentry.

The voices inside the tent went silent, replaced by heavy footsteps coming towards me. The flap was pulled back, and Bruce stood before me. Candlelight flickered within the tent, revealing the other speaker to be Tim.

Without a word, he ushered me inside. I smiled warmly at Tim and sat down on the extra chair in the room. A rug covered the grass floor, and a bed, a desk, and the three chairs were the only furniture in the room.

"We were informed you had a proposal for us…that would be mutually beneficial," Bruce started once we were all seated.

I straightened in my seat, pushing the traumatic memories I had of this man out of my mind. It was rather ironic that he'd hunted me down to bring me here, and yet we'd both ended up essentially trapped.

But none of that mattered now. The only thing I cared about was securing this alliance.

"I know you and your pack were forced into helping Lester because he captured your families," I began, leaning forward. "What you may not know is that Lester has blackmailed me into obeying him in the exact same way. My loved ones have been imprisoned in the same dungeon, which lies beneath this castle, deep underground."

"What difference does that make to us?" Bruce interrupted, frustration hardening his features. Tim put his hand on Bruce's shoulder and he relaxed a fraction.

"My point is that we're in the same situation, and therefore have a common interest—freeing our families," I responded coolly.

"They will be freed. Once you've married him," Bruce said. At least he had the decency to look uncomfortable.

"Lester has already violated your deal twice. Do you truly believe he won't do it again?" I asked pointedly.

"That's..." Bruce trailed off, uncertainty flickering across his features.

"I don't trust him," Tim added, looking at Bruce.

"I can prove that he is planning to betray you once more," I asserted, pulling some papers out of my pocket. "Why do you think he captured only the women and children, while the rest of you were away?"

"Because they couldn't defend themselves," Bruce growled.

"That's only part of it. The women can bear children, and those children can be trained," I revealed. I handed Bruce and Tim several certificates of sale. "Once you were no longer useful, or became uncontrollable, Lester was planning to sell your families to the highest bidder as slaves. Some of the sales have already been finalized."

The blood slowly drained from their faces. Bruce's hands began to tremble with barely controlled rage.

"I'm gonna kill that bastard!" Bruce hissed, veins bulging in his neck.

"Not before I do," Tim growled, his hands bunched into fists.

"There's more. It gets worse. But this knowledge and evidence is our greatest weapon," I said gravely. "We just have to make sure our loved ones aren't caught in the cross-fire."

"What's the plan?" Bruce asked, an edge of steel in his voice.

30

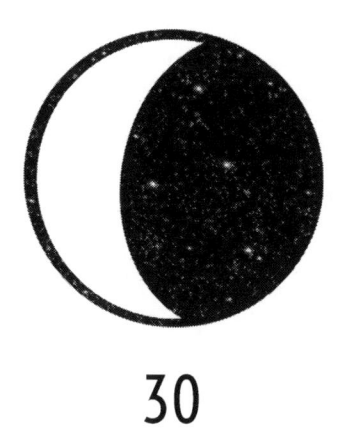

Today was the day. It would either be my ending or my beginning. I had put everything I had into making this plan work. I just had to have faith it would be enough.

Lily, Sophia, and a host of other maids had barged into my room at the crack of dawn, setting upon me like stylish fiends. The dark circles under my eyes had been concealed with face paint. Fortunately for me, the maids had dismissed them as pre-wedding jitters. My lips had been painted a deep red, and my eyes lined with black kohl. Light pink blush had been brushed across my cheekbones, since even the maids knew I would not be blushing naturally during the ceremony.

They brushed my red hair until it shone and proceeded to pull back some pieces from my face, braiding them into intricate patterns that were tied behind my head with a satin bow. Pearl pins were placed to keep several unruly locks from escaping. The rest of my hair was curled loosely, so it cascaded down my back.

And then it was time for the dress.

"Put your back into it, girls," grunted Lily as she and the others pulled back on the laces, tightening the corset as far as it would go.

"I'll still need to breathe," I protested, gasping for breath. "And also speak my vows!" I braced my arms against the wall, trying not to exhale. If they tightened the corset after I exhaled, I doubted I'd ever be able to inhale again. What a pity it would be to die of suffocation from my own dress on my wedding day. Well, if my plan didn't work, I supposed death by dress would be less painful than life as a slave.

I shook my head at myself. No, I was far too stubborn to take the coward's way out. Even if all of my plans failed, I could always make new ones. I would win this game, no matter how long it took.

After the corset came all of the ridiculously fluffy undergarments. Apparently having too much contrast in size between the bride and groom would be uncomfortable for the guests, so the skirts of my dress had been designed to be as puffed up as possible.

Lily and Sophia helped me into each layer, from the hoop frame to the top layers of tulle and lace. Finally, the heavily embroidered dress went over all of it. In keeping with tradition, the dress was made with white silks and linens, with delicate lace patterns on the bodice, sleeves and hemline. Pearls matching the ones in my hair adorned the bodice, which Lester had insisted have the lowest possible neckline.

My shoes were also white, not that they could be seen under the dress. They were flat, with no heel, since high heels would have made me taller than Lester, and he wouldn't like that.

The veil, at least, was beautiful. Intricate floral patterns spanned its length, which began at the crystal diadem on my brow and flowed down my back, ending several yards behind me. Only a duke could afford to spend so much on such an extravagant item, especially one that would only be worn once.

While Lily and the others were busy arranging and rearranging the veil and debating over which jewelry set would look best on me, Sophia went to retrieve my bouquet. By the time she returned, bearing a bouquet of silver roses wrapped in a silk ribbon, Lily had won the jewelry debate. An ornate silver and white diamond necklace was carefully placed around my neck, and matching bracelets and earrings now dangled from my wrists and earlobes.

"Here you are, my lady," Sophia said as she handed me the bouquet. I accepted with a nod, jewels swaying at the slight motion.

The roses had been stripped of their thorns. Most brides would see that as a kind and thoughtful act. But I smiled sadly at the now defenseless flower, which was destined to wilt after its beauty could no longer captivate its picker.

The sun had long since risen and had already reached its zenith in the clear azure sky. The wedding would be held in the afternoon, followed by a grand feast for all the guests.

Now that there was so little time left before the wedding, my stomach was twisting itself into knots. Anticipation and dread filled me. No alarms had been sounded, so hopefully that meant that the plan was still proceeding smoothly.

The guests had already had lunch and were now taking their seats. Even if I'd had the time to eat something, I probably wouldn't have been able to keep it down. Not that Lester would allow me to appear bloated on his big day.

"You look stunning, Lady Serena," gushed Sophia, admiring the jewels glittering at my throat.

"Yes, your hair stands out beautifully against the dress," chimed in a maid with chestnut brown hair.

"Thank you," I smiled warmly. "You all have done a wonderful job."

"We should get you in position now, my lady," said Sophia, after scanning me from head to toe. I was certain not a hair was out of place. She nodded, satisfied.

"Ladies, I need a moment to collect myself," I croaked hoarsely, before clearing my throat. "Alone."

"As you wish, my lady," Lily said, looking a little concerned. I smiled tightly, and they all curtsied before filing out of my room and softly closing the door.

Once I was alone, I quickly stepped over to my dresser. Taking out my dagger, which Bruce had returned to me at our meeting, I carefully arranged it inside the center of the bouquet, the hilt at the bottom and the tip hidden among the flowers. I examined it from every angle, making sure that any flash of metal could be easily explained as the glitter on the roses or the silver thread of the ribbon.

Once that was taken care of, I gratefully sank down into a plush chair, being mindful not to undo any of the maids' hard work. I took a few deep breaths, trying to calm my anxious heart. Today, I needed a spine of steel and a heart of mythril. I looked at my reflection in the gilded vanity mirror. The girl who looked back at me didn't seem like a scared, young girl. She looked like a determined woman, one whose armor was a dress and whose battle paint came in pink, red, and black.

I could do this. *I* had *to do this*. Not just for myself, but for everyone whose freedom hinged on my success today. For all of us, this would be a wedding to remember.

A knock sounded on the door, and I took a deep breath, steeling my resolve.

"Come in," I called, wincing at the slight tremor in my voice.

"It is time for the ceremony, my lady," Lily informed me as she opened the door, Sophia standing right behind her.

I nodded, carefully standing up. Not a hair out of place, I strode out of my gilded cage, Lily and Sophia falling in step behind me. Sophia picked up the veil, so the delicate lace wouldn't catch on something and tear. I nodded my thanks, not trusting my voice.

The walk out of the house and the short carriage ride to the venue passed in a blur. I couldn't help but think of all the things that could have gone wrong, could still go wrong.

And then the carriage came to a stop at the edge of a royal red velvet carpet. I stepped out of my gilded carriage, Lily and Sophia helping me manage my ridiculous dress. They exchanged worried glances, perhaps at my silence. Even the magnificent team of snow-white Arabian stallions that pulled my carriage couldn't draw a single glance from me today.

The red carpet stretched from the edge of my carriage and up the grand stone steps of the Imperial Church. Two grand mahogany doors stood open for my approach, and festive ribbons and banners hung from the carved stone statues of angels and demons that fought along the edges of the roof.

The Lindorian Knights stood on either side of the carpet, at attention. I carefully stepped down onto the pathway that was as red as a river of blood. As one, the knights unsheathed their swords and held them aloft, opposing blades crossing in an archway of gleaming weapons.

Although I knew this part of the ceremony was simply an old tradition, I couldn't help but picture one of those blades sweeping down and dying the carpet a true red. But I made it up the steps and to the open doors without incident.

I paused at the threshold, taking in the scene before me. My attention was immediately caught by the massive stained-glass windows at the opposite end of the cathedral. The sun shining through the painted glass made it glow especially bright in the dim interior. In it, an angel fought with a demon, the angel's spear of light piercing the demon's heart. On either side of this main battle, two smaller window scenes played out. On the left, it showed the bloodied angel standing atop the prone form of the demon, fist raised in triumph, darkness staining the angel's once pure wings. On the right, it showed the gleaming angel clasping hands with the purified demon, whose black, bat-like wings were transforming into soft white-feathered wings.

So good could destroy evil, but not without losing a piece of its goodness to the shadow. But good could also restore what was lost in darkness to the light, elevating both to a higher place of love and light.

Two very different sets of actions, of interpretations, and standards. I wondered which scene I would soon be starring in.

Beneath the stunning stained glass was the less than awe-inspiring sight of Lester in his formal attire, hair slicked back and shoes shining. The Church Officiator stood behind him at the altar.

And off to the side sat the huge silver cage, Fenn lying within it. I kept my face carefully blank even as red-hot fury coursed through my veins. I had guessed Lester would do this, had planned on it even. A final reminder to behave, as well as a means of bragging and showing off his other hunted prize. Feverish blue eyes met mine for an instant, the misery in them nearly sending me to the floor. I tore my gaze away, looking everywhere, anywhere else.

Rows of matching cushioned chairs in the Lindora colors adorned each side of the aisle, seating a sea of unfamiliar faces. Closest to the altar sat Lester's parents, and across the aisle from them sat a family so overly dressed in gold and jewels that they must be incredibly important. I noticed a crown atop the father's head and realized with a start that I was gazing upon the Imperial Family.

I was glad His Majesty was seated right in front, so he would have the best view of what was to come.

I glanced around the room, noting the cleaned up mercenaries standing guard against the walls. Bruce was standing off to Lester's side. He nodded imperceptibly when our eyes met, and relief tore through me.

At my entrance, the choir began chanting and the musicians began playing. The guests all turned in their seats to watch. As I waited, silhouetted by the afternoon sun, the flower girl frolicked down the aisle, sprinkling flower petals all over the place.

Next, my four maids of honor—Chloe, Esther, Emily and Rebecca—swept down the aisle, resplendent in shimmering pink dresses. I had chosen the only four nobles I had met who had actually been kind to me, a commoner.

Lester's lone best man went next. Judging by the way he was ogling my maids of honor, I could truly believe he was a friend of Lester's.

Finally, it was my turn. I lifted my chin high, striding slowly and purposefully down the aisle, not deigning to look at the guests, who likely thought as little of me as I did of them.

I reached the end and stepped up onto the dais beside Lester, who smirked at me.

"All mine," he whispered so softly I doubted even the holy man in front of us heard him.

I simply smiled back, and he looked a little taken aback. As if he'd been expecting fear or anger and didn't quite know what to do with my uncharacteristic reaction.

"I hope you're looking forward to the Lindora tradition of sacrificing a powerful beast to commemorate our union," Lester whispered, triumph written in every line of his face as he glanced at Fenn. "I think I'll have his head stuffed and mounted in our bedroom."

My blood boiled, my vision went red. My calm mask began to slip. If it hadn't been for the timely intervention of the priest, I very well might have stabbed Lester through the heart right then and there.

"We are gathered here today to celebrate the union in holy matrimony of Serena LaRoux and Lester Lindora," intoned the officiator, whose voice echoed off the high, arched ceilings.

We both turned to face him, and the soft murmurings of the guests quieted down. He droned on and on, slowly working his way through the standard verses. I clutched my flowers to my chest, the familiar weight of my dagger in my hand comforting.

Finally, finally, the officiator got to the question I'd been both dreading and eagerly anticipating.

"Do you, Lester Lindora, take Serena LaRoux to be your lawfully wedded wife?" he asked, turning to him.

"I do," he said smugly.

"And do you, Serena LaRoux, take Lester Lindora to be your lawfully wedded husband?" he demanded, turning towards me.

I closed my eyes, taking a deep breath. I looked Lester dead in the eyes, and with the prettiest smile I could muster, I declared, "I could never marry such a monster!"

31

A deadly silence fell over the cathedral. The singing and accompanying instruments petered out and died. The guests sat frozen, shock and confusion written across their faces.

The wolf in the corner raised his head, blank blue eyes igniting with a tiny spark of hope.

"Wha-what did you say?!" sputtered Lester, clenching his hands into fists. His ears and forehead began turning that all-too-familiar shade of red and purple.

"You heard me," I said sweetly. I reached up, carefully took off the ridiculously long lace veil, and set it gently on the ground, while still keeping my bouquet—and my weapon—in one hand.

"What do you think you're doing?" he hissed, advancing a step towards me.

"You'll see soon enough," I stated.

I turned and faced the most powerful people in the room, summoning every ounce of dignity and conviction I possessed.

"Your Majesties," I addressed the Imperial family, curtseying deeply, with one hand over my heart. "I believe it is my duty as your subject to inform you of the misdeeds of the House of Lindora, of which you may be unaware."

At that, the entire hall of people began murmuring agitatedly amongst themselves. Once this whole spectacle was over, I fully expected the rest of the country to be aware of what transpired here within days. If there was one thing aristocrats were good at, it was gossiping.

The emperor, whose expression at my initial outburst had been one of simple surprise, sharpened to one of intense interest. His cobalt eyes narrowed, and he leaned forward, bracing his arms on his knees to steeple his hands together. His purple velvet cape shifted, the fur-lined edges trailing on the floor.

"You have my undivided attention, girl," he spoke, his deep voice carrying to the farthest reaches of the building. "However, should your accusations against the Duke's house be groundless, you will face the full penalty for treason. Knowing this, will you still proceed?"

"Yes, Your Majesty," I answered immediately. "Thank you for your understanding. I know my word as a commoner would not be acceptable alone. Therefore, I would like to present you with irrefutable evidence."

I glanced at Lester as I said the last part, noting how his face had gone suddenly pale. His mother and father, on the other hand, simply seemed outraged.

"What nonsense—" Duke Lindora started, but with a single look from his sovereign, the protest died on his lips.

"You may proceed," the emperor said, gesturing in my direction.

"Thank you," I repeated, curtseying once more. "Wendy, Aly, if you would," I called out to my two friends, who came hurrying forward from where they'd been listening from their stations.

As they hurried towards me, Lester grabbed my arm and growled in my ear, "Aren't you forgetting something? Your mother and that worthless peasant boy and his family are in *my* dungeons. This is your last chance to stop whatever plot you're working on and finish the damn ceremony!"

"You picked me to be your bride because of my appearance. Isn't it ironic that I'll be using what you never cared about, my intellect, to destroy you?" I said seriously.

"You—" he started, his grip on my wrist tightening painfully. Despite myself, I winced.

"Is there some sort of problem, Lord Lester?" inquired the emperor coldly, glancing pointedly at where Lester still gripped my wrist. The empress was frowning at Lester, disapproval and suspicion darkening her fair visage.

"N-no, not at all, Your Majesty," Lester stammered, bowing belatedly, and releasing my arm.

I rubbed the tender spot, grimacing. Wendy and Aly finally joined me, each curtseying deeply with a murmured, "Your Majesties." Wendy carried a stack of documents in her arms. I could tell she was nervous, though I think she was also at least a little excited to be showing off several of her own dress designs to the Imperial Family, since she and Aly each wore one, in addition to my own dress. Aly carried a heavy-looking box in her arms.

"Firstly, I would like to bring your attention to Lord Lester's gambling habits," I began, gesturing for Wendy to hand over a packet of the betting tickets. "As you'll see from the dates on each ticket, Lord Lester has been illegally attending and betting at horse races. And losing a substantial amount of the money that had been intended as taxes and maintenance funds for the territories under Lindora management."

Once the emperor had examined several of the tickets and nodded, I continued, "These represent only a small portion of the whole. Thousands more are currently located in Lord Lester's private study. But where did Lord Lester acquire such large sums? The total sum of the funds lost is far greater than even the Lindora Duchy's total income over the span of a decade. So clearly, this money did not come from there. Some of it was generated courtesy of the people Lester Lindora has illegally sold into slavery, but even that sum is paltry compared to the sum he's gambled away. If you take a look at the date when his bets exponentially increased, it's roughly a year ago, right around the time of the mysterious disappearance of the Verdania Household."

Several gasps sounded from the guests, and I knew at least a few of them were starting to piece together where I was going with this. A glance in Lester's direction showed him trembling with rage. But even he understood that to attack me now would only prove my words true.

The face of Lester's father, the Duke, had gone rigid with rage as he stared at his son. His mother covered her mouth with a bejeweled hand, eyes wide in shock and disbelief.

The emperor crumpled the tickets in a clenched fist. A vein stood out on his forehead. "What exactly are you implying?" he thundered.

"The disappearance of the venerable Verdanias has remained a mystery to this day, even to the inhabitants of Verdain. However, after my own mother sold me to Lord Lester, which is a practice long since made illegal, I stumbled across the Verdania estate. While I was there, I noticed something odd. Although the kitchens lay largely untouched, I found that the armory, the treasury, and just about every easily carried small item of value was gone."

"In addition, the prized Arabian horses the Verdania's had been known to breed, were nowhere to be found, and there was no sign indicating the horses had either been released into the wild or escaped on their own. It was around this same time that Lord Lester acquired a number of fine Arabians and made known his newfound passion for them, as well as for breeding them."

I paused to let this new information sink in, then continued, "But the strangest thing of all were the rumors. There was one rumor I was informed of recently, that Lester Lindora was humiliated at the annual hunting tournament hosted by Your Majesty, by the much younger heir of the Verdania Duchy."

I acknowledged, "But this is all circumstantial coincidence. Or at least, it was. This document here," I continued, displaying the paper Aly handed to me, "is the order for Lindora knights to dress in commoner's garb and exterminate the Verdania family, by any means necessary. Signed and sealed by one Lester Lindora."

Before the last few damning words were out of my mouth, Lester's parents, the Imperial family, and most of the guests were on their feet, yelling and arguing in an unbearable cacophony.

"Lies! Trickery!" cried Lester. "Father, I didn't- I would never—"

A guttural roar of unbridled fury tore through the space, echoing to the high ceilings. Stunned silence descended, and every head turned toward the silver cage in the corner, where the massive black beast had arisen and now stood facing the audience, hackles raised, fangs bared, and vengeance in his icy-blue eyes.

"You worthless woman!" screamed Lester, who began advancing on me. "Your mother, your loved ones are in MY dungeons, and today they all die, in the most painful way possible!"

He grabbed my wrist again, shaking me for emphasis. He raised his hand to slap me, eliciting a harsh snarl from Fenn and looks of horror and repulsion from the guests.

"I will take that as a confession. Guards!" the emperor yelled, but they were too far away. I flinched, bracing for the pain.

A scarred, calloused hand snatched Lester's right arm right before he made contact with my face.

"Now that's no way to treat a lady," growled Bruce, his hulking presence dwarfing even the rotund Lester.

I raised my right eyebrow at him. "That's rather ironic, coming from you," I commented drily.

Bruce grimaced. "I'm sorry fer before. Had to keep up appearances. I couldn't take the chance of losing me wife an' son," he explained, with a quick glare in Lester's direction.

"Apology accepted." Turning to Lester, who was now being held by a pair of Imperial guards, I taunted, "Oh yes, all of those people you were keeping hostage and torturing in your dungeons? They've been freed. You have no more leverage over me, or over your mercenaries. Their wives and children are safe and will never be held in your thrall again."

I stalked up to Lester and took the silver key out of his shirt pocket.

"No—wait, stop! You can't!" Lester whimpered, trembling.

I paused, glancing at him. "You get to face the consequences of your actions now." And with that, I walked over to the giant silver cage.

I stood eye to eye with Fenn. His blue eyes softened, and my heart trembled at the kindness and understanding I saw in them. Quickly, I unlocked the cage door, rushing inside and unlocking the shackles around his legs as fast as my trembling fingers would allow.

The sound of those horrible shackles hitting the floor of the cage reverberated in my soul. Fenn was the one who had been chained up, but it felt like I was being freed as well.

Blue eyes met mine as I reached up and gently removed the silver mask. Tears blurred my vision at the horrific burns on his face where the metal had rested. All I wanted to do was collapse with my arms around him, fingers running through his soft fur.

But we weren't done yet. So I took a deep breath and straightened my spine. "I'm sorry I took so long," I whispered so only Fenn could hear. He licked my hand, and I smiled tightly.

"Come on, let's get you out of this thing," I said louder and exited the silver cage with Fenn right behind me.

Together, we walked back onto the dais, and a hush fell as we passed. Fenn kept his head held high, though I could tell he was still favoring one of his hind legs. We stopped in front of the emperor and Lester, whose parents were animatedly berating and pleading with him to spare their son's life.

"Your Majesty, Your Graces, allow me to introduce Fenrys Yaegar Verdania, heir of Duke Verdania," I stated grandly, gesturing to Fenn.

"And our rightful alpha," Bruce added, looking pointedly at Lester. "But you already knew that, didn't you?"

32

"W-what?! But how...?" Lester stammered, glancing nervously between Fenn and the emperor.

"How did I figure it out?" I asked, taking a step towards him, Fenn growling menacingly at my side.

Lester flinched, his eyes narrowing in hatred. "Let's just say that holding dozens of women and children hostage in your dungeons will cause even the most loyal of servants to talk," I stated with quiet venom.

"A noble like me does not need to justify taking revenge on those who've wronged him," Lester sneered.

"So, you really ordered the assassination of Fenn's family simply because he was more skilled than you? You're a monster!" I yelled. Fenn stiffened beside me.

"I've changed my mind." Lester snarled. "You're not worth the trouble. Guards! Kill her and that damned dog!"

His knights stepped forward, but then hesitated, glancing uncertainly at the emperor, who had been coldly watching the exchange.

"Cease this nonsense at once, or I'll have no choice but to brand you a traitor," he warned.

Lester blinked. But then his face hardened into a mask of determination and hatred.

"Kill them or your families die!" screamed Lester, spittle flying from his purple lips.

The knights lurched into action, and steel clanged against steel as the mercenaries surged to meet them.

"No!" I cried. I'd had Bruce free all of Lester's prisoners, but his guards didn't know that.

All hell broke loose as the nobles who'd been enjoying the show screamed and tried to run out of the cathedral, their ridiculous outfits slowing them down. They pushed and shoved at each other, shouting their ranks at one another in an attempt to get to the front of the horde. As if any of that mattered when the swords started flying.

I gripped the hilt of my dagger, unsheathing it and discarding my bouquet of flowers in one swift motion. I brought it up high to block the downward swing of one of Lester's knights, the impact jarring my arm. He brought his sword around in a wide arc, but I was faster. I stepped in and sliced his sword arm. He dropped his sword with a cry of pain and stumbled back, a look of relief on his face.

A dark shadow lunged past me, and Fenn tossed aside the knight that had been sneaking up behind me. The man hit a column with a loud thud, before sliding to its base. He didn't get up.

Fenn's form suddenly blurred, loud cracks sounding as his form grew taller and thinner, claws retracting into hands, fangs shrinking and muscles shifting. And then all of a sudden, Fenn stood before me in human form, his usual smirk firmly in place. He was also very much shirtless.

My cheeks heated, and I tore my gaze away from his chiseled abs. My heart squeezed at the countless burn marks all over his body. The ones on his wrists, ankles, and face were the most severe. The short time he'd been free of his silver shackles wasn't nearly enough, even for his enhanced healing abilities, to make much progress.

"Fenn," I breathed, blinking back the tears that suddenly misted my eyes.

He smiled at me, but then his gaze went over my shoulder. I whirled, blocking the thrust of the sword that had been aimed at my heart, and countered with a thrust of my own. At the last second, I shifted the blade an inch to the side. The knights might not have attacked if they weren't so worried for their loved ones.

I knew exactly how they felt.

My opponent fell, only for two more to take his place. Behind me, I heard Fenn scoop up the sword my first adversary had dropped and shifted to the side so he could get at one of the knights in front of me.

We dodged and danced in tandem, trading blows with the knights. Lester's knights were skilled, but they weren't putting their all into it, and they weren't accustomed to fighting as a team.

With a swift sidecut, I downed my opponent and took a stab at Fenn's, throwing him off balance so that Fenn could deliver the final blow.

"Thanks," Fenn panted, smiling as if we were training in the field instead of in the middle of a battle.

"I had a good teacher," I replied with a radiant smile of my own.

I scanned the cathedral, noting that most of the nobles had made it outside, away from the conflict, and that there were far more mercenaries still standing than knights. Though I smirked when I saw Bruce battling it out with three knights, a feral grin of delight on his scarred face. Knowing him, if I tried to help out, he'd whine about me depriving him of his fun.

The emperor had ordered his personal guards to surround and protect his family. His son and daughter had buried their heads in the empress' dress, and she was stroking their heads and murmuring words of comfort to them.

To my surprise, the emperor himself had joined the fight, and his prowess in battle was truly frightening. He wielded his saber expertly, neatly cutting down his foes. Where I had avoided dealing fatal blows, the emperor doled them out like sweets. Knights fell at his feet, their pooling blood staining the carpet an even deeper crimson.

But it was his face that I found the most terrifying. There was no expression there, not even one of concentration or exertion. What a terrifying man. At least the knights that dropped their weapons, renouncing Lester and begging for forgiveness on their knees before him were spared.

Several members of the pack had taken their wolf forms and fought with fangs and claws. Some of the mercenaries had managed to capture several knights and tie them up, leaving a wolf or two to guard them.

The fighting appeared to be dying down, though a few knights still fought desperately. If only we could reassure them that their families were fine, but no one would hear me over the clash of steel.

Movement out of the corner of my eye caught my attention, and I turned to see Lester trying to sneak away while no one was looking.

"Oh no you don't!" I snarled.

I lunged forward, Fenn a step behind me, and went straight for Lester. He saw me coming and started scrabbling away, but it was clearly evident he hadn't had to run in at least a decade.

We were on him in an instant. Fenn pinned him down, and I borrowed some rope from one of the mercenaries to tie his hands and feet together.

"You can't do this to me! Unhand me this instant, you lowly curs!" Lester shrieked. "I'll have your heads for this! My parents won't let you get away with treating me like this!"

"Murder is murder, whether you're a noble or not," I stated coldly. Lester flinched at the look in my eyes.

"The 'lowliest' farmer in the land has more honor and character than you ever will. One's strength of character can't be measured by social status or worldly possessions. It's something earned by rising to the challenge of life and overcoming adversity," Fenn added.

"Quite right," rumbled the emperor from behind me. Sheathing his weapon, he stepped onto the raised platform, his steps echoing like thunder. "It would seem your trials have forged you into formidable adversaries," he continued, nodding at Fenn and I. "Fenrys, your father was a good man. My condolences. We must have a lengthy discussion soon."

Fenn nodded mutely.

"But first," he said, turning to Lester, "we must determine an appropriate punishment for this one."

33

"Your Majesty, there must be some sort of mistake!" Duke Lindora protested, helping his wife step up onto the platform.

It seemed that now that most of the fighting was over, the noble couple had mustered up the courage to lift themselves off the floor, where they'd been cowering behind some chairs as their personal guards bled for them. It seemed neither one of them had been truly aware of their son's actions. But could they truly not have noticed any of it at all? Had they paid so little attention to their only son? Perhaps such blatant lack of love and guidance was why he'd turned out the way he did...

"My Lester would never do such a thing!" Lady Lindora added weakly. She clutched her husband's arm for support. I noticed her hands were trembling, and her gilded fan lay forgotten on the floor.

"Let us ask the man himself," the emperor declared, striding forward until he was directly in front of the bound and kneeling Lester. "Do you admit to giving this written order," he said, waving the document in Lester's face, "for the assassination of the noble house of Verdania?"

Lester glanced at his father and mother, both of whom were anxiously awaiting his answer. I could see the gears turning in his mind, looking for an angle, a way to wriggle out of this. The silence stretched out, until I saw an idea spark in his eyes.

"Clearly, I've been framed with a forged document. The funds I acquired around that time were simply due to a fortunate bet I placed at the races," he stated boldly.

"Which is also illegal," the emperor rumbled.

"See? Those peasants are trying to frame my son!" exclaimed Lady Lindora, pointing an accusing finger at Fenn and I.

Fenn stepped forward, his face unreadable. "You must have missed the introduction earlier, while you were cowering on the floor. My name is Fenrys Verdania, eldest son and heir to the Dukedom of Verdania," he stated icily, sketching a mocking bow towards the Duke and Duchess.

"What?!" gasped the Duchess, her hand flying to her mouth. The Duke frowned, furrowing his brow.

"Lord Lester discovered the fact that the Verdanias are a family of werewolves, a fact they endeavored to keep secret. When Fenn returned from the Academy, Lester realized he needed to tie up loose ends," I informed them icily.

"Your Graces, that document, as well as the betting tickets, were discovered in your son's personal study. His official seal is also kept there, in a locked drawer," I said meaningfully. "A thorough examination of the seal will verify its authenticity."

"How did a useless girl like you even get into my study?!" Lester exclaimed.

I smiled. "So you admit what I'm saying is true?"

He blanched. "N-no, of course not."

"Your Majesty, is it really such a surprise that the sort of individual who gambles illegally, forces himself upon his maids, has women and children imprisoned to blackmail others, and buys and blackmails a country girl into marrying him because of the color of her hair is also capable of ordering someone else to kill for him, because of a perceived slight? Even if the targets are also nobles?" Fenn asked, his tone frigid.

The smile dropped from my face as I added, "He also kept the stuffed heads of the Verdanias—and their youngest son— on display in his study, as trophies."

"What nonsense—" Lester shouted. Before he could finish, Fenn had a dagger pressed to his throat. Lester froze, his eyes peering down the length of steel.

The Duchess gasped, whether at his crimes or the blade at her son's throat, I couldn't tell. Perhaps at both.

"You monster! You dare deny it?" Fenn growled. "You must not be aware of this, but werewolves can tell when a person is lying, whether in human or wolf form. Lie, and I will know. Tell the truth, or I will end you here and now."

Some of the wolves glanced over at Fenn's tone of voice, instinctively lowering their eyes submissively.

Lester opened his mouth, and Fenn pressed the blade into his skin, letting a single drop of blood trail down his neck. Lester closed his mouth, swallowing once, twice.

"I don't deny it," Lester whispered hoarsely, his eyes never leaving the blade at his neck. "I ordered the assassination of the Verdania family."

The Duchess crumpled to the floor, wailing like a banshee. The Duke simply stood there, dumbfounded. He stared at his son as if he'd never seen him before, his face as white as a sheet.

Fenn's hand tensed on the blade, eliciting a whimper from Lester. His shoulders were shaking with the effort it took him not to end his family's murderer.

I put my hand on his shoulder. "It won't bring them back," I whispered softly, giving his shoulder a gentle squeeze.

Fenn shuddered, exhaling. Then he returned his dagger to its sheath, standing up slowly.

"The truth at last," the emperor said, nodding approvingly at Fenn. "Ordering the assassination of another noble house is tantamount to treason and carries the corresponding punishment. However, I will also take into consideration the opinions of those who were wronged." He looked at Fenn, and then at me, inviting us to speak.

Fenn paused, turmoil in his eyes. So I spoke up first, to give him more time to think.

"Your Majesty, the crimes that have been committed are unforgivable. So many have suffered or lost their lives to the whims of this man, who was gifted by circumstance with wealth and power. Alas, despite all this, he found it easier to tear others down to raise his own standing, instead of putting in the time and effort, as they did, to attain the same heights.

"Please, do not allow him to take the easy way out once again. In my humble opinion, the most fitting punishment would be for him to serve those he has wronged and to rebuild what he has destroyed. Maybe then he will come to understand the gravity of what he has done, and atone for it."

"Interesting," the emperor mused, stroking his goatee. "And what say you, Fenrys?" he asked, turning his sharp gaze on Fenn. "What would you see done, knowing this fool assassinated your family and had the gall to endanger the Imperial Family?"

I glanced at Lester, wondering about his reaction to what was being said. He was fidgeting with one of his polished leather boots, a look of pure, unadulterated hatred on his face. However, he looked a little more...composed than I'd expected. Did he still believe he could wriggle out of a severe punishment? Surely he was aware that the penalty for just one of his crimes was execution.

Fenn cleared his throat. "Although I do agree that a life of service to others could be fitting," he said slowly, glancing in my direction, "I would honestly rather see the law carried out, for the simple reason that I do not wish to give him the opportunity to take even one more life. Your Majesty, no one else should die, or be miserable, due to one man's ego, simply because of his social status."

Fenn avoided my eyes, so I slipped my hand into his larger one, giving him a reassuring squeeze. He met my gaze, and I nodded at him. He smiled slightly, relief written across his features. Fenn was right. Knowing Lester, he'd likely try to take revenge on anyone who was involved today. And the thought of losing anyone else to him was simply unbearable.

"I am inclined to agree with you, Fenrys Verdania. This scourge on our empire has lasted far too long already." Turning to face Lester, who was still fidgeting, the emperor announced, "I hereby declare that Lester Lindora is to be executed for treason against the crown. His execution will take place three days hence, at dawn. The condemned may put his affairs in order through a regent during that time. The Duke and Duchess are hereby stripped of their titles until further notice, pending a full investigation. Guards, get these fallen nobles out of my sight."

Turning to address the rest of the room, the emperor proclaimed, "All those who aided in the successful capture of this traitor will be handsomely rewarded, regardless of any other factors." He looked at Bruce and his men as he was saying that last part.

I smiled in relief, exhaling a breath I hadn't realized I'd been holding. *We'd done it!* Now that the emperor had been made aware of Lester's actions, none of us would ever have to fear him again. And our loved ones would all be safe from him. I'd be able to see Chris and his family again, and I wouldn't have to hide my hair out of fear anymore!

"Are you sure you want to do this?" Lester sneered from the floor.

A feeling of dread curled in my stomach. He was calm. Too calm. And that was far more unnerving than his usual purple-faced rage. Beside me, Fenn tensed, his eyes narrowing.

"I'm sorry to break it to you, but you're not getting out of this one," I said, my even tone disguising my nervousness.

"Aren't I?" he asked smugly. "You were so close. You managed to find most of the secrets in my office, but there was something you missed."

I bit my lip. I had searched so thoroughly, though. What more could he possibly be hiding?

"What do you mean?" growled Fenn.

"Well, you see," Lester drawled, a wicked glint in his eye, "You weren't exactly the first female I had my eyes on. There was an additional order I gave those assassins that night. I requested that one of the targets be brought back *alive*."

Fenn went absolutely rigid beside me. My eyes widened as the meaning of his words sank in, and the puzzle pieces fell into place.

"You took my sister," Fenn choked out.

"So the mutt can think after all," Lester crooned. Growls echoed from every corner of the room. A bead of sweat stood out on Lester's forehead.

"And I'm the only one who knows where she is!" he added quickly. "Without me, you'll never see her again."

"Well, that does complicate matters," the emperor mused. "However, I'm sure the dungeon master will be able to get the information out of him before the execution date."

Fenn bowed to him, clearly trying to keep his rage in check. "Thank you, Your Majesty. I would be grateful if you would allow me to assist in this matter," he ground out, a dark promise in his eyes.

"No! Y-you won't be able to get me to talk!" Lester yelled. His face had gone deathly pale at the look in Fenn's eyes.

"Won't I?" Fenn said mockingly, imitating the way Lester had spoken so cockily a few moments before. "I think I'm going to enjoy paying you back for the cage, the shackles, the silver mask, the whippings, and of course, what you've done to Serena and my family. There is *nothing* I won't do."

The emperor nodded approvingly at Fenn. "Take him away," he ordered the guards, gesturing to Lester.

But as the two guards hauled Lester to his feet, a glint of silver caught my eye. He pulled a wicked silver dagger out of his boot.

"Die, you filthy animal!" Lester screamed, and hurled it straight at Fenn's heart.

Time seemed to slow down and speed up at the same time as I watched the dagger leave Lester's hand. All of Fenn's many wounds flashed before my eyes. Silver to the heart in this state wasn't something he could come back from.

Before I even realized what I was doing, I'd pushed Fenn out of the path of the dagger. He fell to the floor, the surprised expression on his face quickly turning to horror.

I felt the impact of the dagger sinking into my chest, the cold blade burning like icy fire.

"No! Serena!" Fenn screamed as he lunged forward to catch me, his calloused hands snagging on the ridiculous lace of my dress. My own dagger slipped from numb fingers and clattered to the floor.

"Sorry," I gasped weakly. Red bloomed across my dress.

Fenn cradled my head, his hands shaking. "Stay with me," he begged, his eyes misting. "Someone, find a healer!" he yelled over his shoulder.

"What were you thinking?" he whispered hoarsely, stroking my hair soothingly. Distantly, I heard people running, shouting. Wolves snarling. Lester screaming.

"It was my turn to save you," I murmured, black swirling at the edges of my vision. I reached up shakily, cupping his face in my hand. The roaring in my ears got louder.

"I love you," I breathed out.

The last thing I saw, before the darkness pulled me under, were two precious blue eyes, shining like stars in the night sky.

34

It was cold. So cold. The biting chill had settled deep in my bones, as if I had turned to ice. Not even the worst winters, spent shivering under a thin and filthy blanket, with the winter wind nipping through the cracks in the house, had left me so miserable and frozen.

But then, there was a light. It was weak, and it flickered like a candle in a storm.

"Boil more water!"

"You, go get me more gauze pads!"

"She won't stop shivering!"

"Bring more blankets!"

"What can I do? How can I help?" *For some reason, that voice sounded familiar. I wanted to comfort that voice.*

But why was it so noisy? All I wanted to do was sleep, sleep to make the cold go away...

The noises faded, until I found myself in rolling fields of green and gold, a cool breeze teasing my hair and the warm sun kissing my skin. I was on my back, gazing up at the clear azure sky. The tree above me shaded my face, its leaves whispering of seasons passed and seasons yet to come.

I heard the comforting sound of Soren happily munching on grass nearby. I turned my head to look at him, satisfied with the healthy sheen to his coat. Had I been worried about him? I couldn't quite recall...

"She's lost too much blood!"

"We're losing her!"

"Do whatever it takes to save her. Cost is no object." *I shivered. That voice was cold, calculating. Powerful.*

I blocked out the voices. The voices brought pain. And cold.

I sat up slowly from under the tree. Soren whickered softly, walking over to me. He put his head down, and I gave him a few loving scratches behind the ears. His nose felt like velvet under my fingers.

Movement caught my eye. A strange, fox-like creature was flitting around me on feathery wings. It seemed to glow with its own internal light, and its laughing emerald eyes called to me. Then it turned and dove into the long grasses, disappearing from sight.

I stood up, scanning the field for a hint of a bushy tail. Off to my right, I noticed a house. It was not a shabby shack, like the one I grew up in. It was not a massive castle, like Lester's. Wait, who was that again? Eh, it didn't matter anymore. The house was a nice size, with flowers in the front yard and a few windows. But even better was the large barn next to it, complete with a paddock and a large arena.

It was my dream ranch! A feeling of peace welled up from deep within me, and I smiled contentedly. A home of my very own. I started walking towards it, Soren trailing along beside me, cropping at the grass as we went.

"Nothing we've tried has been effective, Your Majesty."

"Then call for someone more skilled."

"We have, but...but none of them will make it in time, I'm afraid."

"Then there's only one option left," said the familiar voice. "I just hope she can forgive me..." *Something in my chest stirred at the raw emotion in that voice.*

I took a few more steps forward, but then I yelped in pain. I rubbed my left shoulder, trying to ease the sudden stinging. I kept going, trying to ignore the dulling pain.

About halfway to my ranch, I stopped dead in my tracks. A huge, snowy white wolf stood in front of me, blocking the way forward and my view of the ranch. Where it had come from, I had no clue.

But for some reason, it seemed more real than anything else here. Whereas the ranch seemed a little blurry around the edges, this wolf seemed to stand in sharp relief. I glanced at Soren, worried. But he was just as calm as ever, not a tense muscle in his body, as if there wasn't a huge predator right in front of him.

The wolf watched me with emerald-green eyes. When our eyes met, I saw human kindness and intelligence there, and for some reason, I just knew that this creature would not harm me.

Confidently, I walked forward, until I stood right before it. Slowly, I reached out my hand to touch it. The beautiful wolf bowed its head, closing its eyes. My outstretched fingers brushed through downy fur, its warmth taking me by surprise.

Suddenly, that warmth flowed from the wolf through my hand, up my arm to my shoulder and straight to my heart. The heat embraced me, filled me, and I felt strength coursing through every fiber of my being.

Along with the heat came light, a strong light that filled the world with its brilliance, burning away every dark and icy shadow that lurked and lingered.

A soft breeze caressed my cheek, and I shifted, the blankets twisting around me. I slowly opened my eyes, blinking them into focus. The curtains of my room fluttered in the breeze, mid-morning light filtering through.

I frowned, confused. Why was I back in my room at the Verdania estate? I'd just been at Lester's—

Then it all came rushing back to me. The wedding, the fighting. We'd won, Fenn had been freed, but then...but then... I looked down. Gingerly, I lifted the thin white sleeping gown I wore. Bandages were wrapped tightly around my chest, but for some reason, I didn't feel any pain.

I moved my hand to my throat to finger my moon pendant for reassurance, but my fingers found nothing but a slight burn where it normally rested. I panicked and frantically scanned the room. I let out a sigh of relief when I saw it sitting on top of the dresser, the attached Vulclaria feather glowing faintly.

I slowly sat up, expecting a bolt of pain from my chest and my shoulder. It never came. Only a slight soreness remained.

On the contrary, I hadn't felt this good since, well, ever. The sudden trilling of a songbird startled me. It sounded like it was right next to my ear. I looked out the window and spotted the little bird perched in a tree all the way at the edge of the Forgotten Forest. How odd.

Footsteps echoed in the hallway. A hint of pine was in the air. So it must've been Fenn walking down the hallway. *Wait, how did I know that?* The footsteps paused outside my door, and the slight scraping of the doorknob turning gave way to the groaning of the door hinges. Fenn cracked the door open, poking his head in to see if I was awake.

His black hair was all mussed, as if he'd just woken up, but there were dark circles under his eyes in his too-pale face. It was the best sight I'd ever seen.

"Morning," I croaked with a smile. Fenn visibly sagged with relief.

"How are you feeling?" Fenn asked with that lopsided grin as he came in. He padded over to my bed and sat in the chair that was sitting there, as if he'd been there all this time and had only stepped out for a few moments. He handed me a glass of cold water, and I took it gratefully.

"Less dead than I was expecting," I said wryly.

A flash of guilt flitted across Fenn's features, and he stilled, grin frozen in place. A dull thumping filled my ears. My mind drifted back to my fever dreams. I was pretty sure the familiar voices I had heard were the emperor's and Fenn's...but everything was just a haze of red and black and pain.

"What's wrong?" I asked, feeling slightly wounded. Guilt that I was still alive wasn't exactly the reaction I was hoping for.

The thumping noise got louder, faster. I frowned, confused. Was I hearing...Fenn's heartbeat? That couldn't be right—I must still be affected by my injury.

Fenn hesitated, conflict in his eyes.

"Oh!" I exclaimed, realization dawning on me. "If...if you're still worried that I'm afraid of you, because you're a werewolf, don't be. I trust you." I smiled reassuringly and reached out for his hand, capturing it with both of mine.

Fenn met my eyes, surprise in his. "I'm very glad to hear that, Serena," he said, "But that's not what I...that's not what I'm worried about."

Fenn dropped his gaze, and I shifted uncomfortably, unease wriggling through me. An idea, a completely crazy suspicion, tickled the back of my mind. I shoved it down. *Impossible.*

"Why don't you start by telling me what happened after I...after I blacked out," I said weakly, my mind rebelling at the thought of how close I'd come to never seeing Fenn, never seeing anyone I cared about, again. At least in this world.

"Alright," he whispered, giving my hand a squeeze. "After that bastard threw the knife, Bruce and the boys ripped him to shreds. He won't be able to hurt you, to hurt us, ever again," he said with quiet vehemence, his eyes leveling me with their protectiveness.

I nodded, vaguely recalling hearing Lester screaming as I was fading. I didn't know what I expected to feel when he was gone. Satisfaction? Triumph? I just felt...relieved.

"What about everyone we got out of the dungeons? Chris, his family...all those poor women and children? And what did Lester mean about your sister?" I asked, suddenly remembering.

"Safe. They're all safe. The women and children were treated, and most of them have returned to their families. Chris and his family have also been treated, and they're staying here until their ranch can be rebuilt. And your mother...well, it seems she fell ill due to the horrid conditions of that dungeon, but she is currently being tended to in the infirmary."

I smiled, leaning back against the pillows. "I'm so glad...I don't know if I would have ever been able to forgive myself if any of them had died because of me."

"No, Serena. Even if that had happened, the blame would be laid solely at Lester's feet. You are never to blame for the actions of another," Fenn insisted.

Warmth filled me, and I smiled at him. "You're right. Thanks, Fenn."

He nodded, smiling, glad that I understood. But then his eyes darkened, as if he was recalling a memory bathed in sorrow.

"I've arranged for an official funeral for my family. It will be held as...as soon as their heads are returned from the Lindora Duchy," Fenn said thickly.

I placed my hand over his and squeezed reassuringly. "I'll be right there with you to lay them to rest," I murmured quietly.

"And...your sister?" I prompted gingerly after a few moments of silence. I remembered Lester revealing that he'd taken Fenn's sister and sent her somewhere only he was aware of. If only she'd been with the others in the dungeon... Guilt stirred in the pit of my stomach. If Lester was already dead, then that meant...

Fenn closed his eyes and answered, "He, uh, didn't get the chance to reveal more than the fact that she's still alive, or at least, she was the last time he saw her. But knowing Lester, I can hardly bear to imagine what he did to her." Fenn looked away, a muscle in his jaw feathering. His hands formed into fists.

"I guess we'll just have to find her ourselves," I declared, placing my hand over his fist. "Maybe we could get our shadowy, bald buddy Dorent to help us find her." The tension slowly drained away, his eyes softening as they met mine. He nodded, understanding the promise in my words.

Then he sighed, leaning back in his chair, his eyes going a little distant as he recalled what happened next.

"After you fell unconscious, I called for healers, and the emperor offered a handsome reward for saving you. But your wound was too severe. The blade had pierced your heart. Not a single one of the clerics or the healers could save you." Fenn paused, looking down at our entwined hands.

"Then...how am I still alive?" I asked hesitantly, placing my emptied cup on the table.

"I...I had to...change you," Fenn choked out, unable to meet my eyes. "It was the only way to save you." He finally looked up, the turmoil in his eyes clear.

I furrowed my brow. "Ch-change? What do you mean by that?"

"Serena, I turned you into a werewolf."

Stunned, my face went slack, even as Fenn's eyes desperately searched mine. *Was that why I had heard Fenn's heartbeat, the birds in the forest? Why I didn't feel any pain, why my necklace was no longer around my neck?*

The white wolf I'd seen in my dreams, the one that had filled me with warmth and strength, that had looked at me with my own eyes and called me back to the light... A single tear slid down my cheek.

Fenn flinched, shame and despair flashing across his face before he closed his eyes. When he opened them, his eyes had shuttered, his face a blank mask. He made to stand, slipping his hand out of mine.

Startled out of my thoughts, I desperately grabbed his hand before he could leave. A hint of surprise flickered before it was gone again, a crack in his mask.

"Thank you, Fenn," I whispered hoarsely, pouring every ounce of love and gratitude I had into my words. I beamed at him, even as tears streamed down my face.

His stoic mask fell away, hope and joy shining through, and he held me as my gray and miserable world transformed right before my misty eyes into a world of color and boundless possibility once more.

"Thank you, Serena, for saving me," Fenn whispered huskily as he sat down on the bed next to me.

"Well, it was my turn, after all," I murmured, my gaze dipping to his lips.

Fenn gently brushed away my tears. "I'd rather you just repay me in cookies and kisses," he whispered playfully, his eyes darkening to endless pools of sapphire.

"That can be arranged," I purred.

I was smiling when his lips found mine. Whatever the future had in store for us, we could face it. Together.

Thank You!

Thank you for reading The Werewolf's Mask! I hoped you enjoyed reading it as much as I enjoyed writing it. You can buy Daughter of Wind and Moonlight, the next book in the series, here: https://amzn.to/3StzKhe

To be alerted when new books in the series are released, subscribe to my newsletter here: https://k-s-gerlt.ck.page/c4b596cf47

Reviews

Reviews are greatly appreciated, and the best way to support the author and help readers to find new books. If you enjoyed this book, please consider leaving a review so that others can find it as well!

Also by K. S. Gerlt

The Werewolf's Mask Series
The Werewolf's Mask
Daughter of Wind and Moonlight
Son of Fang and Fury
Daughter of Steel and Strife
Son of Prejudice and Pride
The Werewolf's Mask Series Coloring Book

The Kingdom of the Stars Series
To Crush a Star

Want More Content?

If you would like to read an exclusive, unreleased chapter of The Werewolf's Mask, order merch, see character art, and receive updates and release notifications for the next book, please sign up here: https://k-s-gerlt.ck.page/c4b596cf47

About The Author

K.S. Gerlt is an award-winning artist and the author of The Werewolf's Mask series. An avid reader herself, she has always loved diving into the magical worlds within books, from the classics to modern fantasy and adventure. She grew up in Southern California, where her pastimes include horseback riding, ice skating, and painting.

Made in the USA
Las Vegas, NV
26 January 2025

f9bf0b74-f72d-4bc3-8b16-7d6957a9e80aR01